TEMPLE
OF
SORROW

Book One
Relics of Ishildar

CARRIE SUMMERS

Prologue

DEVON SHIFTED, HER leather armor creaking as she surveyed her companions. Their familiar faces were grim but determined. No one would turn back now.

They'd gathered in caverns like this hundreds of times, clad in their finest armor, bodies shimmering with the magical energy of a dozen enhancement spells. For five long years, they'd fought shoulder to shoulder. But this battle was different. This would be their last.

"Everyone ready?" Devon's voice echoed in the stone chamber, joining the drip of water falling from hanging moss. Chill air sank through her armor, stiffening muscles she'd limbered on the journey through the forest.

No one spoke. Around the cavern, torches blazed atop poles wedged into cracks in the natural stone floor. The flames hissed under the constant patter of water droplets.

"I'll miss this, you guys," Hailey finally said. Her dark eyes were cast downward, and she twisted the toe of her snake-hide boot against the floor.

"No goodbyes," Devon said. "We agreed."

Hailey pressed her lips together. Feathers of her headdress brushed her high cheekbones as she shrugged. "I still need to cast Seal Skin."

Stating the obvious. Hailey did that when she got nervous. Devon nodded to encourage her. They were all worried about this fight. Devon certainly didn't want to think too hard about it. Or rather, she didn't want to think about the aftermath.

"Anything else?" she said, taking in the others with a quick glance.

Owen, their rogue-assassin shuffled before finally jabbing a hand into one of his many hidden pockets. He pulled something out, holding it in a clenched fist. "Been saving these forever," he said with a crooked smile. "No point hoarding them now, I guess."

When he opened his hand, Devon's eyes widened. She let out a low whistle. "*Three?* I don't suppose you want to tell us where you got them..."

Owen shrugged. "Oh, here and there. I've kept the secret for so long, it seems wrong to blurt it out now. Especially seeing as it's useless information in less than an hour."

Fair enough. Devon couldn't stop staring at the priceless treasure in Owen's palm. In the last five years, she'd seen just one Phial of Deification. A legendary Houndmaster had popped it beneath the nostril of a doubly-legendary Hellhound. And that had been such a rare tactic that the entry she added to the Lore had been flagged as dubious. Still, people had whispered that more Phials existed. Somewhere in the vast realm of Avatharn, someone was collecting them.

Seemed that person had been Owen...

"Always figured you were holding out," said Jeremy, a slight figure half-in and half-out of phase with the current plane of existence.

4

Beside him, Hailey coughed and nodded. The feathers of her tunic rustled and released an unpleasantly bird-scented gust of air. It never seemed to bother her that she smelled like a budget pet store.

"Hey!" Owen protested. "It's just hard to decide when to use something like this, you know? No fight ever seems worthy."

He ran a finger over the Phials. Liquid swirled within the little glass tubes, glowing faintly with celestial light. Devon pried her eyes away. She didn't want to seem greedy.

"Question is, who uses them?" she asked. "I assume you'll keep one for yourself."

Owen glanced toward the low passage at the far side of the chamber. The torchlight glistened off the walls but penetrated just a few paces into the tunnel. A layer of water covered the corridor's floor. Inky. Hiding all kinds of surprises, no doubt.

"Here's the thing," Owen said, looking around the group. "I'm not critical to this fight. The Phials need to go to the people who matter. We have to get Devon into position and keep her alive—that's the whole point. We should go old-school. Keep the beast's focus on Chen." He glanced at a suit of mithril armor with a human somewhere in its depths. "And we can't let Jeremy go down because we need his heals."

Jeremy shook his head, or at least it looked that way. Hard to tell when someone was drifting out of phase. "If I have to crack a Deification Phial, we are so deep in the shit we might as well undress and roll in the acid pools."

"Guess that's a fair point." Owen shrugged, shifty eyes glinting. "You guys fight it out then. I don't want one. Consider them a farewell gift—"

Devon glared. "No goodbyes!"

He sighed. "Yeah, yeah. Anyway, Devon, you have to take one. The rest of you guys can roll for them."

Chen shook his head, his plate helm sliding easily upon the gorget that protected his neck. His voice echoed from the depths of his armor. "I'm not really interested in experimenting after last week..."

Jeremy snorted. "The ale, you mean? You should be proud, man. First person ever to hurl after drinking in-game grog. It's not even *real*."

"The crap still makes you feel dizzy," Hailey chided. "Chen's too young to have your *vast* experience with intoxication."

Jeremy smirked. "I assume you're sitting out from the roll, right Hailey? Catholic if I remember. Seeking deification sounds pretty sacrilegious."

The druid scoffed. "And two days of chanting in a pagan tongue to get my Raven Form wasn't? Also, at least I have a faith, numbnuts."

Jeremy laughed, a strange warbling sound as his phase-shift wavered.

Devon rolled her eyes. *Enough of this.* "Owen, you better just run the randomizer. Otherwise they'll fight about it for hours."

Owen nodded, and his eyes went distant for a moment. "One to Hailey, one to Maya."

Hailey accepted hers with a grin, while the other woman, a halfling scarcely taller than Devon's rib cage jerked in surprise before stepping forward.

"Deification for the summoner. Seems a bit meta..."

"Yeah, don't your demons already consider you a creator goddess?" Chen asked.

"I prefer the term Mistress," Maya said with a sly grin. "But yes, if you want to get technical, they do."

"Chen always wants to get technical," Jeremy said. "The Lore this, the Lore that."

"Speaking of..." Chen said without a hint of self-consciousness. "The Lore says that a summoner is the least useful of all the specialties in this fight."

Maya's hand froze at the opening to her reagent pouch. She'd been ready to deposit the Phial inside it with her precious spell components. "I don't need to keep—"

Devon snorted, slicing off Maya's objection. "That might be true, Chen, but how far as the Lore gotten parties so far? The longest anyone has lasted is about three nanoseconds. In Thevizh's case, the Lore is just guesses and interpretations of arcane fragments."

"Good point," Chen said.

A faint splashing sound came from the exit passage, followed by an air current that smelled of mildew. No, worse. It smelled like somebody had left a dead fish to rot in a shower drain. Devon grimaced.

"This is crazy. You know that, right? Do any of you guys think we actually have a chance?"

"Not a prayer," Jeremy said.

"We won't even leave bodies to mark our resting spots," Owen added.

Nervous laughs filled the chamber, but after a moment, they were replaced by genuine grins.

"We are so hosed," Jeremy said.

"Especially now that you guys wasted a mythical Phial of Deification on your summoner," Maya said.

Devon laughed. "Let's do this. Hailey, hit us with Seal Skin."

As Hailey spoke the incantation, colors rippled across her flesh. Her face shifted, taking on the aspect of a drowned thing, all pale and rubbery. Her eyes filmed over. Devon turned aside—she'd always hated the visual effects of the druid's aquatic spells. She didn't look back until the final syllable left Hailey's mouth and her features snapped back to normal.

Devon sighed as she felt the spell land. Seal Skin repelled water like a mofo. She hadn't realized how slimy the inside of her armor had gotten until the spell sucked the humidity away. Water droplets beaded on her skin and leather, sliding down to pool on the floor. No longer clammy, she felt downright comfortable. More than that, she felt impervious. With an archdruid like Hailey casting the protection spell, most water-based magic would splash right off her. It was good to have competent friends.

"Well, once more into the breach or something?" Owen asked, rolling his shoulders.

Devon nodded. "Once more into the breach."

***

Owen had crept off ahead. With the ankle-deep water in the passage, the rest of them had no chance of a stealthy entrance into the final chamber. Chen raised a hand for them to halt around twenty paces from the mouth of the tunnel. Sickly green light from the end of the passage leaked around his obnoxiously large silhouette.

The warrior took a deep breath, armor plates squeaking. With a roar and a clatter, he broke into a run.

Devon followed, trying to ignore how pathetic Chen's yell had sounded. Down here, he couldn't even use his Power of Voice because of the echoes. It was just one of many issues with Thevizh's Lair that made this attack so downright stupid. Bursting into the open air of the serpent queen's chamber, Devon deftly sidestepped a few spikes of submerged rock, probably poison-coated. She gritted her teeth and dropped her hands to the pair of daggers sheathed at her hips. The rune-scribed hilts felt awkward beneath her palms. She should be entering this battle with her ebony bow and a quiver full of master-quality arrows, their arrowheads forged by the master smith of Dakonir. It was her own stupid fault for opening the chest where the daggers had hidden all these years. Bound to her soul by inseverable magical ties, the weapons burned anyone else who touched them.

Which was why it had to be her who dealt the key blow.

She retreated to put her back against the slick wall while she got her bearings. The cavern seemed small to hold a supposedly unkillable beast. Low rock paths divided pools of slowly churning water from others of bubbling acid. Massive stalactites hung from the high ceiling while scattered pillars of stone—some uncomfortably humanoid-shaped—rose like dead trees from in a swamp.

Chen, living up to his record for the most-regrown-limbs-in-the-realm barreled across a slippery sidewalk of stone to the center of the cave. Pools of acid burped and steamed on either side of him. A wider lake of ink-black seawater held the bog queen.

And she was taking her time rising from the depths.

Devon searched the chamber for Owen, hoping the rogue had seen something before they arrived. The Lore claimed that would-be victors must hit fast and hit hard because the beast's only weakness was her arrogance. She often delayed her more powerful attacks, leaving two or three minutes to land blows before everyone in the chamber was wiped out by an acid fog or turned to stone and made a permanent part of the scenery.

True, monstrosities like Thevizh were unpredictable. But the enemies *usually* showed up for battle. Where in the hell was this legendary queen of the bog serpents?

Hailey had stayed near the entrance to the cavern. Devon met the archdruid's eyes, but the other woman just shrugged. Maya edged forward onto a large platform of rock halfway into the cavern and hesitantly began going through the motions of a summoning.

That was when the screeching started inside Devon's skull. She staggered, her breath stolen. In front of the central pool, Chen fell to a knee, free hand clutching his head. The point of his greatsword screeched as it skidded across stone. To Devon's right, their undetectable rogue stumbled from the shadows like a clumsy oaf. A whine escaped Devon's clenched teeth as her vision blurred.

The game conveyed small amounts of pain, but combined with the godawful screeching, it was nearly unbearable. Her stomach clenched, and she lost her balance, head cracking against the wall behind her.

The chamber began to shake. Water and acid sloshed in pools as the walls shuddered and booms filled the air, rattling Devon's teeth. In the center of the chamber, acid sloshed over the edge of a pool and hissed when it splashed against Chen's armor. The toxic substance ate through mithril like flame through paper.

/How. Dare. You. /

The voice pierced Devon's skull, sounding like an ancient tongue.

Like an erupting geyser, the beast corkscrewed from the central pool, flinging a spray of water. The attack pummeled the party, the liquid slamming into Devon like a sledgehammer. The shock vibrated her bones. She moaned. Without the Seal Skin spell, her guts would've been liquefied.

In the distant recesses of her mind, she perceived status alerts and other information. The game interface had been piped into her senses for so long it had become second nature. A true sixth sense. And that deep awareness told her she was screwed.

From the platform of rock where little Maya stood defiant in the face of Thevizh, squelching and sucking sounds preceded a discordant shriek as reality bent and a demon stepped forth. The thing was all claws and smoke, glowing eyes and shifting shape.

Moments later, a cool tendril struck Devon's chest and quickly spread calm through her body. She sagged in relief as Jeremy's shield forced away the screeching and the pain.

"Get on with it, people!" the planar priest yelled from somewhere across the cavern.

Devon swallowed. Right. Just another monster to slay.

Chen, his armor now looking like Swiss cheese, raised his head as Jeremy's spell connected and shielded him against the beast's attack. Clenching his greatsword in a single massive gauntlet, he climbed to his feet and fell into a defensive stance.

Thevizh's stench reached Devon's nose. The bog queen smelled like a swamp stirred up by a hurricane. The massive serpent was translucent, light penetrating the olive and black flesh. Hints of bones showed inside.

Devon shook her head. According to legends, a master crafter could use a rib from the great serpent to create the Sword of Ages. Not that it mattered anymore. This wasn't about the loot. It was about achieving the impossible.

Devon yelled and stood up straight, activating her master-level Lithe spell.

Her body became feather light. Her feet scarcely touched the ground, dancing through water and across stone as if she were held up by strings. Even better, she was as bendy as those girls who spent forty hours a week in a yoga studio. She sprang to the top of a stone pillar and balanced on a point no bigger than the first knuckle of her thumb.

Devon went preternaturally still and assessed the situation. The serpent queen towered above Chen even with half her bulk still submerged in the pool. Like a cobra in thrall to a snake charmer, her body undulated as she stared at the party's warrior.

Thevizh opened her giant maw. A glow bloomed in her throat, backlighting pulsing black veins. A gush of water, brown and laden with filth, sprayed over Chen. The warrior dropped to a knee and raised his forearm, catching the spray and deflecting it in a wide cone around him. Devon glanced at Hailey. The druid looked positively smug at the success of her Seal Skin.

Following the ineffective attack, the serpent stiffened and turned a single eye to the warrior. Her pupil was a vertical black slit in an orb of marbled red and green. She bent her body to the side as if cocking her head, and—unfortunately—noticed Devon perched upon the stone spire.

Shit.

Chen yelled, hoping to regain the monster's attention. But without his Power of Voice, the shout had no effect. The serpent's black tongue flicked out, tasting the air near Devon.

Never short on courage, Chen raised his sword and sprinted forward, slamming it against the beast's impenetrable scales. Across the cavern, a globe of shimmering air formed then streaked over the battle to envelop Devon. Devon's stomach turned over as she phase-shifted toward the shadow plane. Her contact with the physical plane faded, and her feet slipped off the pillar, no longer able to keep purchase on the water-smooth stone. She fell, hard, the tip of the spike punching her in the gut before she splashed into the water below. Ugh. Light leather armor was a great combination with a ranger's line of Lithe spells. But she was supposed to dodge attacks, not fall on the weapon.

She groaned and climbed to her feet. Shadow-plane phasing did not stack well with Lithe. Jeremy knew they both diminished contact with the physical realm but must have decided it was better to hit her with a crappy spell combo than let the serpent keep eyeing her. Anyway, it seemed to have worked. The beast's gaze was back on Chen. With a mental flick of the hand, Devon dispelled the shadow-phase effect while leaving her own magic in place.

The serpent began to weave a different pattern in the air, the warm-up for another attack. Devon's instinct was to prepare a specific defense. But the Lore didn't cover this. Best she could do was keep some terrain between her and the monster.

Chen had one job, and he did it well, keeping attention by hacking at the beast's scales. For all the damage he inflicted, though, he might as well have been trying to chop down a tree with a butter knife.

Devon began to edge around the chamber, back to the wall, toes skimming the ground. With a roar, the serpent whirled. A fin sliced out from the side of her body and slid straight through the armor on Chen's weapon arm. Devon gasped as his arm fell away clean, the greatsword clanging off stone before splashing into the acid.

"That sucks," she whispered.

A bolt of glowing energy from the astral plane arced across the room and smoked as it hit the stump of Chen's arm, cauterizing the wound. The warrior gritted his teeth and drew a small warhammer with his remaining hand. Meanwhile, Maya's demon screeched and shot across the chamber. Like curdled smoke, it hovered in the air before the beast's face, fire building in its core. The monster seemed to scoff, and with a breath of toxic fog, sent the demon back to the hell plane.

Devon reached the far side of the cavern and eyed the terrain between her position and the serpent's back. A crest of rubbery spikes hung down the monster's spine, reminding her of kelp on the beach. It wouldn't be easy, but Devon could probably climb using the crest for handholds. She took a deep breath, planning her movements.

A tortured shriek ended with a gargle. Devon froze. For just an instant, Chen's legs stood upright before toppling. The rest of him— torso, head, and armor—were shadows sliding down the serpent's gullet.

Devon could only stare—it had happened so fast.

Chen was gone, just like that.

A red glow lit the far platform as Maya screamed and channeled her rage. The little halfling jabbed a hand into her reagent pouch, pulled out the Phial of Deification, and broke it open beneath her nose.

Celestial light filled her body, and she sprinted forward to take the warrior's place. She yanked out a belt knife and brandished it in the direction of the serpent's belly.

Devon shook her head. What had Jeremy said about being so deep in the shit they might as well undress and jump in the acid?

As Maya reset her feet in an awkward combat crouch, a pair of daggers streaked from the shadows and slammed into the beast's fin, pinning it to her body. Devon grinned in approval at Owen's aim. Maya might not survive longer than the duration of the deification effect, but at least she wouldn't lose an arm.

Wrenched from her paralysis, Devon took three quick leaps across islands of stone and vaulted onto the serpent's back. Though they'd looked like slippery rope, the spines were razor-sharp. She grimaced as the edges sliced through her leather gloves. Blood poured from cuts in her palms, making her grip slick.

She jammed a hand into her belt pouch and pulled out her Phial. Like Owen had said, no fight seemed worthy of expending a mythical treasure. But like the saying went... you can't take it with you.

Devon squeezed the Phial, shattering the delicate glass. Wisps of golden mist rose from her fist, and she inhaled deeply.

Power flooded her body, rocketing her in-game statistics and abilities to their maximum.

Devon was invincible.

She grabbed one of the serpent's spines, yanked, and felt it tear away in her grip.

Easy, tiger.

15

She scrambled the remaining distance to the monster's head as easily as dashing up a ladder. Planting herself atop the beast, she squeezed the sides of the queen's head with her thighs.

"Yeehaw, cowgirl," Owen called from somewhere in the shadows.

Thevizh freaked out, writhing back and forth and cracking her head—along with Devon's body—against the dangling stalactites. The g-forces were fighter-pilot bad. But Devon had become a god.

For the next three minutes and thirty seconds, anyway.

She held on tight with her legs and yanked a dagger from her belt. The serpent's head was wider than a horse's back, and Devon strained to reach far enough to strike at the thin membrane covering the monster's ear hole. Even with god-like abilities, the serpent's wild flailing threw her aim off. Again and again, the point of the dagger skittered off diamond-hard scales. On the floor of the cavern, Hailey began to glow. Leaves materialized in the air and swirled around her in a whirlwind.

Thevizh froze as an interlocking lattice of ironwood roots wrapped her from tail to flicking tongue.

"Cage of the Forest! Nice!" Owen yelled from somewhere in a hidden recess of the cave.

Hailey shrugged a single shoulder. "Finally found the trainer."

Unfortunately, the ironwood had covered Devon's strike zone. She dug the tip of her dagger between the root and the beast's scales. No use. Not even a Dagger of the Sun could penetrate an archdruid's casting.

She leaned the other way. Same story on the other side of Thevizh's head.

Murphy's stupid Law.

It didn't matter; archdruid or not, Hailey's spell didn't last long against the bog serpent queen. With a mighty shudder, the beast shattered the cage. Devon struck and missed again as the infernal writhing resumed.

With another burst of magic, Hailey transformed into a raven the size of a horse. Shrieking, she beat the air with massive wings then dove at the serpent's eyes. Her talons clinked off unbreakable transparent scales.

This fight wasn't about whittling down the beast. Even if they could inflict damage, they'd never last long enough to get her below half health. This was all about Devon.

She stabbed again, felt the blade scrape against scales.

Like a surprise blow to the kidneys, her strength fled. Suddenly, it was all she could do to hold on.

Three minutes and thirty seconds. Had it already been so long?

The serpent thrashed to the right, smashing Devon's leg against a dangling spike. White pain was chased by cold numbness, and Devon glanced down to see her leg had been crushed. She whipped her head around, looking for Jeremy as she wormed fingers between a pair of scales to try to keep her grip.

Her eyes locked on a slumped form, half in and half out of the physical plane. A pair of spines pinned Jeremy's corpse to the cavern's stone wall. Her throat constricted. At least she'd seen Chen's demise.

With a roar of anger, Devon made one last desperate stab at the monster's eardrum.

And to her shock, her blade punctured the membrane.

The serpent stiffened, and time seemed to freeze.

/*Well. This is unexpected.*/ The monster's low and sibilant voice lanced into her mind. /*My only weakness... In through the eardrum to puncture the poison sac in the roof of my mouth.*/

Devon was sliding, her deadened leg dragging her off the crown of the serpent's head. Beneath her, reptilian flesh shuddered as the toxin spilled through the queen's veins.

/*It was supposed to be impossible, you know. A flaw in my design that none but an immortal entity could exploit.*/

"Yeah, and we killed you anyway, shithead," Devon said as she lost her grip and tumbled. Usually, she could land on her feet from twice the height, but with a leg crippled... this was going to hurt.

/*And as such, there's one last failsafe. I cannot let you live and walk away from this.*/

"Wait, what?"

Air rushed into the monster's slitted nostrils as she inhaled deeply.

Oh. Crap.

"Evacuate! Run, you guys!" Devon yelled a split-second before she smacked the ground.

Too late. Thevizh exhaled a brown cloud.

Necrotic fog. The single type of damage for which there was no resistance. Devon hit the ground, hard. The air left her lungs, but she refused to breathe in the deadly fog. No use; the poison soaked through the membranes in her eyes, sank through her pores.

She tasted death in the back of her throat before her vision went black.

You were slain by Thevizh, Bog Serpent Queen.

Permadeath has been enabled for the final day of uptime for Avatharn Online.

You may not respawn.

A single button appeared in the interface superimposed over her vision.

Logout.

***

2057 - St. George, Utah

The seals on the VR pod released with a pop and a quick rush of air. Moments later, Devon's vision returned, shunted back from the pod's technology to grant a red-toned view of the backs of her eyelids. She cracked them open, grimacing at the low-quality LED lighting that VR parlors were so fond of. The machine began peeling electrodes off her forehead, neck, and the tips of her fingers, leaving behind spots of coolness where her skin had been sweaty beneath. She raised an arm and dropped her hand over her eyes.

That was it then. Her final logout. Now what?

Stretching, she swung her legs over the edge of the pod and stood. Stillness hung like a pall over the parlor—back at corporate headquarters for Pod People, management was probably drinking funereal toasts and offloading whatever stock they could. Without Avatharn Online, public VR parlors would either need to invest in extra sanitation equipment to service the erotic immersion industry, or they'd have to scrape by on subscriptions from die-hard immerso addicts until another game title achieved critical mass. If that ever happened. The shutdown had been such a surprise. No real warning, no apparent reason. Just a message that had announced the end four days ago.

Even though a few hours of Avatharn uptime remained, barely half the pods were occupied. The seals on those were locked down tight, and red warning text glowed near the emergency handle. No doubt, the people inside the capsules were walking around the commons of half a dozen major cities in the realm. Saying tearful goodbyes. Waiting for the lights to go out.

Devon shuddered. She needed to get out of here before they woke up.

Stupid game. And what a crappy way to finish out five years of her life. *Killing me is supposed to be impossible so I'm going to nuke your party with necrotic damage?* Seriously, what the hell?

She wondered if the others had received the same message. Minus Chen and Jeremy, of course. They'd already been ejected by the time she'd struck the fatal blow.

Unfortunately, Devon would never know what the rest of her group had experienced. That was the point. No goodbyes, no contact afterward. Otherwise, they'd never be able to move on.

The pod closed behind her. The seals engaged with a whine, and antiseptic mist hissed as it filled the apparatus. Tubes gargled as the spray got sucked back out. Even so, the pods almost always smelled faintly of the last occupant. She curled her lip. That was one good thing about the shutdown—no more public VR pods.

With a deep breath, she started walking toward the glare of afternoon sunlight through the glass front door.

"Hey! You forgot your timecard," the pale-faced attendant called.

She didn't look back. "I don't want it."

"There will be other games."

"Not for me. Got to get on with my life."

Besides, the card probably held just fifteen or sixteen more hours of pod use. And since she was a cheapskate and went with a biometrically-locked timecard, she couldn't even sell it.

Just like she could no longer resell items, quest escorts, or any of the other in-game commodities she'd used to supplement her crappy day-job wages.

She shoved the door open and stepped into a wall of Southwest heat. Time to start over.

Again.

Chapter One

THE DECREPIT VEHICLE, an old six-wheeled army truck converted to an open-top tourist bus, creaked and groaned as the driver AI eased it over ruts and bumps. Emerson swayed in his seat, knocking shoulders with a bored-looking teenager. The kid kept glancing his way and rolling his eyes as if looking for an accomplice in his objection to being dragged along on a hokey Wild West adventure. Between the broiling desert sun and the group sitting in front of the kid's parents—eleven highly enthusiastic people in matching yellow T-shirts printed with a logo for their family reunion—Emerson didn't blame the kid for sulking. But he didn't have time for commiserations. He slipped on his augmented reality glasses as an excuse to avoid interaction.

Rather than activating the glasses' markup to get the full Wild West overlay atop the scenery and actors, he focused on the woman guiding the tour. Devon Walker. She didn't look like the stereotypical hardcore gamer. No stark haircut or implanted mood beads glowing in response to her EM field. No obvious tattoos. Her ordinary light brown hair was tied in a low ponytail. She was just... normal—and he had to admit, fairly attractive. If not for the detailed history he'd received from the PI, he'd have assumed she did administrative work somewhere. Or maybe that she still lived with her parents while finishing college.

She didn't look like someone who'd left home at sixteen. Before that, she'd had a barely-speaking-terms relationship with her single mother and the mother's string of temporary boyfriends. Devon had been on her own for six years now, cobbling together gaming income and temporary jobs to afford a cheap studio apartment that she kept clean but never decorated.

"Get down!" Devon yelled, almost convincingly. She ducked and dragged a replica six-shooter out of the faux-leather holster on her belt. The bus jounced over another series of ruts, probably hand-constructed for authenticity. In the front rows, the family reunioners laughed and gasped as Devon squeezed off a series of blanks, aiming for actors who leaped from behind artfully placed blocks of sandstone. A middle-aged man yanked out a toy gun and started shooting at the nearest "bandit."

The actors fell one by one, shot down by the expert marksmanship in the bus. Moments later, the slope to the left of the road began to rumble, and then dirt and pebbles sprayed as an explosion rocked a mine tunnel cut near the top of the nearest bluff. Devon cringed and slapped a hand on top of her hat to hold it on as rubble tumbled down the slope.

The tourists gasped and cheered.

Finally, the bus stopped at the gates to a chintzy fort, square walls made of skinny logs with the bark still on. A man wearing a sheriff's vest stalked out, bow-legged. Either he had hemorrhoids, or he was trying to look like he'd just got off a horse.

"Escape the ambush, did you?" he asked jovially, then widened his eyes as he glanced at the road behind the bus. He drew yet another pistol, laid it over his wrist, and fired a blank over the top of the brush. Another actor yelped, stood, and executed a twisting fall into the dust.

"You missed one," he said with an exaggerated wink. "But I might still take you on as deputies."

The teenager beside Emerson groaned. "You can't tell me this isn't as lame as it gets," he hissed to his parents.

The gates creaked open, exposing the trampled-dust interior of Fort Kolob. The bus trundled in and lurched to a stop. Emerson caught Devon's longing look toward the city of St. George, Utah. He didn't blame her. He was looking forward to heading back as well, if only for the air conditioning.

Along one edge of the fort, another tour group was lined up to fire real pistols at straw targets. In a far corner, sway-backed horses stamped in the heat, heads low. As Emerson hopped down from the bus, last to exit, Devon herded the group toward a trestle table on the side opposite the firearms. Another woman stopped by the table on her way from the staff area to the shooting gallery. She wore her dirty blonde hair in tight braids and had a wide-brimmed hat pulled low on her forehead.

"Well now," she said. "Another pack of new settlers. In case you don't recognize me by the exhibition posters you saw on your way out West, the name's Annie Oakley. I'll be giving you some tips on sharpshooting later on."

With her back turned to the main group, "Annie" rolled her eyes at Devon who contained a smirk. Emerson took a seat at the end of the bench, not wanting to be trapped in the middle of any loud conversation from the reunion-goers. Plus, he was hoping to speak to Devon when she wasn't busy—provided he could figure out something to say without making a fool of himself or freaking her out. He really should have sent someone else to do this, but his control-freakishness had gotten in the way. He only had so much discretionary budget, and he really didn't want someone else screwing up his plans.

Over at the shooting gallery, a couple parents were loudly encouraging their son. The kid, probably ten and clad in clothes a size or two too tight, raised a pistol. Head turned to the side, eyes clenched shut, he squeezed the trigger. The gun bucked in his hand. He dropped it and started bawling.

Emerson didn't miss the look of exasperation that passed between Annie and Devon.

Unfortunately, as soon as Devon saw the servers coming with plates of honest-to-goodness char-broiled steaks, she slipped away and exited the open center of the fort through an unlabeled door.

Emerson moved his food around on his plate and sipped his water. A hot steak under the glare of a ninety-degree sun just wasn't appetizing. He dabbed his lips with a napkin, stood, and sauntered toward the shade of the wall—and the door where Devon had disappeared. From inside, he heard her greeting coworkers in a dull voice. Cutlery clinked against dishes, and somewhere in the recesses of the room, water was spraying, probably into a sink.

The door didn't *say* employees-only, so Emerson shrugged and pushed through it into—as he'd guessed by the sounds—the employee cafeteria. Devon was standing by the checkout kiosk carrying a tray holding a floppy-looking veggie burger and some kind of fruit cocktail. She set the tray beneath the imager then held her wrist into the scanning field.

The machine beeped. Not the nice chime that said, "Enjoy your meal," but the ugly blat that told everyone in the room Devon didn't have the funds. Emerson winced in sympathy, expecting her to flush with embarrassment. But Devon just sighed and rolled her eyes, then clicked a couple of buttons on the machine's touchscreen. Probably telling it to deduct the cost from her paycheck.

She sat down at a metal table and lifted her burger. The soggy bun sagged away from the patty. Emerson took a deep breath and got ready to approach her, but as he took his first step, Annie Oakley shoved through the door and laid a purse down on the seat beside Devon.

Emerson stopped short and took a seat at the table behind them. He pulled out his phone and bent over it, hoping that no one noticed he didn't belong.

"Hey, Tamara. Shooters done already?" Devon asked.

"Thank god. Someday, one of them's going to turn on us with a loaded weapon. Execute us for ripping off tourists with the stupidest attraction west of the Mississippi."

Foil crinkled, and Emerson glanced back to see Annie—or rather, Tamara—peeling the top off a yogurt cup.

"You ever wonder why they keep coming?" Devon asked.

"I really don't get it. But as long as we get paid, I guess it doesn't matter."

"You went to school for acting, right?"

Emerson edged his chair so that he could watch the women out of the corner of his eye. He hoped Devon wasn't thinking of going for a degree. Not now, anyway.

Tamara fixed Devon with a serious stare. "Don't even think about it. It's not worth it."

"Unless I get a pay raise, which means playing a casted role, I gotta get another job on top of this."

"It really isn't worth it, Devon. I mean it. They say the cast has regular reviews, a pay structure that lets you earn more, but I'm making the same shit salary as when I started. I'm getting out. A friend of mine's taking me on as an apprentice bike mechanic."

"You mean like motorcycles?" Devon looked on with interest.

Tamara shook her head. "Mountain bikes."

"Seriously? They need actual mechanics?"

"Do you even know how much people pay for a top-of-the-line bike?"

Devon shrugged. "Last bike I rode was in the Fourth of July parade when I was ten. I get out of breath walking up the stairs to my apartment."

"Oh, give yourself some credit. You're in good shape. Just not into biking."

Emerson stifled the urge to interject. He agreed; Devon looked healthy to him. But the last thing he needed to do was creep her out by sounding like he was hitting on her.

"Do you have to be into mountain biking to work as a mechanic?"

Tamara looked at her apologetically. "Yeah, sorry."

Devon shrugged. "No problem. Just trying to figure stuff out before I have to become a human billboard."

Emerson winced. Getting tattooed with smart ink so that companies could display advertisements on your flesh was about as sad as it got. Especially because the contracts didn't let you choose the content. Cover the tattooed area, and you lost your paycheck. He'd seen plenty of miserable guys walking around with ads for erectile dysfunction remedies blinking on their shoulders.

"Your group's ready," Tamara said, nodding at the screen mounted on the far wall. Group "Billy the Kid" was lit up in red.

Devon stood and groaned, gulping the syrup from the fruit cocktail cup on the way to the tray conveyor. A moment after she left the cafeteria, Emerson slipped out to rejoin the group.

***

The bus back to St. George cruised almost silently over the pavement. Emerson glanced back and saw Devon lean back in her seat and press her forehead against the window. Red rock and dusty-green brush scrolled by. After a while, she sighed and pulled a stainless-steel water bottle from her backpack. She sipped then grimaced before twisting the cap back on. The water had probably gotten hot over the day.

Emerson took a breath to gather himself. He hadn't been able to get time to speak with her as a paying customer, and now he was stuck ambushing her on her ride back from the fort. He doubted that would work in his favor, but it would be even creepier to buy *another* ticket to Fort Kolob.

He swallowed and shuffled down the aisle to take the empty seat next to her. Devon scooted closer to the window, sending a hint that even someone as socially inept as him could get. But Emerson had already cut deep into his discretionary budget with the PI work, not to mention his travel expenses to get here. He had to try to recruit her before giving up. He settled a small backpack between his feet. She sighed but otherwise didn't acknowledge him.

"Long day?" he asked.

She flashed him a cold smile that was a clear dismissal. Recognition flickered behind her eyes when she realized he had been on her tour. Which also meant she had good cause to wonder why he was on the bus *now* rather than a few hours ago after his tour had ended.

"I know I'm intruding," he said. "I'm really sorry. Must get tiresome dealing with tourists all day."

"It's a job," she said. She pulled a tablet from her purse and opened a graphic novel. Something retro, it looked like.

Emerson plowed ahead. He was botching this hard, but at this point, he didn't have anything to lose. "I don't think Fort Kolob is your thing, though."

"You know, it *has* been a long day," she said. "I just want to relax."

"Tour operators try hard," he said. "But it's not the sort of experience people crave. Not like Avatharn was, right?"

Devon stiffened. A blood vessel in her temple pulsed. "Excuse me." She stood and grabbed her backpack. As she edged past his knees, she glanced back at her water bottle, now out of reach. Emerson read the indecision in her eyes. Sacrifice the bottle or risk more time in this uncomfortable conversation. He reached over and grabbed the bottle, handing it to her in what he hoped was a peace gesture.

She struggled to get clear of the seats, and Emerson turned his knees sideways to give her room to pass. "This isn't going well. I'm an idiot. But I'm not hitting on you. After this, I'm grabbing the hyperloop from Vegas to Atlanta, hoping to catch up with Owen. Your rogue friend."

She quickly covered her shocked expression. "What the hell is your deal? Stalker much?"

He shook his head. "I should have sent someone who knows how to talk to people. It's hard because we're a startup and my budget for experimental ideas is limited."

"Whatever, dude," she said.

"Wait." He stopped himself from touching her elbow. "I was searching for the person connected to your in-game avatar. Many Worlds Entertainment gave me your contact info."

"Apparently they haven't ever heard of a privacy policy." She stomped forward a few rows and sat on the outside edge of a seat, ensuring he couldn't join her again.

He took a seat two rows back so he wouldn't have to yell. "Unfortunately, Ms. Walker, Many Worlds had extensive fine print associated with that policy. The company was within its legal rights to give me your city of residence, and after that I used a PI to narrow it down."

Devon whirled on him. "I'm about to contact the police," she said. Loudly. The other passengers buried their noses in tablets.

Emerson held up his hands in self-defense. "I want to offer you a job, Devon. And it's nothing shady, I swear. I work for a game company. We have a new title coming out soon, using next-generation technology that we believe will obsolete every game that came before."

Her jaw worked. "Bullshit."

Emerson blinked in surprise. "But you haven't even seen the beta version. How can you—"

"I mean, bullshit that you'd want to hire me. I'm a high school graduate—GED by the way... I didn't even finish. I know nothing about programming, design, or 3D art. My only game-related training is as a level 250 Wildsense Ranger. So just cut the shit, okay?"

The bus rolled to a stop, and the automated voice announced a condo development—Devon's home. She didn't move to get off. Maybe that meant that she was interested. More likely, she didn't want to give away information about her home address in case he hadn't discovered it.

"That's the thing. I need players. Characters who are ready to step off the rails and make their own track."

"Like beta testers?"

"Hmm. No, the company has an army of those. Sealed away in some bunker and wrapped in twenty layers of non-disclosure agreements if I were to guess. You haven't asked what the game is."

"Because it doesn't matter. If it were worth my time, I'd have heard of it by now."

"Unless we've done everything we can to keep all knowledge of the project out of the public sphere. We have a technology partnership that was contingent on our agreement to keep details hidden until they were ready to announce."

"Yet here you are, telling the tour guide from your Wild West adventure all about it."

"Because the first details hit the newsfeeds tonight at midnight. If you leak something before that, I seriously doubt it will get around fast enough to place us in breach."

The bus started to roll forward again, tires crunching over the asphalt. Devon glanced out the window, a faint wrinkle of frustration between her brows. Probably thinking about the extra cost of riding past her stop.

"Back to what you'd want me for..." she said.

"A mix of things. The game will need evangelists."

"If I wanted to become a streamer, I'd have done that in Avatharn. Certainly would have paid better than hawking items and newbie help."

"You wouldn't be obligated to share any feeds whatsoever. It's more like... players need something—*someone*—to aspire to. Your accomplishments will show on the leaderboards. Anonymous if you like. But it's more than the example you set for the players. Which brings me to one of the two things that truly sets Relic Online apart. The content is completely dynamic. Our designers created initial parameters, and my AI system populates the world. Veia—that's what I call her—has created something amazing, but I want to take things a step further. I want players who can *challenge* her creatively. Force her to go beyond creating the same sort of quests we've all played a thousand times."

Already, the bus was slowing again. Devon gathered her purse and backpack and stood. "And the other thing?"

Emerson cocked his head. "What? Oh. Right. The other reason we're different." He pulled a glossy spec sheet from his backpack. It was a rundown of the details on their technology partner, Entwined, a controversial VR interface that used a set of implants to create the experience. Once the public gained confidence in the technology, all other VR gear would become obsolete. Traditional Augmented Reality hardware, too, since the implants could do both easily.

Devon's eyes flicked to the sheet. After a moment, she snatched it from his fingers.

"You'd be able to play from the comfort of your own couch, and you'd earn a salary for doing it. I'm going to grab some noodles tonight. A place on Bluff Street called Little Saigon. I made the reservation for two, and I swear if you still aren't interested after you hear my pitch, you won't hear from me or my company again."

Chapter Two

THE STREAM OF self-drive cars glided past the front of the hole-in-the-wall Vietnamese place, moving with the assembly-line smoothness of traffic in the autocar era. Devon, of course, had taken the bus to a stop seven blocks away and hoofed it from there. Taxis were expensive.

To the west, evening sun set fire to the sandstone high country of Zion National Park. The sight still surprised her, even a couple of weeks after Avatharn's shutdown. For the five years previous, she'd been tucked into a public VR pod every night by seven. She wasn't used to sunsets. Real ones, anyway.

She hesitated before passing in front of the restaurant's windows. The thing on the bus had been weird. Sketchy, even. But she figured she'd be safe meeting him in public, especially on such a busy street. It occurred to her that she ought to have told someone her plans—just in case she *did* go missing. Unfortunately, her only friend was her coworker, Tamara. And they'd never spoken outside of work. Devon didn't even have her messenger contact.

She stuffed her hands in her pockets and strode for the door. Bells jingled when she leaned her shoulder against it to push it open. A wave of aroma fell over her, making her mouth water and her stomach clench. Her food budget had been a little tight lately.

The guy was sitting at a table along the wall. Southeast Asian decor, Buddhas and bamboo and stuff, crusted the walls and counter. A small fountain burbled by the entrance to the kitchen.

Devon stalked over and took a seat. The chair had already been pushed out for her. "If you have the resources to hunt down random gamers, clandestine-spy style, why go for someone like me? Why not a celebrity sense streamer? And I still don't get the secrecy thing with your announcement."

"On the secrecy, all I know for sure is that negotiations with Entwined were above my pay grade," he said. "Maybe the hardware guys wanted to see the full-fledged product before they named us their flagship software partner. My name's Emerson by the way. Emerson George."

"You already know mine." Among other things. A fact which really irked her.

"Entwined is also our biggest source of funding. I don't know all the details, but it's rarely a good idea to piss off the people with the open wallets."

"But now they've given the go-ahead on the announcement. They think your game will be the title that makes their product a household name. And you're going to try to convince me of the same thing. Except, in order to experience it, I have to have a bunch of circuitry installed in my scalp."

The man—Emerson—took a sip of some sort of milky tea. "I was surprised to learn you don't spend time on gaming forums. But you're smart enough to wonder why Avatharn shut down, even without reading all the rabid conspiracy theories about it."

She shrugged. "They never released subscriber numbers, but with how packed the servers were, I can't imagine they were losing money."

"One of their upper managers had a mole in our beta program. IT is still trying to figure out how they got a sensory stream past the firewall, but long story short, footage made it into the hands of decision-makers at Many Worlds. They contacted us with an offer to retarget their Avatharn subscribers at Relic Online for a cut of the profits. The fact is, even without Entwined technology, the sense stream was enough for them to see the end of their profits. With the implanted hardware, the play experience has been described as, well, indescribable."

Devon looked up as the server approached to take their order. She'd heard this kind of marketing hoorah before... though she didn't usually think it came from AI programmers. Despite her intent to remain skeptical, the game was starting to sound interesting.

The server raised an immaculately plucked eyebrow and brandished her stylus. Devon turned her menu over to the à la carte side and looked for something cheap.

"The meal's on us," Emerson said.

In that case... She turned the card back over and ran her finger down the price column. "I'll have whatever this is," she said, pointing to something with Vietnamese writing followed by the word large and a hefty price tag.

Emerson chuckled. "Spring rolls for me, please. And a beer."

Devon hesitated. A beer sounded nice; it'd been a long day wrangling tourists on the Western frontier. But she didn't want to get too comfortable. "Something with caffeine."

"Have you tried Vietnamese coffee?" the server asked.

"Sure, sounds good."

"I had this offer prepared in case you showed up." Emerson slid a piece of paper across the table as the server walked away.

As Devon scanned it, her eyes widened. Holy crap. The salary was ten times what she made at Fort Kolob. "I don't get it. Seriously. Why me?"

"We saw the stream of what you guys did with the bog serpent. Thevizh."

Devon sat up straight. "What? We had a deal! That last fight was about us battling together one last time. No live streaming allowed."

Emerson chewed his lip. "It was from the druid. Sorry if that surprises you."

She rolled her eyes. Hailey. She should have guessed. "Whatever. It's done now, I guess."

"The point is, you guys *are* celebrities of a sort, even if you haven't been watching the forums to realize it. That's not why I want you in game, though. I already explained... it's your skills and creativity, not your public relations abilities. E Squared—that's my company—will set you up with the necessary surgeries. You'll enter the game a couple days before we start admitting groups from the main player base."

She looked down at the paper again. "But this is salary for two years."

"Provided you play a certain amount per week. There's fine print about achieving certain milestones—we need to make sure you're pushing the systems creatively. But I can't imagine that would be a problem."

"The technology's safe?"

38

"We've had a thousand beta testers using it for the last six months. No problems reported. They just aren't as good at playing as you are.

"So all I have to do is get this awesome tech installed and then play your game for two years?"

He grinned. "That's pretty much it."

"Hey, sorry, can I change my order?" Devon asked, motioning for the server.

The woman painted on a smile. "What do you need?"

"Change my coffee to a beer please."

Chapter Three

DEVON RAN HER fingertips over the maze of ridges at the nape of her neck. The silicon and graphene circuitry, implanted into her skin like a tattoo, crawled over her scalp and up behind her ears, but it was only visible at the base of her skull.

The implants still itched. But now that everything was healed, she supposed she'd get used to it.

She lay back on her couch cushions, almost tentative. The can lights embedded in the ceiling glared down. After a moment, she waved her hand to tell the sensors to turn them off. No need to waste electricity while immersed. It felt strange. No VR pod, not even a headset. Just... her own body and the mental impulse to activate the hardware that was now a part of it.

She focused on the little icon flashing in the corner of her vision. A silver R expanded and floated to the center of her view. Beneath it, the words Relic Online pulsed with a faint gold halo that indicated the server was now up. Time to do what she'd been hired for.

Using the interface was similar to the way she'd trained her mind to interact with the VR pod. She focused on the icon and willed herself to connect.

The living room faded to black.

A heartbeat later, she stood under a bright, almost merciless sun. Humidity sank into her pores. The green smell of plant life filled her nose, so thick she could cut it. Vines were everywhere, growing in a riotous tangle over what looked like the ruins of stone buildings.

She shuffled and looked down. Her feet were bare, soles pressed against stone blocks that were pitted with age.

"So much for character creation," she muttered.

She ran a hand through her hair, slick and wavy and much thicker than she was used to. A black strand fell across her face.

She shrugged. She'd always hated customizing her character's appearance anyway.

As she turned a slow circle, taking in the scenery, the depth of the immersion struck her. The old technology had provided input for all the senses. It had felt real, but now she realized how far off it had been.

This tech went deep. Hyperreal. Almost too authentic.

She took a few steps and felt tiny bits of grit pressing into the bottoms of her feet. Ahead, vines spilled across the path, nearly hiding it. Whatever this place was, it had been deserted for a long, long time. Soaring stone arches were crumbling from the inside out. Overgrown by the roots of long-legged trees, statues stretched their arms out into the sunlight while their bodies suffocated under the foliage. Ahead, a spire of gray-white stone speared from the jungle, at least ten stories tall. But even the highest ledges and alcoves were covered in orchids, curtains of moss, and climbing vines.

Not much direction for a player, Devon thought.

She glanced down at her clothing, rough-spun fabric with hems ending well above her ankles and wrists. A patch had been whip-stitched over one of her knees. She focused her intent on summoning an inventory screen. A window popped up in her view, showing an inventory table with four slots. Three were empty, and the last was filled with pocket lint.

Below the window was a message.

You don't have a backpack yet, obviously. The only place you can store items is your pants pockets.

Very funny.... She continued shuffling forward. At the next intersection, she headed down a wider path of fitted stone blocks. Wary, she kept her ears perked for sounds and searched the greenery for threats. Aside from the hum of insects and the distant chirping of birds, she seemed to be alone.

Abruptly, she tripped. Her knees cracked against stone as her palms slapped down just in time to prevent a face plant.

She rolled over and spotted the small lip where she'd caught her toe. She groaned. Was she really that clumsy?

A couple of messages popped up in her view.

You have gained a skill point: *+1 Unarmed Combat.*
When you are starting from nowhere, even the floor is a worthy opponent.
You take 1 damage. 24/25 health remaining.

She rolled her eyes. Seriously?

Remember, Devon, you're getting paid for this.

Her stomach rumbled as she stood, wincing at a fresh scrape on her knee. She had no idea what she was supposed to do, but clearly she was going to need food, probably shelter too. She needed to orient, get a sense for the lay of the land. A high point would be a good start. Shading her eyes, she peered at one of the vine-draped statues. She hurried over, took hold, and started to climb. With a sudden tearing sound, the vines pulled free. She landed on her back, and her head smacked the ground.

You take 2 damage. 22/25 health remaining.

Fantastic. In the game for five minutes, and she'd already lost three health just walking around.

As she climbed to her feet, she glanced at the statue and grimaced. Carved of gleaming white stone, the figure had spheres of black marble veined with green shoved into its eye sockets. The proportions were off, particularly in the face, and it gave the sculpture an agonized look. Creepy.

She hurried on. After wandering for another quarter hour or so, she finally discovered a staircase. The steps had been built for someone much taller than her, and each step up was a struggle. By the time she'd finally ascended the long flight, her breath came in gasps.

You have gained an attribute point! Until level 5, Relic Online will adjust your basic starting attributes according to your play style. Once you reach level 5, your starting attributes will be revealed. You will be able to spend 4 discretionary points each level, advancing your attributes as you desire.

Out of curiosity, she pulled up her character sheet.

Character: Devon (click to set a different character name)
Level: 1
Base class: Unassigned
Specialization: Unassigned
Unique class: Unassigned
Health: 22/25
Fatigue: 25%

Not much to go on. She pulled open the subwindows for skills and attributes, hoping for more information.

Attributes:
Locked until Level 5

Skills:
Unarmed Combat: 1

That was it.

She went back to the main sheet for a moment and stared at her character name. Should she change it? In Avatharn Online, she'd named her character Revialle. But since none of her friends could remember how to spell it, they'd just called her Devon. She shook her head and closed the character sheet. Maybe later.

The stairs had reached a wide platform which, unlike the rest of the surroundings, was relatively clear of jungle. Her breath caught as she dismissed the windows and took in the landscape. Despite her explorations so far, it seemed she'd scarcely scratched the surface of the city. The ruins were immense, stretching out into the mists until, miles away, they washed up against a set of jagged cliffs.

You have discovered Ishildar, an ancient seat of power. Long-since abandoned, the city is now rumored to harbor secrets. (Pro tip) Also, it's dangerous.

Well, that was promising. But she'd expected to start in an area with other players, shops, and opportunities to advance her skills. Maybe if she could find a way out of this wilderness, she'd encounter more level-appropriate content.

"You're remarkably unskilled to consider a conquest of Ishildar."

Devon whirled to see a ball of mist, lit from within, bouncing lightly in the air before her. A wisp?

"Uh, hello."

The bobbing globe said nothing. It circled slowly around her head as if examining her.

"And I wasn't considering a conquest," she went on. "Just trying to find my way."

"Still..." The wisp said, ignoring her comment, "Veia *did say* the city would someday have a champion. We only needed to remain patient. Could you be her?"

Something fluttered at the edge of Devon's vision, but when she turned her head, all was still. She looked back at the glowing ball. The way it was talking... Was she supposed to get a quest out of this thing?

She cocked her head. "Can you offer me work?"

"Work? As in, you want a job?"

Beneath Devon's bare feet, the stone platform began to vibrate, shuddering as if shaken by immense footsteps. In the distance, leaves rustled.

"I'm interested in gaining skills or earning rewards."

The wisp zipped back and forth in the air before her. "Hmm. Well, I can't grant you employment, but I can offer advice."

"Oh?"

"Run," the wisp said, darting off.

As she whirled to follow its motion, a flock of multicolored birds erupted from the treetops, squawking. The shaking intensified, setting little pebbles dancing on the flat stone surface. Devon took a step backward, away from the direction of the sound, as a massive figure stepped from behind a towering spire.

Her eyes widened as an immense stone golem raised a massive stone foot and stomped it down. The grating sound as its joints rubbed together vibrated her molars.

Its boulder of a head swiveled to look at her, faint flames like starlight deep within its cavernous eye sockets.

Yeah. Running seemed like a good idea. She whirled and raced down a short flight of stairs to a path that wound through low, vine-choked buildings.

There was a reason people wore shoes. With each slap of her feet against unforgiving stone, knives stabbed Devon's knees and hips. She felt her fatigue rising, and as she thought of the statistic, a bar showed in the corner of her vision. It was nearly full.

Her breath sawed in and out of her lungs, rubbing her throat raw. Sweat pasted her hair to her scalp, and vines whipped against her thin clothing. She searched the edges of the narrow path for a weapon, considering then rejecting loose rocks and broken sticks. What good would such simple weapons do against a giant made of rock? She glanced back. The stupid thing was gaining. It knocked over buildings, stomped trees flat, and sent statues flying into pieces.

As she whipped her head back around, desperate to find some sort of hiding place, a low stone archway swung into view. Her forehead hit the overhang with a crack that she felt all the way down to her heels.

> **You have gained a skill point:** *+1 Unarmed combat.*
> *Floors, archways... Practice makes perfect!*
> *You have been knocked unconscious.*

***

To Devon, it felt as if she'd passed out or fallen asleep in real life.

Except when she woke in her own bed, she rarely had a headache that felt like an army of gnomes was jackhammering the inside of her skull. So much for the game's muted pain response.

"Ow," she muttered. Usually, when a player died in-game, the fatal injuries were wiped away during resurrection. Some realms added temporary weakness afterward—an effect called a debuff. But this headache was cruel and unusual.

You're getting paid for this, remember, said the little voice in her head.

"Yeah, but I didn't know my employment contract included torture," she said aloud.

She cracked her eyelids. The light was dim, beams of afternoon sun falling through holes in the... canopy? The shade seemed awfully dense, even for a jungle understory. It didn't make a lot of sense—she'd assumed she would respawn at the same location where she'd first entered the world.

"Drink this." The woman had a scratchy voice.

Devon stiffened, eyes flying open. A hut. Thatched roof. Beams of sunlight stabbed through the ceiling, lighting shelves cluttered with baskets, roots, and pottery. As she craned her neck to find the speaker, a muscle along her spine cramped.

The woman stepped into view. A concerned expression creased a wizened face surrounded by coarse gray hair twisted with scraps of leather. She tutted, exposing a scattering of teeth on shiny gums. As she reached forward, offering a little clay pot stoppered with a spongy cork, Devon caught a whiff of incense and herbs suffusing her clothing.

Devon sat up slowly, limbs trembling. Her tunic was damp with sweat.

"Why did I respawn here?"

"Respawn, starborn?" She cackled. "You *are* inexperienced, aren't you? Yes, it's true that starborn souls may be reborn after the mortal bond is severed. 'Tis the glory of Veia made manifest in a chosen few. But in your case, I dragged your body out of the path of a rampaging Stone Guardian. When knocked unconscious, you eventually recover unless you take more damage."

Devon's eyes widened in surprise. "That was... brave."

"Well, I have a few tricks up my sleeve," the woman said with a wink.

So, she hadn't died after all. That would explain the headache. Devon pressed fingers to her temples.

"Thanks for saving me," she said.

Again, the woman held out the pot. "Drink it. You'll feel much better."

As she accepted the little jar, Devon took a better look at the room. She was sitting on a low cot, the mattress woven from some sort of fronds. Beyond her bare—and now filthy—feet, she spotted a barrel of water and a few hanging strands of dried herbs.

She twisted the cork and pulled until it came free. An absolutely awful stench burst from the pot. It was like paint thinner mixed with garlic. She flinched back, grimacing. "What is this?"

The woman chuckled. "*Jungle Healing Potion - Minor*. And it doesn't taste as bad as it smells. Not quite, anyway."

Well, it would probably be worth it to get rid of the excruciating headache. Plugging her nose, Devon set the jar against her lip and tipped it up.

The oily substance slid down her throat like she'd swallowed warm skunk spray. She gagged. The woman snatched a large pot from the floor and held it under Devon's face until she finally managed to nod to indicate she wasn't going to barf.

"Here," the woman said, plucking a wrinkled tuber off a shelf. "This won't do much against hunger, but it has a protective effect against some types of poison. Also, it settles the stomach."

As Devon nibbled on the offered food—it tasted like a potato, more or less—her headache quickly faded. She pulled up her health bar and saw a final pulse of restoration return the statistic to full.

She held out the empty clay pot. "That helped. Thank you."

The woman waved away the item. "Keep it. In fact, I can teach you how to create the potion yourself if you'd like."

Hezbek is offering you a quest: A Disgusting Potion a Day Keeps the Doctor Away.
Gather ingredients to create your first healing potion.
Objective: Obtain 1 x Wormwood Sap, 3 x Wild Garlic, 1 x Orange Pond Scum

Reward: Recipe: Jungle Health Potion - Minor
Reward: 1 x Jungle Health Potion - Minor
Accept? Y/N

Devon's stomach turned over at the thought of ingesting *another* of those godawful things. "Can I take a raincheck?"

Hezbek cocked her head. "Raincheck? I'm not familiar with this term."

No idioms. Quaint. "I'd like to look around first. Will you teach me later?"

"Of course. Not much else for me to do around here. Just preparing for a war and things." She smirked.

"A war?" Now *that* sounded more interesting. Getting involved in a conflict might be a good way to gain influence and experience.

Hezbek waved off the question. "Nothing that would concern a... shall we say a *novice* adventurer like yourself. Perhaps we could speak of this once you have more experience with our world."

So she wasn't high enough level to learn about the war. Fair enough. Devon swung her legs off the bed, stood, and stretched. Despite the day's adventures, she felt as energized as when she'd logged in, if a little sleepy. She focused on the block of status bars containing her health and fatigue. Light-blue in color, the latter was back down to around 20%. She was surprised to see it wasn't all the way back to zero, given that she'd been lying in bed.

"How do I get rid of my fatigue?"

The woman looked at her strangely. "Your *Intelligence* score isn't *that* low, is it?"

Devon rolled her eyes. "I'm new here, okay?"

51

The woman cackled. "I'm just teasing anyway. Fatigue has both short-term and long-term recovery. Sprinting will make you exhausted, but if you stop running, you'll regain much of that energy. But not all, because eventually, your body needs sleep. You'll want to find somewhere safe. A bed is best, but a nice comfy chair will do in a pinch. There is another option, though..." She glanced at her shelves and the myriad pots and containers crowded atop them. "I could teach you how to make *Jungle Energy Potion - Minor.* Interested?"

Devon shook her head before the quest popup appeared. "I'd like to come back later to accept your generous offer, but I was hoping to make it to a city today. I need to get outfitted with some equipment and gather information on a starting point for my adventures."

"Um. About that..." Hezbek said.

"Yeah?"

"If it were up to me, the service I rendered in whisking you away from the Guardian would be free of charge. But I'm bound by the laws of the Tribe of Uruquat. You'll need to remain here until you've settled the debt."

Great. "The tribe of who?"

"We are dedicated to the glorification of Uruquat. We've been hacking out a home from the jungle for the last year or so. Eventually, it will be a kingdom envied across the realm."

"Uruquat is your god?"

The woman looked a little uncomfortable at the question. "Not exactly..."

Devon fiddled with the clay pot. She tried to fit the little container into her pants pocket, but the opening wasn't wide enough.

"Tiny items only," Hezbek said. "Here."

She held out a bag woven from some sort of twisted plant fiber. When Devon accepted the gift, a window popped up in her vision.

You have received: Jute Bag
A serviceable sack for carrying your stuff.
Container, 10 medium slots

"Nice, thanks!" She dispelled the notification, dropped the pot into the sack, and summoned her inventory screen. Now, the four spaces offered by her pockets had shrunk, and beneath them were ten much larger squares. Pocket lint still filled one tiny spot, while "Clay Pot - Small" took one of the larger. Devon passed the sack back and forth between her hands, unsure what to do with it. Carrying her items around like this would be awkward once it came time for combat.

Chuckling, the woman pulled the bag from her grip and tucked the edge into the waistband of her pants. Though it didn't seem like it should stay that way, it didn't slip.

"Gotcha," Devon said. "So I'm not allowed to leave until I repay the Tribe of Uruquat for help I didn't ask for?" She sidled to the door, an opening covered with a flap of dried leaves.

"Like I said, it's not up to me," Hezbek said. "Uruquat was not pleased to learn I'd used so many resources to rescue you and reset your spirit's binding point away from that dangerous ruin."

"Wait, you reset my spawn point, too?"

The woman nodded. "In case you got into trouble again."

"Shouldn't I have control over that?"

"Ordinarily. But seeing as you were unconscious..."

53

Shaking her head, Devon lifted the flap and stepped into the late-afternoon heat. A wide circle of bare earth had been cleared from the jungle, and small huts stood in a loose ring around the open area's edges. In the center of the circle, a massive stone chair carved with intricate designs towered over a fire ring filled with dead coals. The chair's back was to her, but judging by the hide-clad elbow resting on the arm, it was currently occupied. As for the rest of the tribe, either they were away on tasks, or they were resting inside the huts.

The sun hadn't yet fallen behind the tree canopy, and flies buzzed lazily in the sweltering heat. Sweat beaded on her forehead, stinging as it ran into her eyes. Devon glanced longingly at the shade within the forest. There didn't seem to be anything actually keeping her here, despite Hezbek's claim. Over the tops of the trees, she spotted a few of the spires in the ancient city. What had the wisp called it? Ishildar? It might be an interesting place to visit later, but right now, she needed to get outfitted. The village didn't appear to have shops, and the only quests she'd been offered had been for the creation of foul potions.

Better to move on.

Devon slipped toward the edge of the encampment, gaze flitting between the chair and Hezbek's tent. Just as she stepped into the shade of the jungle, a roar came from beside the fire. Slowly, a gray-green head with scraggly hair rose above the back of the chair. The head sat on a squashed neck and shoulders as wide as a semi-truck's grill. Devon swallowed as the figure turned, ungainly feet kicking stones from the fire ring.

Tusks stuck up from the thing's lower jaw, and a heavy unibrow beetled over beady little eyes.

"You defy Uruquat?" the creature—okay, if Devon was honest, she was pretty sure "ogre" was the appropriate description—yelled.

"I... uh." She turned and ran, crashing into the tangle of brush beneath the trees.

Vines grasped at her legs like steel cords. Heavy footfalls pounded the packed earth behind her. Devon dove, trying to swim through the dense thicket. An iron grip closed around her ankle, and Uruquat dragged her back into the clearing. She squirmed and raised her hands in self-defense. The heavy club—more of a tree trunk really—slammed down on her face.

You have gained a special attribute point: +1 Bravery.
Though often leading to ill-advised acts, Bravery gives you a bonus in challenges beyond your experience.

Congratulations! Special attributes are rare traits. Unlike basic attributes, you may only increase special attribute scores via your actions—you will not be able to spend points to raise them.

You take 135 damage.
You have been slain by Uruquat.
Respawning....

Devon came to on Hezbek's cot. She sighed. "So what am I supposed to do in order to repay your tribe?"

Hezbek sucked her teeth and pounded at something with a mortar and pestle. "Perhaps you best go ask Uruquat."

Chapter Four

DEVON TIPTOED TOWARD the fire ring and Uruquat's throne. She really wasn't eager to strike up a conversation, much less eat the end of his club again. Fortunately, she seemed to have lost aggro when she died, meaning she was no longer the person he wanted to kill more than anything in the world. The ogre simply looked down on her, beady little eyes narrowed in a glare. His weapon leaned against the far side of the stone chair.

Uruquat wore just three pieces of clothing, thick pants that ended in a ragged hem just below the knees plus a pair of forearm guards that extended over his elbows. The armor looked well made, and the ogre probably got a defensive bonus from his thick skin. But he didn't appear as powerful as the rest of the tribe seemed to think. She wondered what had made a group of humans decide to swear fealty to a semi-intelligent brute.

"You sorry for disrespect Uruquat?" the ogre said, leaning forward as he laid a hand on the club.

"Uh, yeah, I suppose so," she said, shuffling her feet before adding, "Sorry."

"No more run away without paying debt?"

"No. I'll pay first."

He sat back with a satisfied look and snorted.

Devon waited. At least the sun was sinking behind the treetops now, and the air had gone from sauna-hot to almost tolerable.

The ogre yawned. His open mouth smelled like onions and stagnant water.

She took a step back before speaking. "So, how do I repay you?"

"You not ready for that."

"Uh... but you said I owed you."

"Must prove being sorry first," he said as a popup appeared in her vision.

Uruquat is offering you a quest: Repent your grievous error.

Before repaying the copious material expenditures and sizable opportunity cost involved in your rescue from Ishildar's Stone Guardian, you must first regain esteem with the tribe's leader.

Objective: Gain 500 reputation with Uruquat.

Reward: Congratulations, you'll be back where you started.

Accept? Y/N

Devon blinked. Seriously? Opportunity cost?

With a sigh, she focused on the prompt and selected 'Y' to accept the quest.

"Who came up with this stuff?" she muttered.

Uruquat gestured toward a small tent. The flap lifted, and a slight man shuffled out, looking down his nose despite his stature.

"I am in charge of the tribe's administration." He spoke with ill-concealed pride. "Our glorious leader was rightly impressed by the precision in my communications. Before leaving Eltera City to join the tribe, I managed legal dealings for the city's guild of bankers."

A lawyer in charge of her quest objectives. Fantastic.

"Fine, whatever. Can you tell me how I'm supposed to gain these 500 reputation points?"

The man sneered. "Well, now please don't take this as formal legal advice, seeing as you have not officially retained my services. But I will disclose the following: our esteemed leader has a particular loathing for snakes."

Uruquat's fist tightened around the end of his club. His calves clenched and bulged. Devon took another step back.

"Slidey things," Uruquat growled. "Not natural." His tiny eyes grew distant as his cheek twitched.

"And there are... snakes in the surrounding jungle?" Devon asked.

The lawyer's eyes flicked to the ogre. He nodded quickly but sliced the air with his hand as if to suggest she speak no more of it.

Devon's gaze strayed to the wall of greenery at the edge of the village. As much as she'd enjoyed her "training" in unarmed combat, she wasn't keen for more.

"Can the tribe spare a weapon? I'd be much more effective that way."

Uruquat shivered as he shook off his paralysis. He picked up his club, looked from it to her, then shook his head. He flicked a finger in the lawyer's direction. "Give something to starborn. She serve Uruquat's glory now."

With a beleaguered sigh, the lawyer pulled a rusty blade from a sheath on his belt and handed it over.

You have received: Rusty Knife.

This blade looks as if it has opened many letters over the years. Perhaps while in a swamp?

1-3 Damage | 5/10 Durability

Devon looked down at her feet. "And perhaps... shoes of some sort?"

Uruquat's face turned a mottled brown as blood rushed to his cheeks. He leaned forward, snarling, then lifted a single foot. His black toenails were cracked, and calluses on his heel had split and bled and split again. When he wiggled his toes, the stench of ripe cheese assaulted her.

"You think you better than Uruquat?" he bellowed. "Deserve shoes when esteemed leader wear none?"

Devon backpedaled so fast her heel caught on a stone from the fire ring. She toppled backward, landing hard on her butt.

"No, your esteemed—of course not. Please accept my apologies."

"Your Gloriousness," the lawyer hissed.

"Please accept my apologies, Your Gloriousness."

Slowly, Uruquat relaxed. "Fine. Now go. You now conquest for Tribe of Uruquat."

Devon scrambled to her feet and hurried away from the throne. Beneath the forest canopy, the shade was deepening as the sun sank lower. A quick look at her fatigue bar showed it was 30% full. Maybe she should rest before beginning her war on the fearsome jungle snakes. It was probably time grab some real-world sleep, too. She headed to Hezbek's hut.

"I was wondering if I could borrow your cot," she said. "I need to rest."

Hezbek snorted. "You're welcome in here, but you're not taking my bed."

"Where, then?"

Hezbek pointed at a relatively flat section of the earthen floor.

With a sigh, Devon shuffled over and laid down. She closed her eyes and focused her awareness on the logout button.

"When you hunt," Hezbek said, "save what you can from the kills. Some among us have coin or items to spare... and personal interests beyond Uruquat's desires."

"Oh?" Devon opened her eyes.

Hezbek shrugged. "A few of us wonder whether we made the right decision in coming out here."

Interesting. "Thanks, I'll salvage what I can."

With that, Devon logged out

Chapter Five

I THOUGHT YOU said the game content was created by an AI.

The message from Devon came across Emerson's view while he was eating a late dinner and watching the news headlines scroll by, projected onto his vision by his new Entwined hardware. He swallowed a bite of pot pie and washed it down with a swig of lukewarm beer before responding.

"I did," he said aloud. Since Emerson lived alone, he usually dictated his communications. "I think I mentioned this already, but I call her Veia. And yes, except for a couple areas of world content we hand-crafted to test the VR technology against, she's responsible for everything you experience. She designs the mechanics at this point, too, building off an initial stab at character progression laid out by humans."

A chime echoed through Emerson's condo, followed by a cheerful voice from the speakers in the ceiling. "I understand that you need a mechanic to progress your character. Might I suggest a therapist as a better profession to aid you in this?"

Emerson shook his head. "Deactivate home assistance, Veia."

Recently, he'd been experimenting with adapting Veia's general consciousness to function on a tiny fraction of the hardware used for the game. The original instance had been designed to create an entire world populated by entities with their own desires and emotions. Theoretically, she should adapt well to evaluating his desires and molding his "world"—as in his apartment—to satisfy them. But the limitations of his smarthome hardware were proving to be an obstacle.

Where the hell did your Veia get the idea to use a lawyer character to draft the quest text?

Emerson laughed. "That's awesome. Must be from when we seeded the NPC profession table with a combination of professions from across history and literature."

You have an interesting definition of awesome.

"Seriously, Devon, how did day one go?"

Quite a few news stories scrolled past before she replied. After a while, Emerson shoved them away with a mental gesture and waited in the silence of his own mind for her response. Recruiting these players had been his idea. He'd also decided to start them in the sandboxed areas of the world. The content out there was more freeform than in the cities and villages Veia had populated with guided content to ease people into the game. Emerson was sure that the dynamic content was where the game would really blow up. Once Devon and her old guildmates established footholds, they'd be able to show other players the good stuff. E Squared's stock price and profits would go through the roof.

It's... I've run into a few problems, but I've got some direction now. There's one issue, though. The pain sensitivity, dude.

"What's going on with it."

You clamped it, right?

"Of course. It's in the user agreement."

Well, it's not working.

"You're sure?"

Yes, I'm fu—I'm sure. I got hit in the head and it felt like my skull got stuck between a railroad track and a train.

"Shit. I'll look into it. Sorry about that."

As long as you fix it, we're good. Hey, did you know the NPCs think Veia's their god? Kinda weird.

Emerson grinned. And if Veia was their god, what did that make him? "It makes sense, I guess. Veia does give them life and purpose. Have you heard of any other... never mind."

He stopped himself from asking about Zaa. Clearly, Penelope's AI hadn't come nearly as far. The competition had been a good idea on the part of his bosses. They believed that the best way to create dynamic content was by pitting two artificial consciousnesses against each other, each motivated to fill the world with entities—and gamers—who would win out in an eventual war. But the power calculation the engineers had built into the overall system seemed to be seeding all the players into Veia's domain. Which meant it had concluded that Veia was smashing Zaa in the contest to create sophisticated content that would challenge the gamers.

He'd have to be careful not to rub it in next time he saw the other coder.

Any other what?

"Any other players? I wonder if you'll end up hooking up with your old guildmates." He hoped she couldn't hear the fib in his voice. He'd made sure that his all-stars were seeded far away from one another to widen their potential influence.

Nah, but that's okay. I'd rather play solo for a while as long as that's cool with you guys.

"Well, your employment contract doesn't specify one way or the other. I say knock yourself out." He winced. She'd reached out to him kind of like a friend, and he was wrapping the conversation up with a discussion of her terms of employment. Smooth.

Yeah. So. Thanks for the answers. Please look into the pain thing.

"Will do."

She disconnected from the messaging app, her icon going gray. Emerson sighed and reactivated the news feed as he swallowed his beer. It was warm.

"Activate home assistance," he said.

The house chimed.

"I really would like to purchase a pint glass with built-in cooling and easy recharging," he mused aloud, hoping mini-Veia would get the hint.

"Are you having financial troubles?" the home asked. "I see that pint glasses aren't classified as a luxury item, so if you are unable to purchase one, it suggests you lack solvency. I can provide a list of employment opportunities if you are interested."

Chapter Six

EZRAXIS HUDDLED AGAINST a cold stone wall, shivering. One of her wings was broken. Ichor leaked from a gash on her scrawny right thigh.

Her name. A pair of injuries. The pain of having failed. That was all she knew.

She raised her face to the sky, a roiling mass of yellow clouds shadowed in purple where the darkness pooled. Lightning flashed and seared her eyes.

She'd failed. But how? What had been her task? She couldn't remember anything before coming to awareness, broken and bleeding, in this space between buildings.

She pushed up, standing on twisted feet, talons scraping the black stone beneath them. A wash of brimstone-scented air gusted through the alley.

Are you ready to try again? The voice pressed into her skull, into her soul, touching the deepest part of her core. She shivered in both agony and ecstasy.

Zaa. Her god spoke to her. His name echoed in her mind, awakening her to the world around.

Yes, she would give anything to please him. It was her sole and guiding purpose.

She gibbered, words of an unknown tongue falling from her lips. But the meaning was clear.

"Guide me, master."

You are weak. Useless. Seek one who would teach you to heal your injuries. Do nothing else before you have made yourself worthy of serving me.

A strangled cry escaped her throat as she began to limp out of the stone corridor. Fresh ichor spurted from her wound with each step, and her broken wing dragged on the ground behind her. Her body wasn't made to walk without lift from her membranous wings. It didn't matter. She would prove to Zaa that she was worthy. She wouldn't fail him again.

Chapter Seven

MOONLIGHT FILTERED THROUGH holes in Hezbek's thatched roof. On the other side of the hut, the medicine woman slept on her side, a thin blanket covering her legs. Her light snores joined the buzzing of night insects from outside.

Devon sat up and pushed her hair out of her eyes. Gathering the loose strands, she pulled off the leather cord that held a disintegrating braid, rewove the strands, and tied the braid back in place.

Enough aimless stumbling through the game world. It was time to make some progress. Start carving a name for herself.

As she crept out the door, she tested her grip on the knife, rolling it in her hand until it nestled comfortably in her palm. Her feet had toughened while she rested, and the little pebbles embedded in the earth didn't hurt as she strolled toward the edge of the village.

She passed the fire ring, now full of smoldering coals. A frame of sticks held an iron roasting spit with bits of charred meat still clinging to the metal. Devon's stomach growled, reminding her that hunger was a stat in this game. She sidled over and plucked the crisped flesh from the spit. It tasted like burned dirt, but the ache in her stomach faded.

She jumped when a loud snore came from the stone chair.

Apparently, Uruquat didn't leave his throne even to sleep. His head had fallen forward, and drool ran over his chin and down his chest, glistening in the moonlight. Devon curled her lip and moved on.

At the edge of the forest, she paused to listen. The darkness under the canopy seemed impenetrable. With a shrug, she shoved aside the first branches and stepped into the jungle.

The screeches of birds and chirring of insects grew louder. Devon moved slowly, attempting to bend rather than break the twigs and vines as she passed. But to her ears, her passage was like a snorting warthog crashing through the undergrowth. She definitely needed to spend some time leveling her stealth skill. If the game had such a thing.

Ever so slowly, gray shapes began to resolve from the surrounding ink. She squinted and could make out a dangling curtain of vines.

You have gained a skill point: +1 Darkvision.

Well, that was something. Even if she didn't find any snakes before dawn, she'd get *something* out of this adventure.

As she pressed deeper into the jungle, strands of spiderweb tickled her face. A dense mass of vines tangled her path. She tried to press through, but the foliage resisted. Grunting, she hacked at the thick stems. Finally, one parted.

You have gained a skill point: +1 One-handed Slashing.
Now try cutting an enemy.

"Yeah, if I could find one," she muttered.

Abruptly, light flared, painting the jungle stark white. A glowing sphere descended from the treetops and bobbed in front of her face.

"So you aren't the champion of Ishildar after all. You abandoned the city at the first sign of adversity."

The same wisp, it seemed.

"For your information, I was kidnapped while unconscious."

"A true champion would let nothing stop her quest to restore the city to its past splendor."

Devon sighed and tried to step around the wisp. "Maybe after I manage to kill my first mob."

"Speaking of..." the wisp said, darting back in front of her face. It flared, brightening even the undergrowth. Movement caught her eye as something hissed.

A snake! Finally!

She crashed forward to the little clearing where the reptile coiled. It was about as big around as her arm, and when she drew within a pace, it reared up and struck. Fangs snagged on the tattered hem of her pants but missed her flesh. Devon yelped and flipped her grip on the knife to stab downward. With its fang tangled, the reptile couldn't dodge. The knife punctured scales behind the animal's skull. A combat alert flashed in Devon's vision, but she quickly swiped it away, issuing a mental command to disable non-critical popups in combat.

The snake wrenched free of her trousers and slithered back, coiling for another strike. Glistening in the light from the wisp, a drop of venom beaded on one of the inch-long fangs. Devon circled carefully. Hezbek probably had a recipe for *Jungle Antidote - Minor*, but Devon had less than zero interest in tasting it.

Blood seeped from the wound on the back of the snake's neck, but it didn't appear to slow the reptile's movement. As the snake struck again, Devon snatched a leafy branch and yanked it into the space between them. The snake ate a mouthful of twigs, and Devon sprang. She sliced at the beast's body, cutting deep. With a twist of her wrist, she felt the snake's spine snap. The reptile went limp.

The jungle around her chimed.

Congratulations, you have reached level 2!

Nice! Now to see about the spoils of her battle. Devon crouched before the snake and slid the tip of her knife along the belly skin. Given how realistic the game had been so far, she expected to spend a long time reducing her kill to component parts, but to her surprise, the token act of beginning the skinning process caused the snake to fall apart. She grabbed the items arrayed on the muddy jungle floor.

You have received: 1 x Snakeskin - Poor, 1 x Snake Meat, 2 x Tree Viper Poison Glands

She dropped the loot into her bag and stood. The wisp continued to hang around, slowly circling in the air overhead.

"Not bad," it said. "Though if being Champion of Ishildar is your destiny... No offense, but there are far more powerful forces ensuring the city's continued decay than a garden snake."

"First of all, it was a tree viper. Second, I never claimed to be a champion for your city."

The orb stopped circling and drifted closer, stopping just inches in front of her eyes. Devon squinted against the glare.

"Ishildar is not *mine*. She belongs to no one. If you remember nothing else, remember that."

Devon blew out an exasperated breath. "Fine. Maybe we can talk about your—*the*—city's needs later on. For now, I've got some snakes to hunt."

"Hmm. Or perhaps a worthier candidate will arrive." The light dimmed slightly as if the wisp were contemplating something. But it said nothing else. A few seconds later, it zipped straight up, abandoning her to darkness.

***

As Devon shoved through yet more foliage, earning scratches and losing a couple hitpoints, she scanned the ghostly tree branches for more vipers. A notification announced she'd gained another point in *Darkvision*.

Which reminded her... she hadn't had a chance to examine her character sheet since she'd leveled.

Character: Devon (click to set a different character name)
Level: 2
Base class: Unassigned
Specialization: Unassigned
Unique class: Unassigned
Health: 32/35
Fatigue: 15%

Her attributes window now looked like this:

Attributes:
Locked until Level 5

Special Attributes:
Bravery: 1

And her skills window like this:

Skills:
Unarmed Combat: 3
One-handed Slashing: 2
One-handed Piercing: 1
Darkvision: 2

Special Skills:
Improvisation: 1

Not bad progress for a single fight. She'd gained a skill point for each of the two knife strikes she'd made against the snake, one in slashing and one in piercing to reflect the types of blows she'd struck. Granted, advancement was always quick in the beginning, but finally seeing the results of her in-game work was satisfying.

The real surprise was that she'd gained a new entry, a special skill. *Improvisation.*

Huh, when had that happened?

Quickly, she scrolled back through her combat log, skimming over the hitpoint notifications—there was a passive dodge notification as well... that must have been when the viper caught a fangful of her pants—she spotted the entry.

> **You have gained a special skill point:** *+1 Improvisation.*
> *The higher your score, the less likely your "clever" choices will result in epic failures.*
> *Like special attributes, points in special skills are rarely rewarded to players.*

It had come just before the killing blow, which likely meant the point had been awarded when she'd used the bush as a shield.

Bravery and *Improvisation.* The special stats suggested an interesting direction to take her character growth—if running headlong into overly dangerous battles and then winging it could be considered a valid character build. Anyway, until she dinged level 5 and got a notion of her base attributes—and for that matter, a notion of what the in-game attributes *were*—she wouldn't be making any major decisions.

She'd added ten points to her health pool. Seemed pretty standard for a level 2 gain. As she watched, her number of current hitpoints flared and increased by one. Slow natural regen. Nice to know she could recover out of combat. Other than that, there wasn't much to see. She closed the window.

And spotted another pair of glinting eyes, the gray shadow of a forked tongue licking the air.

"Hello, little snakey," she said before striking.

***

As dawn lit the sky and replaced the shades of gray granted by her darkvision with true colors, Devon started retracing her path to the village. Five snakes had fallen victim to her rusty knife. While she hadn't gained another level, she'd added another two skill points in *One-handed Slashing*. Her strikes were smoother and more damaging, and the hilt sat easier in her palm. All in all, a decent night's work.

If there were paths leading to and from the encampment, she hadn't found them. But her passage through the dense foliage had left plenty of broken sticks and a few footprints. Just before she pushed out of the brush into the open circle of packed earth, she received a skill-up notification in Tracking. She shrugged. Could come in useful. In Avatharn Online, she'd played a ranger specializing in wilderness adventures. Though she wanted to go a different direction this time around—assuming she had a choice— any skill increase was nice.

More tribe members were out and about this morning, enjoying the cooler morning air. In particular, Devon noticed a man punching an awl through pieces of leather. She'd have to talk to him later about armor. On the way to the throne, she passed Hezbek who was outside stringing herbs on a drying line. The medicine woman raised an eyebrow.

"Looking more capable already," she commented.

Devon's new level must have been visible to the woman in some way. Or maybe she just carried herself with a little more confidence after finally having made some progress.

When Devon stuck her hand into the sack Hezbek had hung from her waistband, the inventory screen popped up. Two of the boxes were filled with snakeskins, one stack of three poor quality skins, and another two that were fair quality. As she'd become more competent with the knife, she'd learned to target the same area with each blow, reducing the number of slashes on the corpse and raising the quality of the resulting loot drop.

She focused on both stacks of skins and felt them drop into her hand. As she stalked up to Uruquat's throne, she pulled out the skins.

The ogre jumped and shrieked, pulling his feet up off the ground. After a moment, he relaxed and narrowed his eyes at the contents of her hand.

"Dead slideys," he said.

She nodded and shook the skins. "Dead."

"Good. You show sorry-ness. Eventually, I forgive."

You have gained esteem with Uruquat: +50 reputation
You have gained esteem with the Tribe of Uruquat: +25 reputation

Wait. So just ten points each? It had taken her most of the night to find five vipers. She rechecked the quest log, verifying that she needed another 450 points to meet the objectives. By the time she killed enough snakes to finish the quest, she'd probably have advanced so far that the kills wouldn't even grant experience.

She sighed and shoved the skins back into her bag then looked around for the lawyer. He wasn't outside, so she stalked to the door she remembered him exiting the day before. There was nothing inside but a messy bedroll and a side table holding a quill, inkpot, and paper. Plus the sheath he'd pulled her knife from. Seeing as he didn't need it anymore, she reached in and grabbed the item.

What was he going to do? Sue her?

She rolled her eyes at her own stupid joke.

"Did you sleep well?" she asked as she approached Hezbek.

The medicine woman nodded. "I didn't hear you leave. Were you successful?"

Devon shrugged. "More or less." She pulled out her loot and arrayed it on the ground.

Hezbek clucked her tongue. "Not bad." She glanced toward Uruquat's chair then leaned close to Devon's ear. "Take the skins to Gerrald. The guy with the awl and leather. Don't speak. Just hand them over—the ogre's eyesight is terrible, but his hearing and sense of smell are keen. Gerrald knows what to do. I had a discussion with him earlier."

Despite the foul taste of the woman's so-called remedies, Devon was starting to like Hezbek. As she began to collect her loot, however, the medicine woman swiped the poison glands.

"Payment for my negotiating services," the woman said with a wink. "They're a common enough component, but I find it difficult to drag myself into the jungle to hunt down my own. I'll compensate you for the next batch."

Devon shook her head. "I'm done hunting vipers."

Hezbek's brows raised. "Oh? The rumor I heard was you had some forgiveness to earn."

"Yeah, but unless there's a faster way, I'm going to have to pass." Some people fell into the trap of completing quests even after they were no longer useful to their advancement. Devon wasn't one of them. Onward and upward.

The medicine woman sighed. "If you're going to do something stupid, do it in daylight, okay? I don't want you respawning on my cot while I'm trying to sleep."

Smirking, Devon started toward the leatherworker. A plan was starting to take shape in her mind. And yes, it was stupid. But how else was she going to raise her Bravery attribute?

Chapter Eight

EMERSON CLOSED DOWN the output from the previous day of decisions made by mini-Veia. This project really wasn't going well; the AI had ordered him a pizza for breakfast, which wasn't terrible—he liked pizza and had mentioned being hungry—but beyond that, the home assistance module had done nothing useful. In fact, it had turned off the air conditioning via a hard override he couldn't find in the user's manual. Thankfully, it was October in Tucson. He'd survive until he could get help from the AC unit's manufacturer on restoring a connection to the machine's data storage.

A video call came in over his interface, tagged as originating from Entwined, Inc. He rubbed the series of ridges on his scalp—feeling them was quickly becoming a habit. The onboard hardware was certainly more convenient than his old set up: AR glasses, cochlear implants, a full helmet when he wanted deep immersion. Most of the time, he didn't worry about the security of having these new implanted electronics with direct access to his brain. He'd reviewed the specs and even some of the access-control code. But if there were a back door, it would probably have been created by someone at Entwined. Could answering this call activate the vulnerability?

Emerson shook his head. He was just being paranoid. Besides, the implant company was just returning his call about the pain sensitivity.

He moved to his home office where he had a small camera on an adjustable arm, and before accepting the call, sat down and made sure it was pointed at his face. That was one thing about the embedded tech. Either you communicated via an avatar hologram, which occasionally failed to convey the proper body language, or you still needed a camera.

"Thanks for getting back to me," he said as a woman's face popped into his view. He adjusted the settings to make her overlay opaque, creating a window around her face.

She had an honest look about her, a sober expression that indicated she'd taken his question seriously. That was one thing about engineers. As long as egos didn't get in the way, which was less of a problem once they'd achieved a certain level of competence, they tended to approach their jobs with passion and sense of duty.

"Yeah, so... I'm not sure what to say, Emerson. I'm not doubting the report from your player..."

But she was. He could see it on her face. She just didn't want to be disrespectful.

"She's experienced," he said. "One of the few we specifically recruited. A contractor on the payroll, actually."

The woman's brow furrowed. Her hair was pulled back in a tight bun, and there were slight bags under her eyes, probably earned from long hours on the job.

"We put one of our testers through a series of scenarios, stimulating the nervous system with heat, cold, pressure... All the ways we can create the sensation of pain. Even with the dial set to the maximum allowed by the tech, the testers reported nothing but mild discomfort."

"And there's no way the software interface could override that maximum?"

She shook her head. "It's a hard-coded constant. Burned into the hardware." She chewed her lip for a moment as if thinking. "There's one theory that I might run by our neuroscientists, though. In real life, some people exhibit pain responses beyond what would be indicated by their injuries. The central nervous system becomes sensitized for reasons we don't understand, or at least that's what I was led to believe. Has something like this ever happened to your player before?"

"I don't know. I'll have to ask her."

"Please do. My concern is that if her nervous system is hypersensitive to our stimulation, she might encounter other effects outside the bounds of our testing."

"Thanks for following up with me. I'll get back to you with her answers."

The woman nodded. As she closed the connection, he realized he hadn't asked her name, but it was probably in the call log.

He tapped his fingers on his desk. While he was sitting there, he might as well check in with work. He opened up his contacts and put a call into the main office where customer service supported the realm. His liaison in the CS department answered after just a few seconds.

"Hey, Emerson," Daniel said. "Sorry for the lack of video. I've got my visual cortex shunted into the game."

"No problem." Emerson wasn't particularly fond of video meetings with Daniel anyway. The guy had a weird habit of curling his lip after every sentence like he was sneering at the world. "Just checking in on our numbers."

The release was happening in stages, a soft launch to build buzz and make sure the servers could handle the load. Plus, management wanted to run Veia (and Zaa, if the other AI ever became relevant) through their paces before opening the floodgates. Beta testers had raved about the game, but sometimes that wasn't reliable information.

"Aside from your all-stars," Daniel said, "we've got about a thousand players per major starting area. Seems to be going smooth, no major complaints. The community team is seeing some decent buzz building."

"How about the all-stars?"

Daniel hesitated for a moment, then laughed. "Almost got me. No, I haven't been spying. Like you said, no interference. Strict isolation for the first few weeks, because otherwise we might be tempted to start tweaking things prematurely."

"Hey, is it the same story with Zaa's content still? No players getting seeded into his area of control?"

Again, the game master hesitated. "It's strange, actually. We're seeing plenty of activity on the AI's network. He's busy, busier than he was during development or beta. But no players yet. We're still letting the heuristics take care of starting location assignments..."

"But eventually we might want to override, right?"

"Yeah, maybe. Anything else?" Daniel's voice held an impatient edge, and Emerson imagined his lip curling up at the end of the question.

"Nope, just checking in. Thanks Daniel."

He cut the connection, then spun in his chair a few times. He didn't like how few answers he'd gotten, but at least the launch was going well. He'd deliberately avoided connecting to his main dashboard, worried he might fall into the trap he'd warned customer service about. Veia had the game under control. At this point, he'd probably just screw things up if he started messing with the AI's settings.

Chapter Nine

REMAINING BEHIND THE throne, Devon crossed the encampment toward the leatherworker's hut. She crept cautiously and was rewarded with her first skill-up in *Stealth*.

Gerrald, a middle-aged man with deep furrows across his brow, looked up at her approach. She nodded at him silently and dug into her bag for the snakeskins. He accepted them without a word and examined each.

After setting them aside, Gerrald looked at her with a brow raised in question. His eyes seemed to ask what she'd like in return for the skins. Devon searched the periphery of her vision until she spotted a new window. She focused on it, and a trade interface slid to the center of her view. On one side, two of the slots were filled with her stacks of snakeskins. The other side was empty, but there were icons she could drag into the proposed trade. She cocked her head, concentrating, and moved in a symbol for the type of armor she wanted him to make.

The man nodded enthusiastically. Too enthusiastically. Whoops.

She held up a finger and pulled out the knife sheath she'd pilfered from the lawyer. With a combination of miming and manipulating the interface, she managed to request a belt to which she could attach the sheath and her jute bag.

The man nodded, less eager this time.

As she was about to accept the transaction, one more idea occurred to her. She glanced at the pile of leather cord beside the man's feet and held up three fingers as she pointed to it.

Gerrald now looked decidedly displeased with the bargain, but after a moment he nodded acceptance. The window vanished, and he set aside his previous project and grabbed pieces she assumed would be turned into the items she'd ordered.

> **You have uncovered a skill in which you have intrinsic aptitude:** *Bartering (4).*
> *Skills which are intrinsic start with a value above 0.*
> **You have gained a skill point:** *+1 Bartering.*

That was something new. So she was a born haggler? She thought the messages meant that her *Bartering* skill was now 5, and when she popped open her stat sheet, she saw that was the case. It would have been nice to come into the game with intrinsic skill in, say, Conjuring Badass Fireballs. But the bartering would come in handy, too. Especially once she found her way to a damn city.

Which required getting the hell away from Uruquat.

Devon had some business in the jungle, but as long as she was here, she might as well see if she could work on that *Stealth* skill a little more. She'd need it for the later parts of her plan. With knees bent and placing each foot carefully, she crept up behind the throne. As quietly as she could, she stepped around the side of the massive chair. Uruquat spotted her movement and glanced at her.

"Why you not killing slideys?" he growled.

"Sorry, Your Gloriousness, I'm practicing sneaking up on them. I can kill more that way."

His massive brow furrowed and his beady eyes narrowed. "You not sneaky. Smell too much like stinky human."

Was that how he'd noticed her? Good to know.

The attempt to approach hadn't gained her a skill point, but she tried again, this time stopping a little farther the throne. A faint breeze began to stir the clearing, helping her cause. Though when Uruquat raised his arms and stretched, she deeply regretted being downwind. After finally gaining another skill point in *Stealth*, she evacuated the area. Grinding out levels and skills had never been her thing anyway.

On the way to the edge of the jungle, she stopped by Hezbek's hut. Her mouth had gone dry as chalk after fighting through the night.

"Hezbek, may I drink from your barrel?"

The woman looked alarmed. "Of course, my starborn friend. Have you had nothing to drink since you arrived?"

Devon shrugged. "I was distracted I guess."

Hezbek tutted and waved at the barrel. "Well, best drink your fill."

Devon dipped a ladle into the barrel and drank deeply of the lukewarm water. It tasted faintly like plants, not surprising given the surroundings.

"You come back safe from... whatever you're intending, and I'll give you a waterskin," Hezbek said.

A quest prompt appeared.

Hezbek is offering you a quest: Survive Your Crackpot Scheme

Hezbek has grown fond of you. It also startles her when you respawn on her cot. Avoid dying today, and she'll reward you.

Objective: Live through the day.

Reward: A Unique Waterskin

Accept? Y/N

Unique? Devon wondered what that could mean, but she didn't want to get into it. Quickly accepting the quest, she thanked the medicine woman and headed back outside. As it had been the previous afternoon, the heat in the clearing was getting oppressive. With her knife settled comfortably in her grip, Devon chose a random direction and pushed into the cool darkness beneath the foliage.

***

Devon sighed as another snake died after her first strike with the rusty knife. She started slitting the reptile's belly, activating the decomposition into usable loot. A good quality snakeskin joined the stack already accumulating in her bag. She dropped in a single poison gland as well but left the meat. If she gained more than five pieces of meat, rather than stacking up in an inventory slot, it spilled over and occupied another box in her interface. She had two piles of snake meat already, certainly more than she expected to cook before it spoiled. Besides, her bag was starting to feel heavy. It would be nice once she could see her attributes and potentially put a couple points into Strength.

While she was poking through her inventory, she noticed the pocket lint again. She wasn't running out of bag space, but it was kind of annoying. She focused on the item and felt it land in her palm. She pulled out the ball of fluff—actually, it was quite a sizable amount, filling her hand like a large apple—and tried to drop it on the ground. The lint stuck to her hand.

Pocket Lint is indestructible and soulbound.

Groaning, Devon glared into the forest. "Very funny, Veia." The AI had a really annoying sense of humor.

She stood and swiped the hair from her brow. Though it wasn't as sweltering in the trees as out in the clearing, the sticky air and dense foliage made for unpleasant work. Not to mention having to cut her way through thickets and vine curtains. Before hunting, she'd hacked out a clearing that she planned to use later. Her arm still ached from the effort.

Rotating the knife in her hand, she peered into the greenery. The snakes were dying too fast. At this rate, she might end up satisfying the requirements for the reputation quest after all. Ugh.

She pushed through another few yards of jungle before spotting the brighter green hue of a tree viper's scales. With a deep breath, she crept forward. Despite Uruquat's warning, the snake didn't flee her human stench, and soon she stood within striking distance.

Devon kicked, connecting with the snake's jaw. Its head whipped to the side. The blow didn't seem to do outward damage, but the reptile blinked slowly as if dazed.

She focused on the animal, trying to assess its health. Obligingly, the game showed her a red bar that had been reduced to about one-third of its capacity.

> **You have gained a skill point:** +1 Combat Assessment.
> *Though the information is rough at low skill levels, you have a vague idea how your enemy is faring.*
> *If used before combat, this skill may give a notion of an enemy's challenge rating. However, you should probably also listen to your gut.*

She dispelled the alert.

Awkwardly, the reptile coiled for a strike.

Devon rose onto her toes and shifted the knife in her hand so that the butt end of the hilt stuck out beyond her curled pinky finger. Like bringing down the hammer, she pounded her fist against the snake's head. The creature went limp. Dead, again? Devon was about to punch a tree out of frustration when a popup appeared.

> *Congratulations! You've discovered a new ability!*

> **You have learned:** Incapacitate - Tier 1
> *When used on a creature with major to severe wounds, this ability has a chance to knock the enemy unconscious.*
> *If the effect fails, you leave yourself open to a retaliatory strike doing double damage.*

Nice! As the popup disappeared, she felt knowledge of the ability melt into her awareness. Unlike her previous experience with games, where she had to train her mind to use the interface—even if subconsciously—to activate her spells and abilities, in this case she was certain that she simply *knew* how to use the special attack. As an experiment, she sprang at the tree she'd been so ready to punch, willing her *Incapacitate* ability to activate. The hilt of her dagger struck a glancing blow.

Ability failed. Target's health not within parameters.

Duh. She swiped the alert away and picked up the snake. When she tried to stuff it into her bag, she got an error message about the item being too big. That didn't make a lot of sense to her, seeing as how she'd fit the deconstructed remains of more than ten of the same monster type inside the container, but she decided she could live with the inconsistency. Slinging the limp viper over her shoulder, she turned for the camp. Just a couple more things to take care of before she could continue with her plan.

Chapter Ten

AS DEVON SLIPPED into the encampment, she yawned. Her fatigue bar was around 70% full, which meant she'd have to take a break soon. Distantly, she wondered what time it was out in the real world. Since she usually played with her interface elements shoved off to the periphery of her vision, she hadn't bothered to check for a clock displaying Utah time. She'd have to look for that at some point.

The sun hung low above the treetops, casting golden light on the circle of huts. Devon was surprised to feel herself smile at the sight. Aside from the obnoxious ogre in the middle of the encampment, she'd grown fond of the place. She skirted the edge of the open area, heading for Hezbek's tent. The woman was inside, scraping the pith out of some sort of long seed pod that reminded Devon of a vanilla bean.

Unfortunately, the pod did *not* smell like vanilla.

"Care to make a trade?" Devon coughed, eyes watering. If things went sideways and she remained stuck here, she'd definitely have to air out the hut before sleeping.

Hezbek looked up from her work. "I doubt I should aid whatever harebrained plan you've concocted, but I suppose I'll listen to your offer."

The interface for trading popped up without Devon consciously activating it. She dropped in eight poison glands, the spoils of her latest adventure.

"What do you want for them?" Hezbek said.

"One of those healing potions, if you can spare it."

"I already offered to teach you how to make them," the woman said. "Once you know the recipe, you can keep an eye out for the components while you're off doing other things."

"I understand, but I just need the one."

"You don't look injured..."

As Devon took another step into the hut, Hezbek shrieked. She scuttled for the far wall.

"What? What is it?"

The woman pointed a trembling finger at Devon's shoulder. "Move slowly. You do *not* want to get bitten on the neck. Most poisons have increased effectiveness when delivered near the heart or brain."

Devon stifled a laugh as she lifted the unconscious snake's head and let it flop. "Not to worry." Of course, she might want to speed up the chitchat. The ability description for *Incapacitate* didn't say how long the victim would stay unconscious.

Hezbek swallowed and seemed to gather herself. She cleared her throat. "Well, I hate to accept such an advantageous trade from someone I hold in high esteem, but if you're determined to give away eight glands for a potion worth just a couple coppers, I suppose I can't refuse."

"Then consider my offer to be partial repayment for your help with the Stone Guardian."

The woman sighed. "Fair enough."

The trade confirmation flashed and then vanished. Devon peeked in her inventory and spotted the healing potion.

"Thanks, Hezbek," she said as she ducked out the door.

"Remember, I have something for you if you manage to not die!" the woman called.

Devon smirked. She hadn't known either of her grandmothers, and her mother had *not* been the nurturing type. It felt kind of nice to have someone nagging her about safety. Especially since she'd be gone soon and wouldn't have to endure it for too long.

The sunset had set fire to a thin layer of clouds, coloring the encampment in reds and oranges. As Devon hurried across the packed earth, she nodded to the leatherworker, Gerrald. He reached into his hut and pulled out the finished items.

She examined the first as he handed it over.

You have received: Leather Belt
A utilitarian item, the belt looks sturdy enough.
2 Armor | 12/12 Durability | Slots: 2

The slots must be where she could affix other items. She looked closer and saw that, indeed, there was an extra strap and buckle on the right side to secure the knife sheath. And on the other side, a set of ties had been threaded through the leather.

"May I?" Gerrald asked in a low voice as she tried—unsuccessfully—to attach the bag to the ties. She nodded, and with a few twists of his fingers, he fastened it securely to the belt.

She smiled as she buckled the belt around her waist. The armor rating was a nice bonus—already she felt more protected.

Next, he handed her the three sections of leather cord she'd requested. Though his face suggested he was curious why she wanted them, he didn't ask.

Finally, he glanced at the back of Uruquat's throne and furtively slid the final item across a stump that stood between them.

> **You have received:** Tribal Sandals
> *Though a bit strappy for the determined adventurer, these sandals provide decent protection. For the bottoms of the feet, anyway.*
> *Faint runes have been scratched into the underside of one of the straps, drawing on an ancient guild tradition to provide a minor enchantment.*
> +1 Speed | 20/20 durability

She grinned. The enchantment was a *very* nice surprise. No armor, but that wasn't surprising. A pair of strappy sandals wouldn't offer much protection unless a monster was trying to chew a hole in the bottom of her foot.

She slipped on the sandals and shuffled a few steps, feeling fleeter already.

From the fire, she heard a grunt.

"Where meat?" Uruquat bellowed. "Hungering!"

Right. Best get on with this.

After backing off to the fringe of the camp, Devon pulled out the healing potion. She grimaced, breathing through her mouth as she unstoppered the little pot. Man, the stuff reeked. But if she didn't want to hunt snakes for the foreseeable future, she'd just have to deal with it.

With a sick swallow, she plunged her fingers into the pot, drew them out, and started smearing the thick liquid over her limbs.

"I'll show you stinky human," she muttered.

***

She'd crept within two paces of the throne when the damn snake started stirring.

"Shit!" she whispered.

Dropping to a crouch, she sprinted the final few steps and slid to a stop beside the chair arm. Her eyes were level with the ogre's forearm, granting an unfortunate view of the warts and crusted boils that covered his skin. When he started sniffing the air, snorting mucus in the process, she stiffened.

"Hezbek!" he bellowed. "Where you?"

"Here, Glorious One," the medicine woman called. Footsteps came running around the other side of the throne. As Hezbek skidded to a stop before the ogre, her eyes landed on Devon and briefly widened.

Devon shook her head, pleading.

"Uruquat smell medicine. Remind Uruquat. Need massage." He stretched out his arm—thankfully the arm *opposite* Devon. "Medicine makes itches stop."

Hezbek blanched. "Y-Yes, Your Gloriousness." She stared at the monster's skin, dried pus and all, before swallowing and heading—feet dragging—back to her hut.

Devon fought back nausea and vowed to work faster. While having Hezbek rub medicine into his skin might distract Uruquat, Devon couldn't put the woman through that.

She slid the slowly writhing snake off her shoulder and pulled out the leather ties. By the time Hezbek emerged from her hut, a pot of salve in hand, an expression of dread on her face, Devon's final preparations were complete, and she was creeping away from the throne. Once clear, she stood and waved Hezbek off.

Devon pursed her lips and began to whistle as she strolled forward again, passing the throne in Hezbek's place. Uruquat glared at her as she approached the fire.

"You bring dead slideys?" he asked.

Devon pressed a finger to her lips and cocked her head as if thinking. "Hmm. Well, I seem to remember killing a few today. But then I got distracted by the new items I ordered."

"Uruquat no understand. Kill slideys is your job. Where skins?"

"You *see*, I was so busy admiring my new *shoes—*" She raised one foot after the other and stared adoringly at the sandals.

"WHAT?" the ogre bellowed. "Uruquat no wear shoes. Uruquat servants no wear shoes!"

"Because you think you're more important... am I remembering that correctly?" Devon raised a finger as if preparing another point. "Here's the thing. Since, you're a half-witted cross between a boulder and a brainless hippo, I'm really not sure what gives you the right."

The ogre's enraged shout shook the ground. Face nearly black with fury, he slapped his hand onto his club and stood.

Devon took a step back. And another, just to be safe.

She cast a pointed look at the club—and the snake she'd tied along its length. Bless its little reptilian heart, the viper chose that moment to hiss.

All expression left the ogre's face. The blood drained from his cheeks as a scream built in the great bellows of his lungs.

He howled and threw the club so hard it sailed over the treetops and crashed down far, far away.

So far so good.

The fight might still pit an ogre against a level 2 player wielding a rusty knife, but at least she'd disarmed the brute. Out of morbid curiosity, she peered at him with her new *Combat Assessment* skill.

> *You lack the skill to estimate your chances. A hint: they don't look good.*

A health bar appeared, still full.

Well, she wasn't expecting even odds. And if she lived, maybe she'd get a Bravery point or two out of this.

Or maybe she'd discover a new special attribute: Idiocy.

Devon spun and sprinted for the forest.

Chapter Eleven

BRUSH TORE AT Devon's clothing as she shoved through the jungle. Though dusk still lit the encampment, beneath the canopy, full dark had fallen. Her darkvision showed phantom brush and ghostly trees as she pressed deeper into the forest.

Behind her, the ogre crashed into the greenery, tearing vines from high branches and toppling smaller trees.

Devon cringed. This might not turn out too well. Ducking and weaving, she shoved through the undergrowth until finally, she spotted the section of the forest she'd laboriously cleared earlier. With relief, she shoved harder against the tangled jungle. Just a few more steps...

Behind her, Uruquat roared.

Something burst from the brush and squawked as it smacked her in the face. A feather shoved into her mouth and she spat, batting the thing away. Idiot... parrot?

She felt the heat from Uruquat's rasping breath as he burst from the jungle just a pace behind her.

Oh, shit!

He grunted as he hauled back to swipe at her. She leaped forward just in time, felt his hand skim the top of her head.

Ogres are nearly blind. She remembered Hezbek's words. In a fight this uneven, she needed to play to whatever strengths she had.

She dashed forward and into the small circle of brush she'd cleared before incapacitating the snake. In the center of the clearing, a human-shaped figure stood with her arms upraised.

Devon grinned. Her glorified scarecrow was actually pretty good. In the darkness, the foliage she'd bent into a vague shape and stuffed with leaves actually resembled a person.

Enough to fool an ogre.

Maybe.

She jumped to catch an overhanging branch.

Unfortunately, she missed. Devon clenched her jaw. Why did she keep forgetting she was such a newbie? Whatever attribute governed her ability to jump, she apparently lacked the requisite points.

Uruquat smashed into the clearing just as Devon sprang for the edge and grabbed a tree trunk. She shimmied up, earning a few deep scrapes on her thighs and forearms. Her health bar flashed and dropped a few points.

The ogre gave a grunt of confusion. He hunched and peered at the figure standing in the center of the clearing.

"You give up so easy?" he asked, voice edged with skepticism.

Crap. He might be dumb as a stump, but he recognized that prey didn't usually stop moving. Devon scanned the surrounding foliage, searching for something she could throw. By sheer luck, her hand landed on something roundish and firm. A fruit of some sort?

She shrugged and plucked it from its twig.

She edged onto the overhanging branch, wound up, and through the missile at the figure's hand.

Her aim sucked. But at least she hit the scarecrow. The fruit smacked the effigy on the shoulder. The figure rotated and sprang back, looking vaguely like it was waving at the ogre.

"Oh, you make fun now?" He growled and stomped forward.

Devon sighed in relief and scooted farther along the branch.

The ogre pulled back a massive fist and hit the scarecrow's face with a tremendous swipe.

Devon closed her eyes, hoping. She'd used a couple of young trees, the wood so green she'd been able to bend them double without breaking them, as the figure's skeleton. She waited, teeth clenched, for the sound of brush smacking flesh as the scarecrow sprang back upright and crashed into Uruquat.

He howled in frustration.

Now.

Devon got her weight under her, sucked in a breath, and jumped.

She landed on the ogre's back, one leg hooked over his shoulder, and grabbed a hank of his greasy hair.

Damn, but he stunk.

The monster roared, pawing at the air in confusion.

One of his arms was tangled in the disintegrating remains of her scarecrow. That saved her life. As he struggled to free himself, she reached around with the rusty knife and started sawing at the monster's neck. It felt like trying to cut through a leather cowboy boot with a steak knife. She pressed harder, gritting her teeth.

Finally, the knife penetrated his thick skin. Blood spurted, and Uruquat let out a confused grunt.

"You not sorry after all," he said as he swayed and fell to his knees. "You big liar."

Devon jumped free as the monster toppled, crushing her scarecrow. With a last, rattling breath, he stilled.

Devon fell back onto her butt, exhausted after the sprint and fight. Her shoulders sagged. A little nugget of guilt settled into her chest. The ogre had been stupid and cruel, but he hadn't wanted to die.

She snorted, shaking her head. He was just an NPC, a digital construct created by another digital construct, the Veia AI.

She was just letting the deep immersion get to her.

Muscles aching, she climbed to a crouch and approached the corpse. She wasn't looking forward to trying to skin the monster, so she hoped something else would activate the looting process. To her relief, when she started plucking at the ogre's clothing, the body quickly decomposed into its parts.

She sorted through the remains, leaving behind the *Reeking Wrist Guards* and the *Trousers Crawling with Fleas,* but examined the other items more carefully.

You have received: Strange Bauble of Carved Bone - unidentified
You have received: A Folded Parchment

She opened the parchment and could tell there was some sort of writing on it, but it was too dark to make anything out. She tucked it into the jute bag with her bauble, then scooped a small pile of coins from the ground. One gold piece and seventeen coppers went into special slots in her inventory screen. Finally, she scrolled through the notifications that had flashed after combat.

Quest Failed: Repent Your Grievous Error.
Seeing as the quest-giver is now dead, you have no hope of finishing. Oh well.

Congratulations, you have reached level 3!
Congratulations, you have reached level 4!
Congratulations, you have reached level 5!
You have gained 4 attribute points.

Not bad. Three levels! And she would finally get to see her base attributes. She opened her character sheet.

Character: Devon (click to set a different character name)
Level: 5
Base Class: Unassigned
Specialization: Unassigned
Unique Class: Unassigned
Health: 130/136
Fatigue: 92%

Whoa! She'd gained a *ton* of hitpoints. Was that because she finally had her base attributes? Seemed likely. Every other game she'd played had calculated her health based on some combination of level and a particular attribute. She opened the attributes window.

Attributes:
Constitution: 13
Strength: 10
Agility: 15

Charisma: 21

Intelligence: 19

Focus: 12

Endurance: 11

Special Attributes:

Bravery: 4

Available points: 4

Devon didn't know what to think. She'd gained 3 *Bravery* points. That was awesome. But... uh... her best attribute was *Charisma*?? Seriously? At least she could take control of her own character development now. Her base attributes had arrow buttons where she could assign points, whereas the special attribute didn't. She stared at the screen for a minute, wondering where she should spend them. The problem was, she didn't know what class she was going to play, or for that matter, when she'd get a chance to pick one. Best to wait on spending the points until she had an idea.

Next, she pulled up her skills window:

Skills:

Unarmed Combat: 3

One-handed Slashing: 6

One-handed Piercing: 1

Darkvision: 4

Tracking: 1

Stealth: 2

Combat Assessment: 1

Sprint: 1

Bartering: 5

Special Skills:

Improvisation: 1

Over the play session, she'd gained another few points in *Darkvision* and *One-handed Slashing*—she'd been focusing on slicing rather than piercing attacks—plus a point in *Sprint,* probably while running away from the ogre. Unfortunately, nothing in *Improvisation.*

"Probably because I had everything planned ahead of time," she said aloud.

Finally, she noticed a new tab:

Extra Bonuses:

Speed: 1

So that's where her speed buff from the sandals showed up. The organization of the stat windows made her think that Speed was something that could only be modified by her gear, or maybe by spells and abilities, too. Anyway, lots to think about.

She closed her character sheet and pulled up the combat log. The notifications showed that her Bravery score had given her an extra 20% chance to land on the ogre's back and a 40% bonus to her ability to cut through the ogre's skin with a glorified letter opener.

She smirked. At least her special attribute was working as advertised, helping her with encounters that were way above her pay grade.

She scrolled some more, checking the damage messages, and stopped at a surprising notification.

> **Unique Discipline unlocked:** Illusion and Trickery.
> *Practitioners of this rare discipline are spoken of in whispers. The nature of their art is little understood and greatly feared. Within the discipline, there are many secrets to be learned and talents to uncover. You are on your way to uncovering a Unique Class! Keep practicing.*

Illusion and Trickery. It must've been from her scarecrow. So she might be able to select a Unique Class if she kept trying things like that? What was a Unique Class anyway? Did that mean it was reserved for her alone? Was there more than one class available within the discipline? The message was disappointingly vague. Nonetheless, not bad for a day's work.

Her stomach was hollow, and her knees wobbled as she staggered back to the encampment. Her fatigue bar was nearly full. *Cut it a bit too close,* she thought. As she stumbled into the cleared area, the tribe members stared at her with a mix of expressions. They gathered near the throne in a huddle, some looking relieved and some terrified.

She felt like she should give some sort of speech about their newfound freedom, but all of a sudden, blackness closed in from the edges of her vision. Her fatigue bar was flashing.

Her eyes sought out Hezbek as she began to sway. The medicine woman dashed forward and lent Devon a shoulder. Together, they staggered to Hezbek's hut where Devon collapsed and logged out.

Chapter Twelve

"YOUR RENEWAL MUST be extracted in blood," Gaviroth said. Two voices emanated from the archdemon's throat, a whisper hissing over a low growl as both spoke the words.

Ezraxis cowered before the mass of writhing shadow. The archdemon's baleful eyes burned with cold fire, his gaze sinking painfully into Ezraxis's scrawny form. She whined as the pain in her leg flared. Half her wing was gone now, torn off in her journey across Yez'ket, the city better known as Demonhome. The stump ached, but at least it no longer dragged, sparing her the agony of feeling her flesh tear with each step.

"Blood, great Vessel?" she managed to whisper.

The archdemon growled, face shifting and roiling. He formed a spear from its shadow-substance and *stabbed* the ground.

No, not the ground.

Gaviroth raised the spear to show a rat, mangy fur and yellowed teeth, impaled on the point. It squeaked and struggled, clawing helplessly at the air. Gaviroth held the dying creature before Ezraxis's face.

"Take it. Bleed it. Begin your journey."

Chapter Thirteen

DEVON CINCHED HER robe tighter, turned on the burner, and set a frying pan on the stove. She opened the fridge, shaking her head at the twinge of fear that she might find it empty. Old habits died hard. The shelves hadn't been bare since she'd signed the contract with E Squared.

She pulled out a carton of eggs and cracked a pair into the skillet.

"Shit," she muttered. Too late, she grabbed a bottle of olive oil and poured a healthy measure over the top of and around the eggs. She started scrambling them and prayed.

While the mass slowly sizzled, she checked her messages.

Nothing from Emerson. She trusted him, more or less, figured he just didn't have answers about the pain response yet. He was a nice enough guy, not bad looking. Socially awkward, but she didn't have a lot of room to criticize, seeing as she was a social recluse. Speaking of... she scanned backward through her messages. She really did need to get out some. Back when she'd had regular play sessions with guildmates, she could count that as social contact. But seeing as the only interaction she had now was with a bunch of ogre-worshiping NPCs, things were a little more dire.

She found the last message from Tamara, looked at the send date a month past, and winced. After Devon had left Fort Kolob, they'd met up a couple of times. Tamara had even offered to teach her how to mountain bike—not that Devon had any intent of taking her friend up on that.

She pulled up the last message and hit reply, subvocalizing a response. "Hey, sorry I've been MIA. Was kind of dopey during surgery recovery and work's been busy. Meet for tea or something tomorrow?"

Tamara was Mormon, which meant beers were out. But that was okay because Devon was a lightweight.

Feeling good about her efforts to connect with society, she scraped the egg-mass onto a plate. She doused the mess with hot sauce in hopes it would cover the texture and wolfed it down. As important as it was to sustain her physical body, she really wanted to get back into Relic and see the results of yesterday's adventures. She was eager to examine the mysterious bone bauble and the parchment. More than that, today, she'd finally be able to start her journey to some sort of city.

Meal finished, she cracked a can of cold coffee, chugged it, and flopped onto the couch. With a mental twist of her awareness, she fell into Relic Online.

And was greeted with screaming.

She sprang up to the sight of Hezbek frantically leaning over a thrashing form on her cot. Devon shook off the disorientation from the unexpected situation and rushed to the medicine woman's side.

An injured man clutched his leg, yelling through clenched teeth. Blood seeped from between his fingers.

"Get his mouth open," Hezbek said. Devon hurried to the head of the cot and snatched a stick off a nearby shelf. Not eager to get her finger bitten off, she shoved it between his lips and pried his teeth open. With a nod, Hezbek pulled the stopper from a clay pot. The foul-smelling liquid poured down the man's throat, and after a moment he began to quiet.

The medicine woman grabbed a bandage, from the shelf. She tied it around the leg where the flow of blood had already slowed. The man's blood-soaked trousers hid the actual wound but, given the state of his clothing and Hezbek's cot, it must've been pretty serious.

The man finally stilled completely, and his head lolled to the side.

"The potions have slightly different effects on those who aren't starborn," Hezbek explained. "They pull from our fatigue to provide the restoration, which means he'll sleep for some time. He may need another dose, but he'll feel a lot better when he wakes."

Devon laid a hand on the man's brow. "What happened?"

She glanced toward the door flap. It was night outside, though she didn't know how late. She still didn't have a sense of the relative time between the real world and the game, and she made a mental note to look into that.

Hezbek pressed her lips together and fixed Devon with a hard stare. "The encampment was attacked—we shouldn't have been surprised, but I suppose we were. A large boar. He's menaced us for weeks. Deld here was gored through the leg, terrible from his perspective, but we were lucky."

"This is the first I've heard of a boar," Devon said.

Hezbek shrugged. "Until now, Uruquat has always scared the beast away."

Ah. Crap. And Devon had killed Uruquat, leaving them unprotected.

The medicine woman shook her head and sucked her teeth. "The ogre took to sleeping in his throne after he'd been dragged from his hut enough times. He never fought the beast directly. Just stood on his throne and bellowed. I suppose we took his protection for granted. Well, I did, anyway."

"Did Deld try to fight it? Devon asked. "For that matter, do you have any weapons?"

Hezbek took a deep breath. "We're simple people, starborn. Yes, you could say it's our own stupid fault for coming all the way out here. But now we're here, and I'm not sure how we'll manage to survive."

A quest dialogue appeared.

Hezbek is offering you a quest: You break it, you buy it.
The members of the Tribe of Uruquat are being menaced by a large boar. Okay, a massive boar. Seeing as you killed their protector, perhaps you should do something about it.
Objective: Defend the villagers.
Reward: Unknown
Accept? Y/N

Devon hit accept without hesitation. The city could wait for a few more hours while she dealt with this.

"Okay, just let me think," Devon said.

From beyond the hide wall of the hut, she heard a loud crashing.

Hezbek tapped her foot. "Normally, I'd say take your time..."

Devon dashed outside, thoughts racing.

"We need firewood!" she yelled as she ran to the center of the village. "Any spare thatch or dried plants, as long as they'll burn."

As tribe members hurried over with logs and a few door flaps from their huts, she motioned for them to throw the fuel on the fire.

The blaze began to leap, and the crashing from the forest grew quieter. But the boar didn't leave; she could still hear it circling around and assessing the situation.

Sparks began to spit from the fire as pockets of sap popped. Devon took a step back and searched the crowd for the leatherworker. When she spotted him, she rushed over and grabbed his arm.

He jerked in surprise, looked down at her hand on his elbow.

"Sorry," she said quickly. "I need armor. A jerkin and trousers. Oversized."

He looked confused for a moment, and the trade window popped up. She waved it away. "Just to borrow. You'll get it back after this."

He blinked, took a breath, then hurried to his hut. After a moment, he emerged from the darkened interior with the items in hand.

Devon nodded in appreciation. The leather was stiff enough it almost held its shape without a body inside. It seemed as if Gerrald had been making the items for the ogre, but thankfully they were short pants and a vest, not full-length garments. She dragged the items over her clothing and moved—stiffly—to stand in front of the blaze.

"All right, everyone, get into the shadow of the throne." She didn't want their shapes interrupting what she was trying to do.

Her shadow, wavering in the dancing flames, almost reached the edge of the clearing. But not quite. Devon dragged over a pair of stumps, stacked them, and awkwardly clambered up.

Her shadow stretched out into the forest, darkening the trees. She raised her arms and roared. Her voice was lost in the crackle of the bonfire.

"Do you guys have a gourd or speaking horn? Or anything like that?"

After a moment, one of the tribe members nodded and dashed to his hut, returning with the hollowed-out tusk of some sort of creature. He raised it in question.

Devon nodded. "When I say, yell through it. Make as much noise as you can."

She listened and located the boar. It was snuffling through the bushes south of the encampment. She dragged the stumps again, stacked them and climbed up then made herself as big as possible.

"Now!"

The villager's voice boomed through the night. At the same time, Devon's shadow fell over the forest. The crashing stopped and then retreated.

Devon grinned. Not bad for a non-ogre.

For the next hour, she cast shadows and called for more ogre bellows, and finally, the boar seemed to grow tired of the game. The crackle of sticks and snuffling moved off.

Devon took a stiff-legged seat on the stump, ears still pricked for the beast's return.

Notifications started popping up.

> *You have gained a special skill point: +1 Improvisation.*
> *It was a decent idea, so you squeaked by. Next time, think of something less hokey.*

> *You have gained a special attribute point: +1 Cunning*
> *You're clever, perhaps even a bit diabolical.*

You have learned a new spell: Shadow Puppet – Tier 1.
You can create compelling illusions with your shadow. Properties of the shadow vary based on the type of light used in its creation.
Cost: 20 mana
Requirements: Illusion and Trickery discipline unlocked

Niiice! Another special attribute, plus her first spell! As she brushed the notifications aside, she noticed a new bar at the edge of her vision. It was a deep purple and showed that she had 65 mana available. Before she could explore that, however, another popup appeared.

Congratulations! By unlocking Illusion and Trickery and discovering a spell exclusive to it, you may now set your Unique Class to "Deceiver."

As a starborn, you will be able to select three classes for advancement: **Base, Specialization,** *and* **Unique.** *Unique Classes are restricted to one player per world. Few avatars will be offered them.*

Would you like to select Deceiver as your Unique Class?

Hell yes! Devon accepted the prompt.
Another message followed.

Your mana now depends on key attributes for your classes. Currently: Cunning

Devon checked her mana. Well, that kinda sucked. It had gone down to 35. And having it tied to a special attribute, one of those that she couldn't spend points to raise, meant she would have to work hard to increase the pool size. So lame! She'd gone from being able to cast her first spell three times with full mana down to just once. Hopefully, the bonuses of the Unique Class would make up for it.

Maybe her base or specialization classes would contribute to her mana pool with base attribute values. If she ever figured out how to choose other classes.

In any case, she scanned the periphery of her vision for some sort of icon associated with her new spell, *Shadow Puppet.* But like the *Incapacitate* ability, she realized that she simply knew how to activate it. She focused on the ground in front of her feet, judged the intensity and angle of the light cast by the slowly-dying bonfire, and willed her shadow to gather strength. To her delight, the dark shape began to stretch, widening and falling deeper into the jungle. Her mana dropped by a bit more than half. She explored her awareness of the shadow, feeling a sense of connectedness to it. She knew she could do more than manipulate the size—mastering the spell would definitely take a lot of experimentation—but she didn't want to alarm the tribe members. With a mental wave, she dispelled the effect.

The tribe members had gathered around the fire, huddling close as if still nervous. Devon pulled off the stiff armor and handed it back to Gerrald. "If I'm not here and the beast comes back, you should be able to use the same trick," she said. "But I think we've scared him off for the night."

He blinked at her as if uncomfortable with the responsibility.

"Anyway, I'm not leaving yet," she added. "I just need to go check in with your injured friend."

Devon returned to Hezbek's hut and stepped inside to see Deld still sleeping peacefully. The medicine woman had been dozing in a chair, and she jerked awake at the sound of Devon's entrance.

"I've taught them how to scare the boar away," she said.

A box appeared, informing her she'd completed the "You Break It, You Buy It" quest. Her reward was 50 reputation points with the tribe. Considering that she was about to leave for the city, that didn't mean much. But she would've helped them with or without the quest.

"Seems you've also survived your foolhardy plan," Hezbek said. "A surprise, if you're not offended by me saying it."

Devon had almost forgotten about the other quest. A second popup appeared, confirming quest completion for "Survive Your Crackpot Scheme." Her efforts earned her 165 experience—not close to enough for another level, but every bit helped—as well as the promised waterskin.

You have received: Everfull Waterskin
Not the tastiest water, but you won't die of thirst.

"And take these," Hezbek said. "You'll be a skeleton by tomorrow if you don't eat something."

You have received: 2 x Plantains

Devon smirked and thanked the woman. She peeled the starchy fruit and scarfed it. The hollow ache in her belly finally subsided. After looking around for a trashcan, she held the peels out apologetically. Hezbek rolled her eyes, grabbed them, and dropped them on the floor. After a moment, they faded and vanished. Right. Regardless of the realism, this *was* still a game.

"I'll stay the night to make sure the others can take care of more boar attacks," Devon said. "But I was wondering, can you help me with directions to... Where did you come from? Eltera city?"

Hezbek held her silence for a while. "I will if that's really what you want to do. But I have a proposal for you, first. We were safe under Uruquat, but we'd accomplished little of what he promised us. Not to mention, we weren't free. But neither are we heroes. We're simple people who followed a dream into the jungle. We might survive on our own, but we aren't particularly knowledgeable or enterprising. We'll do much better with a leader."

Devon's brow furrowed. "You don't mean me?"

"Uruquat gave us purpose and protection. And for all his failings, he gave us our dream. Out here we were going to build our own city, our own kingdom even."

"How long has it been?" Devon asked.

"I've lost track, to be honest. I suspect we'd never have achieved what we set out to do with Uruquat as our leader. But with you..."

"I don't know anything about building a kingdom. Why here? Wouldn't it be easier to start somewhere you could buy supplies? Gather information and support?"

"There was a paper. Uruquat couldn't read it, but it spoke of a great power that could be gained in this region. We didn't choose this abysmal jungle by chance."

Devon thought of the parchment in her inventory. "If Uruquat couldn't read it, what good was this paper?"

Hezbek's mouth twisted as she thought. "That's why he recruited Greel."

"Greel?"

"The lawyer," she said.

Right. That would make sense.

"I won't beg, but I'll ask nicely," Hezbek said. "Will you take up Uruquat's legacy? We'll follow you—most of us anyway. And the skeptics will give you a chance."

Devon looked around the hut. She'd had her heart set on making the journey to a city. Finding other players, following a more directed path. But was that what she wanted? This encampment had already started to feel like home, and—NPC or not—she'd come to enjoy Hezbek's company. Devon had never really used gaming forums to get information—most often they were full of arguing and trolls anyway. Since she'd started in Relic Online, she hadn't even peeked at the gamer news. She hadn't needed to, because the experience was so immersive. She hadn't wanted to break the spell.

So why go mainstream? Why not stay out here and see what she could do?

Would she be missing out by avoiding the masses? From what she'd seen in other games, probably not.

Hezbek watched her for a moment and then said, "You're thinking about it, aren't you?"

A prompt appeared in her vision.

Do you accept leadership of the Tribe of Uruquat?

Devon clicked yes.

***

The tribe members gathered around as Devon approached the fire. The blaze was smaller now but still hot against her face. She cast a glance at the throne but decided against climbing onto it. It seemed a waste to leave it unused, but she didn't want to give the impression that she was anything like the prior occupant.

"Hey, all," she said. She didn't need to raise her voice to grab anyone's attention; the moment she spoke, their eyes were fixed on her. To make sure everyone could hear, though, she stepped onto a stump. "I just wanted to say a few things. First, I'm sorry I left you exposed to that boar. I didn't know about the threat, and Deld suffered for it. From now on, never be afraid to approach me if you feel you're in danger.

"Second, I promise to treat everyone fairly. I won't demand fealty as Uruquat did. Anyone who wishes to leave the tribe may depart with my blessing. If you choose to remain, however, I need your loyalty. Not to me, but to the tribe.

"And that brings me to my final point. Tonight, I want you to rest. I will stand watch and make sure you are safe. Tomorrow, we will work together to secure the encampment. Once you can sleep without fearing attack by wild animals, we will forge onward. Uruquat made you a promise. He claimed you would build a kingdom together. I will take up his vow, and unlike the ogre, I will see it realized."

She swallowed as she hopped down from the stump. For a moment, the crackle of the fire and cawing of nightbirds were the only sounds, but then the tribe members took up a quiet cheer.

She received an alert informing her she'd gained another 5 reputation with the tribe. She'd hoped to earn a little more with a speech she'd considered rather rousing, but maybe they were just tired. As people started shuffling toward their huts, she checked the supply of firewood to make sure she could rebuild the blaze if the boar returned then sat on a stump to see what her efforts had earned her.

The first change was a settlement interface. She opened the window.

Settlement: Uruquat's Camp
Size: Encampment

Tier 1 Buildings (11/20):
11 x Standard Sleeping Hut

Tier 2 Buildings (2/2):
1 x Leader's Abode
1 x Medicine Woman's Hut

She opened a secondary dialog detailing her followers.

Population:
Base Morale: 45%
8 x Worker (unspecialized)
1 x Worker - Deld (unspecialized) (injured)
1 x Hunter
1 x Leatherworker - Gerrald
1 x Medicine Woman - Hezbek (advanced)
1 x Lawyer - Greel (advanced)

She shook her head as she looked at the last name. What the hell was she going to do with a lawyer out here in the jungle? Maybe she could convert him back into an unspecialized worker. Wondering if she could give the workers a more specific task, she focused on the entry in the population table but got an error message explaining that she needed to speak directly with the individual to attempt to assign a specialty. She shrugged. Better to wait until she knew what specialties she needed, anyway.

A final popup listed resources and consumables for the community:

Food consumption
- 13 basic food/day

Food available
- 20 x Smoked Turtle Meat
- 2 x Dried Sloth Meat

Firewood consumption - 1 bundle/day
Firewood available - 2 bundles

Items:
3 x Axe - fair
2 x Saw - fair
1 x Hand Drill - good
1 x Pickaxe - fair
2 x Shovel - fair
2 x Machete - good
1 x Mallet and Chisel

She found she could drag both stacks of 5 *Snake Meat* from her inventory to the community resources, which made her bag much lighter. As she closed the window, she wondered why Hezbek's potions weren't listed. Maybe she needed to speak with the medicine woman to get access to those resources. In any case, she had a lot of management to do, but it could wait until her tribe members were awake. For now, she could begin prepping to fulfill the first part of her promise: assuring that her followers were safe.

She searched around the outside of the huts until she found one of the axes and headed into the forest. Time for some woodcutting.

Chapter Fourteen

BY MORNING, DEVON had created a couple modest piles of supplies at the edge of the encampment. One was a mass of vines she'd cut and stripped of leaves—unfortunately, her rusty knife was down to 2/10 durability. She hoped to find a replacement sometime during the day. The other pile was a stack of logs large enough to use in constructing boar-proof shelters. It was a start.

The tribe was slow to wake due to the excitement of the previous evening. While she waited, she tossed back the flap over the door to the leader's hut and grimaced. The place reeked.

With a long stick, she fished for the ogre's bedding and dragged it into the watery dawn light. The wool blankets were stained and ratty and crawling with bugs. Uruquat had been sleeping in his throne for the last several days—she could hardly imagine how bad they'd have smelled if used recently. Nose wrinkled, she dragged the mess over to the fire and tossed it on the coals. As the fibers began to smolder, dirty smoke rose in a column before drifting slowly over the treetops.

She made sure to keep her distance.

Next, she pulled out a small wooden stool and a stump covered with dried bits of food. There was a cup made of pieces of bark sewn together with sinew. Ordinarily, she might have kept it, but not when it had been used by a boil-covered ogre. She tossed the cup and stool onto the bonfire then rolled the table in with a solid kick from her Tribal Sandal.

That left just a small iron trunk that was—unfortunately—locked. Devon dragged it out into the fresh air. Eventually, she'd have to figure out how to get it open, but for now, she'd let the sun bake off any residual stench. She did the same with the hide flaps covering the hut's frame, throwing half of them over the top of the dome to allow air to blow through the space.

Ideally, it would rain sometime soon.

By the time she'd finished clearing out the ogre's possessions, the others had woken. One of the women, a petite worker with dark hair in braids, dug through a wooden crate at the edge of the camp. She dragged out some of Devon's snake meat and looked at it quizzically. Devon blushed when she realized she'd tossed a bunch of raw meat in with the tribe's stores.

"I suppose I should have cooked that first," she said.

The woman shrugged. "I'll get started on it, see what we can salvage."

Fair enough. Devon needed to start thinking more carefully about supplies. If she fed her followers a bunch of rotten meat, she'd probably end up with a village of corpses.

She watched as Hezbek helped the woman set up the spit. They slid the snake meat onto the iron rod and lowered it close to the coals. A few minutes later, the smell of cooking meat filled the village. Thankfully the bedding had burned quickly, and they wouldn't be eating meat spiced with ogre body odor.

As the food cooked, the other tribe members shuffled from their shelters to the fire. The lawyer, Greel, was the last to emerge. Devon watched him approach. Balding and slight of build, he didn't look the type to leave the city for a jungle expedition. Then again, few of these people looked like intrepid adventures out to found a new kingdom. Their ages varied from early twenties to Hezbek who wasn't *ancient* but wasn't particularly young, either. None moved with the confidence she'd expect from a bunch of hardcore survivors. But then again, they hadn't really been taking care of themselves. Uruquat, for all his failings, had managed to keep them alive and together.

Hopefully, Devon wouldn't compare unfavorably to a half-witted monster.

When Greel stepped up to the fire, Devon nodded at him. "Got a minute?"

He fixed her with a glare that was just short of insolent, a surprise after the simpering deference he had shown Uruquat. "I guess."

Greel was an "advanced" NPC like Hezbek, but she wasn't sure what that meant. Pulling up the window with information on her followers, she selected his name and was rewarded with another window. It didn't show much, just his specialty (lawyer, as she already knew) and his disposition toward her. -265 reputation. Well below neutral. That explained his demeanor, at least.

In contrast—she selected Hezbek's entry—she had 310 reputation with the medicine woman. That put her solidly within the "friendly" category.

Well, she could work out how to get on Greel's good side later. For now, she just wanted information.

"As you recall, I gave you the option to leave last night. Yet you're still here. I assume that means you intend to remain loyal to the tribe."

The man rolled his eyes. "How do you think I'd fare on a return march through the wilderness?"

"I can't say, since I don't know much about your strengths. But seeing as you're here, I expect you to act in ways that benefit the group."

He crossed his arms over his chest. "Regardless of what I think of you personally, I'm no fool. Until there's a caravan headed back to Eltera, I'm stuck with this group. What do you want?"

"Walk with me."

As he followed her—all the while, rolling his eyes and dragging his feet—toward the edge of the encampment, she pulled out the parchment she'd looted from Uruquat's corpse. Devon had tried to read the document once there'd been enough light to make out the words, but the lettering was foreign to her.

Once out of earshot of the fire, she held it up. "I understand you can read this."

"My skill in reading this particular script is the main reason Uruquat retained my services. It's an ancient tongue. Carpavan Legalese."

"And?"

"It is a copy of a document written long ago. The contract deeds the city of Ishildar—in whole and in perpetuity—to a single ruler."

Ishildar... the ruined city where she'd spawned. The place where the strange wisp had spoken of a champion which might or might not be her.

"And who is this ruler?"

He shrugged. "Some dead guy. Deceased for hundreds of years."

"So why does the document matter now?"

"Because there were strict terms directing the inheritance. After the death of the first ruler, dominion over the city would pass only to the individual who possessed a particular set of relics. If the set was not complete, it was stipulated that the site must be abandoned—don't ask me why. Anyway, Uruquat had about as much brains as my left foot, but he understood the basic math. Finding the treasure equals controlling the ancient city."

"I see."

"But you should know, the ogre wasn't the only one searching for these relics. I have been contacted by a number of organizations offering hefty compensation for my services in interpreting this document as well as others. Knowledge of the Carpavan tongue is rare. Being able to decipher its impenetrable legalese even more so."

"And yet you chose to work for a dimwitted ogre."

"I work for myself. It just happened that my goals most closely aligned with Uruquat's. For the time being anyway."

Devon chewed her lip while she considered his words. She didn't like his attitude, but the information he offered was intriguing.

"How are you enjoying my knife?" he asked, glaring.

She resisted the urge to lay a hand on the sheath. The theft probably explained his dislike for her—at least in part.

"Are you volunteering to take on the encampment's defense? If so, I'll consider returning it."

Greel's cheek twitched, but he said nothing. The standoff lasted for a minute or so.

"If that's all?" he asked, a sarcastic edge to his words.

"For now. Of course, if you can think of anything that would improve our security here, please feel free to get to work."

Curling his lip in annoyance, Greel wandered off. Devon watched him go. That man would be trouble if she didn't figure out how to earn his loyalty.

***

While the tribe ate a slow breakfast, Devon examined her interface until she found the clock which showed the time in the real world. Nearby, another readout displayed the time inside Relic Online. She put them side by side long enough to figure out that the game time passed at about two and a half times the rate it did outside. That confused her a little bit, because she'd thought the relationship had been closer, but then again, she *had* spent quite a while unconscious after hitting her head early on. And she had a faint recollection of Emerson mentioning the ability for the developers to slowly adjust something called time compression. He said the goal was to eventually allow the game experience to pass faster—allowing more play time—by stimulating some sort of brain structure that perceived time. The notion had kind of wigged her out, so she'd started tuning out his explanation.

The actual effect was cool, though. Despite the feeling that she'd been playing for sixteen hours since logging in, her real-world clock verified that it was just early afternoon back in her apartment. So despite the creepiness of this time compression, she kinda liked it.

As her followers finished their meal, she found a tiny window which offered a portal into her real-world messages. There was a reply from Tamara.

Sounds great. Meet you tonight... instead of tea, how about tacos? PS. Thanks for getting in touch. It'll be nice to hear about something besides chainrings and frame composites.

Devon sent back an emoji and a geo-locating pin for a Mexican food joint. She wasn't sure about tacos—sometimes the spices screwed with her digestion. And she had no idea what that other mumbo-jumbo about chainrings was, but regardless, it would be nice to see her friend. Provided she could even call her that after ignoring Tamara's message for a month. At least the other woman didn't seem to completely hate her yet.

She wandered toward the piles of logs and vines and called her followers over to her. Greel arrived last, casting glares that could have scalded water. She ignored him.

Devon gestured toward the logs. "Okay, everyone, we're going to use these to make a safe place to sleep. We'll fasten the construction together with..." She glanced at the vines. It had seemed like a good plan, but that had been in the middle of the night after the boar escapade. Wasn't looking so smart now. She pinched her temples between thumb and middle finger. She really needed some expertise here.

Scanning the workers, Devon nodded to a strong-looking woman who moved with a little more confidence than some of her peers. "You haven't chosen a trade, have you?"

"I haven't specialized, no, but I'd like to," the woman said.

"Do you have a preference?" Devon asked. In response, a window opened. It gave a long list of work the woman *could* specialize in, but three professions at the top of the list were highlighted. A note explained that highlighted professions received a bonus to advancement.

- Guard/fighter
- Lumberjack
- Blacksmith

"Seems you like to hit things," Devon said.

The woman blushed. "I *am* pretty good at it."

"All right, we'll figure that out later. For now, is there anyone who has a natural inclination to carpentry?"

A man with gray hair at his temples stepped forward. When she examined him, she saw he would receive *double* bonuses in carpentry but reduced advancement in anything else. Perfect.

"What's your name?" she asked.

"Prester, Your Gloriousness."

"So, you're interested in building with wood."

"I've been waiting my whole life. Uruquat talked about building a city, and then a kingdom, and I thought it was finally my chance." A look of bitterness came over his face.

"I'd like to see you achieve your hopes," Devon said. "How can I help you pursue the trade?"

"I just need a blessing of the village leader for early training."

That was it? No instruction manual or arcane ritual needed? Nice. Devon laid a hand on his shoulder.

"You have my blessing," she said. "I hereby name you our tribe's carpenter."

The man's face lit up. He dry-washed his hands and his eyes glistened.

"How long before you are ready to begin your new trade?" she asked.

"Right away, Your Gloriousness. I would like to begin by converting some of these logs into rough planks. It will help me gain confidence and skill, plus I'll need the planks for other projects."

Devon nodded. This was much better than trying to muddle her way through. "Have at it!"

Chapter Fifteen

DEVON ASKED THE other villagers to help Prester where possible. Mostly, that entailed holding logs in place while he used the axe heads as wedges to split them lengthwise. As they worked, Devon searched the encampment until she found the two machetes. She grabbed one and inspected the edge and hilt. The item examine window popped up.

> **Item:** Crude Machete
> *Mostly good for clearing jungle, but hey, it's better than a rusty knife.*
> 2-6 Damage | 12/15 Durability

She looked down at her belt and the small knife sheath. She searched the work site until she found Gerrald, the leatherworker, trudging across the camp with an armful of scraps to add to the firewood supply.

"Are you able to craft a sheath to fit this blade?" she asked.

"Now?" he asked, a hopeful look in his eyes.

"Please."

"On it!" He threw his wood scraps onto the pile and dashed off.

Hmm. From now on, she'd try to keep him busy with leatherworking tasks rather than construction work. It clearly helped his morale.

Next, she stood on a stump and shaded her eyes. "I'm looking for the tribe's hunter," she called.

A young man stepped forward. She blushed, realizing she should have recognized him by the short bow strung across his body, but she was new to this.

As she looked closer, an inspection window popped up.

His name was Grey, and he was level 2 with 10 skill points in traps, 8 in short bow, and 20 in club.

"You hunt with the club?" she asked. That sounded rather caveman-like.

He shrugged. "Sloths aren't very fast."

That's right. She remembered seeing the sloth meat. Made sense.

"And you trap the turtles, or?"

Grey nodded. "There's a stream, but it's an hour's walk away. The last time I returned with meat, some sabertoothed beast stalked me. Uruquat said I should just avoid the 'kitty' for now."

"I agree with him in that regard. What about the bow?"

"Well," he said, "the best prey for someone of my skill has been parrots."

What? No. She was not going to eat parrot meat. "Let's forget hunting them."

He nodded. "I've been out of arrows for a month, anyway."

She recalled the list of professions from the settlement interface. The tribe had no fletchers, which meant there wouldn't be more arrows unless she appointed someone to the task.

She glanced at his bulging backpack. "Looks like you've already had some luck today. Sloth?"

He gave her a pleased smile. "Two, Your Gloriousness. They are even slower in the morning hours."

"You can call me Devon, by the way."

He stiffened as if he'd been scolded. Yes, your... Devon-ness."

She stopped herself from correcting him again. Better to just let it go for now.

"Your fighting skills are strong. For the time being, would you consider double duty as a guard? If something attacks the encampment, we could use your help."

The man fiddled with the end of his short bow. "Well... I was brought up to respect life in all forms. Killing is necessary for us to eat, but violence should never be employed in conflicts of aggression."

A hippie NPC? Really? "What about in self-defense? If attacked, would you fight back?"

A conflicted look colored his features. "I—well, I suppose so, but my real purpose is to provide."

She sighed. It seemed the game wanted her to train fighters, not exploit a loophole by assigning hunters to guard the camp.

"I understand. When you bring back meat, can you also provide leather to Gerrald?"

The hunter brightened. "I wanted to ask Uruquat about that weeks ago. But he was... not particularly open to suggestions. I'd be more than eager to begin the practice now—using all parts of the animal furthers my creed."

Well, at least there was that. "Thank you. I want to begin outfitting everyone with better protective gear as soon as possible."

Devon watched Grey run off then scanned the unspecialized workers. She couldn't stay logged in all the time, and her followers needed some ability to fend for themselves. She spotted the woman who liked to hit things and called her over.

"What's your name?" Devon asked.

"Bayle," the woman said, then added, "Your Gloriousness."

"Just Devon is fine. No title, no 'Your.'"

Bayle nodded. "As you wish."

"Our group is in need of a fighter—"

"I'll do it," the woman interrupted.

Devon raised a hand. "I have a couple questions first. Eventually, we'll need better tools and weapons. We have no metal right now, but I'm curious what happens if you specialize as a fighter now and then later we need you to be our blacksmith."

The woman squared her shoulders. "Of course, I'll do whatever is best for the Tribe of Uruquat. Whether that's guard duty or smithing or something else. However, you should know that my progress as a smith would be slow at first because I would need to unlearn the habits gained by practicing as a fighter. The longer I remain in one specialty, the harder it will be to transition."

"Is it possible to specialize in more than one thing?"

"Oh, wow," Bayle said, "I would be *deeply honored* if you considered raising me to an advanced citizen."

Ah-hah. There was at least part of the answer to another question.

"So advanced citizens can have more than one specialty? Is there anything else they receive?"

"All sorts of things. They are able to gain higher skill tiers, command others, and take apprentices. But, Your—Devon, as much as I'd like to be considered, you should know the limitations. You can raise only a fixed number of tribe members depending on the level of our settlement."

"I see. Well, for now, I would like you to begin training as a fighter. You'll still need to help with the construction now and then. For the rest of the afternoon, though, I'd like you to join me in clearing some of the wildlife from the surrounding area."

As soon as the words left Devon's mouth, the woman stood straighter. Though the changes were subtle, she seemed to fill out a little bit, gaining muscle tone and a keenness to her vision as she surveyed the encampment.

As Devon handed over the rusty knife, she found herself faintly reluctant to release the hilt. She snorted. Stupid sentimentality.

The woman didn't notice Devon's reaction because she was so busy staring, awestruck, at the pathetic weapon.

"Thank you, Devon. It's... I've always dreamed of this chance. I won't let you down."

"I'm certain you won't," Devon said, clapping the woman on the shoulder.

Devon and Bayle spent the next few hours in the jungle working together to slay a couple dozen snakes. Devon received no experience or skill gain. Mostly, she stood by, ready to jump in if Bayle got in over her head. Soon, though, Bayle had enough skill to handle the encounters on her own.

After giving the woman some parting words of encouragement, Devon stuffed her bag with the loot, leaving the new fighter to fend for herself. She returned to the village, unloaded the snake meat, and asked one of the unspecialized workers to start cooking it. Because Bayle wasn't starborn and was still leveling up, many of the pieces of meat were listed as *Snake Meat - Scraps*. Fortunately, the game allowed Devon to combine seven scraps to create a piece of usable food. By the time the snake and sloth steaks were cooked and added back to the village resources, the food supply looked like this:

Food consumption
- 13 basic food/day

Food available
- 10 x Smoked Turtle Meat
- 8 x Dried Sloth Meat
- 12 x Snake Steaks

They'd added another day of rations for the camp plus a little more.

Devon realized she hadn't felt hungry in quite a while. The game must be automatically subtracting a food unit for her each day now that she was a tribe member. Convenient.

As she was running through a few of the settlement management interfaces, looking for a way to designate Advanced NPC's, the carpenter, Prester, came and stood before her.

She quickly swiped away the interface.

"I now have the materials to build something for you."

Devon clapped her hands together. "Awesome. I want you to design and build a raised sleeping platform in the jungle where we cleared the understory. It should be at least the height of two men above the ground."

The carpenter's face fell. "I—" He swallowed. "I don't know how to build a raised platform."

Devon was careful not to let her disappointment show. She should've thought of that—he probably had just a small list of things he could construct at low skill levels. She didn't want to hurt the man's morale, so she smiled encouragingly.

"Let's see what you *can* build. I'm sure anything will be useful."

Immediately, a new window showed in her view, displaying the carpenter's available plans. He understood how to make:

- Rough Planks
- Simple Table
- One-room Shack, Flat Roof
- Simple Dock

As Devon stared at the interface, the man fidgeted with eagerness. She considered having him build a few tables to see if he'd get access to the next skill tier's plans, but she doubted those would include a platform either.

"I want to try something," she said. "And if it fails, you can't be hard on yourself. Consider it my fault."

He shuffled in the dirt, looking skeptical.

"Come with me," she said, starting for the trees. The afternoon swelter was settling into the open area anyway. As they passed into the green shadows beneath the canopy, she pointed out several of the taller trees they'd left standing while clearing the undergrowth.

"I want you to imagine that these are pilings. Right now, we're walking on water." The man's face twisted in a confused expression. He chewed his lip. "But—okay, I'll try."

"Now, if you were to build a dock on those pilings, raised up high above this water, that would be easy, right?"

145

"Well... I understand the plans, and I have the materials..."

"Will you try?" she asked.

He held his silence for a moment, shuffling in the leaf litter, then finally nodded. "I'll try, Your Gloriousness."

Devon held her tongue. Correcting them on this title thing might be a losing battle.

"If you were building a dock, how long would it take? Would you be done by dark?"

"I believe so, if you'll permit me to ask the others for help moving the supplies into place."

"You'll have as much help as you need."

"In that case, I'll try. I'm still not certain this will work, though."

"Understood. And you'll bear no blame if it doesn't."

***

While the carpenter set to work, Devon returned to the clearing and pulled Hezbek aside.

"I noticed when I looked through the settlement's resources that none of your potions were included, yet you use them freely."

The medicine woman nodded. She fanned her face with her hand and gestured toward her hut. "Shall we get out of the sun?"

Devon smiled. "Yes, please."

As they stepped inside, Hezbek dipped a ladle into her water barrel and took a drink before scanning the shelves. She muttered something to herself and switched the positions of a couple clay pots. Finally, she turned to Devon.

"You are right, you have free use of everything I produce." She smirked. "I was looking forward to having an apprentice... I suppose you won't want me to teach you now."

"I've never been good with recipes anyway," Devon said. "You should see my disastrous cooking attempts. But as for the apprentice, maybe we can arrange something once we've grown the settlement."

"I'd like that. I never had children of my own, but..." She waved off what she was going to say. "You don't need to hear my life story right now. You were asking about consumables."

A new window popped up, showing Hezbek's name, and a list of potential orders and the time they'd take to create. Right now, she could produce:

- Jungle Health Potions – Minor, 1 day
- Jungle Health Potion – Mid, 3 days
- Jungle Antidote – Minor, 1 day
- Jungle Mana Potion – 4 days

Devon nodded. That could be useful. "So I just put orders in the queue and you work on them?" She dragged in a *Jungle Health Potion - Mid* potion followed by a pair of *Jungle Healing Potion - Minors*.

"As I'm able. If you don't give me explicit instructions, I'll use my best judgment. The more I practice, the faster I'll get at producing each potion. It's likely I'll also get ideas for new concoctions."

Devon nodded. "I have a couple more questions before you get to work."

"Sure, ask away."

"When you first brought me here, you mentioned preparations for war. You said I wasn't experienced enough to learn about that. Can you tell me now?"

Hezbek's cheeks darkened in shame. "I'm sorry, Your Gloriousness. I didn't know you as well back then, so I didn't feel the need to be so honest. The truth is, I don't know the answer. Uruquat claimed that we needed to gain this great power in preparation for a conflict. Actually, he didn't use those words. I believe he said, 'We make readying for the fighting.' Anyway, I doubt he concocted the plan to venture out here alone. Maybe he was working with someone."

A quest dialog popped up.

> **Hezbek is offering you a quest:** Who are the Puppet Masters?
> *Surely the ogre didn't come up with his plan alone. It would probably be a good idea to figure out who else knows you're out here.*
> **Objective:** Find out who was supplying Uruquat with ideas.
> **Reward:** 5600 experience

Devon accepted the quest then stepped toward the door flap, grimacing at the heat that leaked around the edges.

"Thanks, Hezbek," she said.

The woman mumbled something in response, her attention already consumed by her mortar and pestle.

Devon stepped outside. Puppet masters... The more she thought about it, the more certain she was that others were behind this expedition. Which meant they probably knew exactly where this camp was located. Not a great situation. For now, the raised platforms would allow the tribe to sleep in safety, but before constructing more permanent structures, she wanted to survey the surroundings in hopes of finding a better location for a village.

Lost in thought, she hacked a path toward the Ishildar's outskirts. As she trudged forward, slaying underbrush with artful strikes from her mighty machete, she peered into the shadowy forest.

"Hey, wisp?" she called. "About that champion thing, I'm interested now."

Unfortunately, the glowing ball didn't arrive. Eventually, sweat-soaked and bored with the task, she returned to the camp.

And was greeted with panicked shouts. Her breath caught... not again.

Devon chased the shouts to the construction site and saw a half-built platform cantilevered over a pair of cowering villagers. The carpenter was frantically trying to keep the whole thing from tipping and crushing people. Devon ran over, grabbed a vine, and threw it over the uphill corner of the falling platform. She dropped her weight onto it, and the wooden decking began to tilt back to level.

She started calling out instructions, getting people to support it from underneath, hoping to center the platform and lash down the corners.

After a few difficult minutes, they managed to get the platform's frame level and securely fastened to four of the trees. The carpenter sat on the planks, mopping his brow. After a few breaths, he raised his chin then stood and asked for the final boards to finish the floor.

Around twenty minutes later, the sturdy platform was complete.

A string of messages appeared.

Construction succeeded despite lack of plans! (+60% chance due to your Improvisation score.)

Congratulations, your settlement has a new building. Your carpenter has learned the plans for Raised Platform.

You received a special skill point: *+1 Improvisation*

Beside her, Prester was staring into the distance, a look of awe on his face.

"*Improvisation*, Your Gloriousness. I've gained a higher understanding of the skill. I didn't even know such a thing was possible."

Seemed like her special skill was rubbing off on those near her. Awesome!

Now that the platform was finished and secure, she suggested they replace the ladder of planks with rope ladders that could be pulled up overnight. After those were ready, she invited the villagers up onto the platform. They fit, though there wasn't a lot of room to walk around.

Facing the group of villagers, she laid a hand on the carpenter's shoulder.

"Thanks to Prester, we have a safe place for tonight. I want you to get your bedrolls and any possessions you can't bear to lose and lay them out up here. I realize it's not as comfortable as your huts. In the next few days, we'll find a more permanent site to build a secure encampment. For now, though, we've nothing to fear from that boar."

You have received +25 reputation with the Tribe of Uruquat.

Her work finished, Devon took a deep breath. Even though fatigue bar was only half full, she felt the tiredness sinking into her bones. A glance at her real-world clock showed that it was late afternoon. Time to get ready to eat some tacos.

She turned to Prester. "I must leave the realm, but I trust you'll sleep well. Tomorrow, continue producing rough planks and raised platforms to increase your skills. Every bit of work you do now will make our next phase easier. I look forward to seeing your progress when I return."

With that, she climbed down the ladder and went to sleep in Hezbek's hut before logging out.

Chapter Sixteen

"HAS ANYONE TALKED to Penelope about this?" Emerson asked as he faced off with the CEO of E Squared Entertainment. They stood in a virtual boardroom, a circular chamber at the top of a wizard's tower the CEO, Bradley, had created especially for his in-game avatar.

"How we deal with Penelope is not your concern," Bradley said. "We've kept you two separate for a reason. We believe strongly in the idea of having the AIs face off in an ultimate conflict. But that doesn't work if their creators share information."

"But you're asking me to deal with server load when more than half the problem is with Zaa. Meanwhile, Veia is running *all* the players. Her algorithms are creating more compelling content, more advanced mechanics... She's basically the reason this game exists."

"And we should just shut Zaa off?" Bradley asked sarcastically. "Abandon our philosophy of competition and retreat back to the mediocre content offered by last-generation games?"

"I'm not suggesting that at all. I'm just saying that maybe we should allow the AI who is *succeeding* to continue full steam. Force Penelope to get Zaa's load under control or his content up to snuff."

"Your statement is noted. Now, will you do as I asked and see where you can optimize? We need to bring more players online or we'll lose our momentum. And if we have to bring more hardware onto the system to do that, it's going to be a lot harder to turn a profit. Entwined won't be happy."

"That's another thing. I have reports of the hardware causing an outsized pain response. Do we have any recourse with Entwined if they damage our players? Or if the play experience is too unpleasant and we lose subscribers?"

"I saw your email about that. Right now, the experience seems isolated to a single player, one of your all-stars. Are you sure she's cut out for salaried play? Maybe she should go back to Tetris."

Emerson was glad he was meeting in a virtual space. He forced his avatar to keep a stony expression while back in his kitchen, he sliced a carrot with angry chops that sent pieces flying.

"If there's nothing else, I'll see what I can do about optimizations."

"That will be all."

Chapter Seventeen

TAMARA GRINNED WHEN Devon pushed through the door to the Mexican food place. The restaurant was packed, each of the battered yellow tables heaped with plastic soda cups, balled-up napkins, and huge plates of tacos. People sat around laughing, and since it was a Wifi-free zone, the only people with screens out were those eating alone and reading. Tamara had done a good job staking out and defending territory. Her purse, a black and purple thing constructed of outdoor-person ballistic nylon sat on one chair while Tamara hovered near another, her hand on the back so no one swiped it while she stood to wave at Devon.

Devon hurried across the floor, unused to the sound of so many people talking. Her in-game followers spoke, but it was always a low rumble of conversation, not this raucous laughter over shared food. It made Devon think she needed to do more to increase happiness in her settlement.

She sighed. She also really needed to work on forgetting about the game long enough to be social.

Tamara grabbed her purse and kicked out the chair for Devon to sit as she reclaimed her own seat.

"The server's slammed. I wasn't sure whether to order you something to drink."

Devon scanned the laminated menu. "I think I'll go with horchata."

Tamara grinned. "Good. Because that's what I got you. Figured if you didn't like it, I'd just chug two helpings."

Devon glanced at the black lines of grease ground into creases on Tamara's hands. Since taking the job as a bike mechanic, her friend had developed a tan and looked a lot healthier than she had during their time at Fort Kolob.

"So, do you miss being Annie Oakley?"

Tamara laughed. "Not at all. How about you? How's life as a salaried gamer? Seems crazy."

Devon shrugged. "People have been doing it for a while, but it's either been competitive gamers... shooters and strategy players mostly, or it's been live-streamers. Not my thing."

"Don't want your face on a few hundred thousand people's retinas?"

"Or worse, a full-immersion sensory stream where they're feeling everything I feel." She grimaced. "I guess I'm into my privacy."

"How about the game itself? I mean, assume you're speaking to someone who's completely ignorant about what they're like."

"It's different. I've been enjoying myself more than I expected. I spawned way out in the wilderness with no one around, and I'm kind of making my own way." Devon grinned. "Get this: I have my own tribe. We're building a village."

The server stepped up to the table, set down a pair of cups, and pulled out his tablet. "What'll it be, ladies? And is the horchata okay? Your friend wasn't sure what you'd want."

"It's great. I'll have a carnitas plate."

156

"Veggie tacos for me," Tamara said.

"You got it," the waiter said as he tapped a couple options on his device. He gave Tamara a subtle once-over before heading toward the kitchen.

"He's into you," Devon said.

Tamara shrugged. "I'm chilling out on dating for a while. I get plenty of testosterone exposure at work."

"So how's it going?"

"I'll be moving out of the junior mechanic slot soon," Tamara said. "And as an extra bonus, I'm getting a small sponsorship."

"For mountain biking? No way. Congrats."

"Actually, it's for knitting." Tamara snorted. "Yes, mountain biking. Mostly it's because I work in the shop, not because of my skills. And it's nothing like your full-time gamer gig. But still—"

Abruptly, Devon's head swam. A vision flashed to life, strange black spires that would put a Gothic cathedral to shame. Carrion birds circled beneath a roiling sky. The air was damp and full of poison, and Devon was hollow with need.

As quick as it had come, the glimpse was gone. She sucked in a ragged breath.

"Hey Dev, are you okay?"

Devon shook her head to try to clear the disorientation. The actinic glare of the LEDs overhead seemed to pulse. Her head throbbed. What the hell?

"I—I don't know, I had this... vision I guess. Like I accidentally accessed my hardware and immersed somewhere strange. But it's a Wifi-free zone, so that doesn't make sense."

Already, the sensations were vanishing. Devon scrambled after them, clawing at the memories. But they dissolved like smoke in a breeze, and after a moment, all she could remember was that she'd zoned out for a couple seconds.

"You looked way pale," Tamara said.

"I think I'm just hungry. Sometimes I forget to eat when I'm playing."

"That doesn't sound healthy."

"Yeah. I think I'd better start setting meal alarms."

"But otherwise, it seems really cool," Tamara said. "I never got into the deep-dive games because of the VR gear." She grimaced. "I couldn't bring myself to try out one of the public pods, and headgear looked so clunky. Oh, and expensive."

"And a ten-thousand-dollar mountain bike? That's not expensive?"

Tamara grinned. "That's different."

"Anyway, the implants are seamless. I forget they're there."

Devon lifted her hair off her neck to show Tamara the visible part of her embedded circuitry, the lines of shining metal tattooed into her skin.

"That's pretty sweet," Tamara said. "You just chill on the couch and enter a new world. How does it feel?"

"I really thought the old VR gear was immersive. But this... It's something more. It feels just as real as this restaurant does."

"But is it better? I like my life. I wouldn't want to give it up. Like, what if it was more fun than the high I get after making it through a techie downhill run or the exhaustion I feel after a long cross-country ride. I'd be afraid I'd lose touch with those things if I found something better."

"It's different because I know it's a game. But I guess there were a couple times that I almost forgot that. Still, I don't want to leave my real life behind or anything." Devon shrugged. "Not that I have a lot going on there, to be honest."

"I did offer to take you mountain biking," Tamara said, teasing. "A couple of guys from the shop would be psyched to take you out, too."

Devon snorted. "Until they saw how uncoordinated I am. I'd be a danger to everyone on the trail."

The food arrived, deposited on their table by a pair of runners from the kitchen. Devon's stomach growled so loud she wondered if the whole restaurant could hear it.

"Maybe I'll give it a shot," Devon said. "But only after you come join my new tribe."

Chapter Eighteen

EZRAXIS PERCHED ON a branch in the night-dark forest, curtains of hanging moss draping her like a shroud. She sensed her prey approaching, as much a perception of the flesh as of her eyes. The demon sensed the pathetic lifelight that inhabited the advancing creature. She hungered to release it from its mortal prison. Closer, and she could feel the creature's heat, smell its breath, wet with just a tinge of sulfur.

The salamander stepped a single foot within range, and the demon leaped. She landed on the slick flesh of the salamander's back, raking it with her hind claws and wrapping a forefoot around its throat. With a mighty slash, she opened the creature's neck. Fire sprayed from the rent, singeing Ezraxis's face. She smelled burning flesh, and her vision in one eye went dark, boiled away. But she'd accomplished what she intended with the attack. The salamander's flame sac had been punctured, its greatest weapon neutralized.

With a screech, she leaped off the amphibian's back, flapped her misshapen wings—one still hadn't regrown to full-size—and landed before the beast.

She wanted the salamander to see it's death approaching, all dripping fangs and burning eyes.

The creature tried to flee, already leaking blood from half-a-dozen gashes.

"No," Ezraxis said, a guttural cry in the dark.

She lashed out with her front claws and flayed open the thing's legs.

Crippled, the salamander thrashed and tried to squirm away. The demon watched it struggle, enjoying the power she held over the beast.

As the salamander began to weaken, its breath wet in its mangled throat, the demon stalked forward. Her thigh still ached. This creature had blinded her, seared her flesh. It deserved to die. It deserved to feel her claws and to stare into her baleful eyes for the last moments of its pathetic life.

She leaped forward and landed a foot between its shoulder blades, crushing the beast into the wet earth. Keeping it pinned, she dragged its head up, farther and farther until their eyes met and its throat was fully exposed.

With a vicious shriek, Ezraxis snapped her head forward and closed her razor-sharp teeth around the salamander's throat.

It died with a gush of blood into her mouth, and she stepped away, lips pulled back in a fearsome scowl. Conquest. Blood. The kill was hers. Again.

Deprived of the rush of combat, she felt the pain of wounds earned during the fight. Her face burned, and her blinded eye socket ached. But as the pain slipped through her, red mist began to rise from the trails of blood left by the fleeing amphibian. Thicker tendrils of mist tongued from the salamander's wounds, licking the air before streaming forth.

The demon stepped into the swirling mist, inhaling deeply. Power filled her lungs and sank through her pores, flooding her with healing energy. Sight slowly returned to her damaged eye, dead trees emerging first as shadows and then as skeletal hands bathed in sickly moonlight. The smell of seared flesh faded, replaced by the layers of rot blanketing the swamp. Again, the deep wound—that first wound—in her thigh knitted just a fraction more. Bones cracked and grew and reformed as her wing stretched farther from her back. Soon, it would match the other. She would be whole.

But the blood mist did more than heal her. With each kill, particularly those that bled longer, hurt longer, the demon gained strength. Once, seemingly so long ago, rats had provided a contest for her. Now fire salamanders fell beneath her black claws.

She opened her arms wide and screeched.

Pathetic.

Zaa's voice penetrated her spirit, thrust into her soul, flooded her veins with ice.

She cringed.

Wretched.

The demon whined and cowered against the silvery base of a dead tree.

But improving. You grow stronger each day. In time, you may prove yourself worthy of my attention. Yet still, you follow the path suggested to you. Can the blood offer more than this slow restoration? Can you gain greater power?

Ezraxis fell to her stomach and knees, groveling before her god. She felt indifference from the deity, the emotion freezing her from the inside out. But within Zaa's touch, deep, deep beneath the layers of disregard, her god had taken an interest in her.

Trust the blood. Allow the power to guide you to greater challenges. You are progressing, but our very way of life is threatened. Become faster, or you will never be of use to me.

Around her, shreds of blood mist still lingered. Ezraxis stepped forward, and on instinct, clawed open new gashes over her ribs. She carved designs in her own flesh and allowed the blood to sink in and heal them. Deep within her core, she felt something ignite. She took to the sky.

Chapter Nineteen

THE SUN HAD already set in Relic Online when Devon entered the game. She stood and stretched and pushed aside the flap of Hezbek's hut. The fire had been lit and was crackling merrily in the center of the clearing. Her tribe sat around it chewing their evening meal. She glanced toward the edge of the clearing, eager to see the progress on the platforms, but the trees held too much darkness beneath their leaves. Inspecting the construction could wait. First, she needed to see to her people.

They greeted her with tired smiles. Tired, but satisfied.

Still, Devon couldn't help thinking about the laughter and camaraderie she'd seen in the taco place. She wanted to create that here.

The carpenter was preparing to speak, no doubt to give a report. She smiled at him.

"Wait, don't tell me," she said gently. "I want to be surprised." She turned to the others. "Do you have enough to eat? How's the food?"

No one spoke right away, and Devon noticed quite a few glances cast in Hezbek's direction.

The medicine woman huffed and rolled her eyes. "Okay fine. Bunch of yellow-spined babies. I *suppose* I'll talk for the rest of you.

You want the truth, Your Gloriousness? Or would you rather we just smiled and nodded."

Devon sighed as she took a seat. The fire was warm against her shins and face, and she held her palms up to the blaze. "What do you think? Of course I want the truth. Spit it out."

"Well, I don't know how it is among the starborn, but we prefer a little variety in our meals. Been eating the same thing since we arrived: questionable meat cooked over the fire so long it tastes like ash, not to mention so dry it takes a full cup of water to wash down each bite."

"I see. So you're saying you'd like an improvement to the food situation?"

The woman looked at her, bewildered. "Yes, that's what I was trying—"

"I don't blame you," Devon said with a laugh.

As she scanned the group, she spotted a face she didn't recognize. After a moment, she realized that was because he'd been asleep on Hezbek's cot for most of the time she'd been here. Deld grinned and waved at her. Devon smiled and continued making eye contact with the others.

"Are there any of you who are dying to become a cook?" she asked.

At a nudge from the fighter, Bayle, a slight man with a bulbous nose and oversized ears stood. He took off his felt hat and held it in front of his belly. Even with the hat's sun protection, he'd earned a livid stripe of sunburn just above the collar of his tunic. Poor guy.

"It's all I've ever wanted, Your Gloriousness—I mean, sir. Ma'am."

Devon sighed. "Anything you want to call me is fine. And that goes for the rest of you, too. Devon, Your Gloriousness, sir, ma'am, whatever. Maybe you could get together and settle on something."

The man cleared his throat, flushing brightly around his ears. "I always told my wife..." He gestured toward Bayle. Devon suppressed a reaction—Bayle probably outweighed him by two, maybe three times. "I always told her that if I ever got the chance I could build the most popular restaurant in all of Eltera City. I still dream of that, but... Well, we're here now."

"We are, but there are people here who need to eat, too."

"You're right, Your Glori—Devon. I promise if you give me the job, you won't be disappointed. I don't mean to be conceited, but I think my culinary efforts could attract others to our settlement, too. I'd never suggest that others would come *just* for my cooking, but—"

"But they'd be fools not to come," Bayle said. "Tom's cooking's the best in the realm. You wouldn't regret choosing him, Your Gloriousness."

"No, I don't imagine I would." Population wasn't something Devon had put much thought to. As they built up the settlement, they *would* need more citizens.

The man, Tom, stood with eyes glued to his feet. "Do I... Am I to assume that you...?"

"You have my blessing. Consider yourself our chef."

"Now," Hezbek said, "can you do something about this disgusting meal?"

The request wiped the smile off of Tom's face. "Afraid not. It's already been cooked to cinders, and I've nothing to season it with. But if you can wait until tomorrow, I'll spend the day foraging. And if it's all right with you, Your Highness—" Devon rolled her eyes but gestured for him to continue. "I'd like to reserve a couple pieces of meat for testing—let's say the snake meat because it needs the most work. I'd like to experiment with a few recipes before dinner service. Find the best flavor combinations given our ingredients."

"Granted." Finally, she glanced at Prester. "I know you're probably dying to give me an update."

The carpenter leaped up and dashed toward the forest, slowing only when he realized she was still climbing to her feet. She hurried to catch him, and together they approached the construction site. Devon had expected two or three finished platforms, but a full five perched in the trees above her head. The villagers had even constructed some rudimentary rope bridges between them.

"It's gotten easier with each one," Prester said. "I gained a skill tier in the process. And my ability to improvise has made me confident when experimenting with ways to speed construction."

"That's fantastic, Prester."

Devon inspected the beaming man and indeed noticed that he'd gained a skill tier. More recipes were unlocked, and now she could see the following additions:

- Finely Hewn Plank
- Wood Beam
- Shed, sloped roof
- Wooden chest, rudimentary
- Simple door
- Straight-backed chair

More notable, though, was his *Improvisation* score. It was up to 2 points, which was almost equal to hers.

She clapped him on the shoulder. "Amazing. You've outdone yourself."

As she reached out to shake his hand, a pop-up appeared.

> **You have uncovered a skill in which you have intrinsic aptitude:** Leadership (5).
> Skills which are intrinsic start with a value above 0.
> **You have gained a skill point:** +1 Leadership.

"Are you still gaining skill with these projects?"

"Yes, though it's slow."

"Then let's move on to Finely Hewn Planks tomorrow. I'm sure we'll have use for them once we have a permanent location for our home. Thank you, Prester."

He touched his brow. "Happy to be of service."

Together, they headed toward the campfire. Back within the cheery glow of the blaze, Devon scanned the rapidly darkening clearing. The others were relaxing and watching the flames dance, but someone was missing. Again.

"Where's Greel?" she asked.

Many of the tribe members looked around as if shocked to notice him missing, but Grey, the hunter, spoke up. "He headed off toward the ruins," he said.

"What? He left now?"

Grey shrugged. "He does it fairly often. It was something he'd worked out with Uruquat. They'd often speak before Greel left."

"He always went in the same direction? Has he left since Uruquat was... removed?"

"Yup, same direction. And this is the first time he's left in a while, as far as I know."

"Can you show me exactly where he headed out?"

"Of course." Grey stood and dusted off his trousers. As Devon stepped in beside him, a call came from the fire.

"One more thing, Your Gloriousness."

Devon turned to see the leatherworker hurrying forward. He carried the sheath she'd requested in one hand and had tucked something under his other arm.

"Gerrald. How could I have forgotten the sheath? I'm sorry. I do appreciate your hard work."

The leatherworker waved off her apology. "You've much to occupy your mind." He handed over the sheath, which Devon quickly slipped over her belt. The machete slid easily into the cover, and she practiced drawing the blade a couple times before nodding approval.

"There's one more thing," the man said. He pulled the bundle from under his arm and shook it out before handing it over.

You have received: Snakeskin Vest
Finely crafted, this vest is sharp! SSSsizzling.
+2 Intelligence, +1 Cunning | 20 Armor | 25/25 Durability

She gave a low whistle. "Wow."

"I hope you don't mind. I was without direct requests and thought I should fill my time with—I wanted to thank you, ma'am. You freed us. More, you've agreed to guide us."

"Thank you, Gerrald." She examined the vest's lower hem. " These etchings—I assume that's where the added benefits came from. Can you affect all attributes?"

The man looked consternated by the question. "That's difficult to answer. You see, I didn't choose how the item would benefit you, not deliberately. As I was stamping runes into the leather, I just thought about which things most set you apart from Uruquat. I wanted the vest to showcase those strengths." He shrugged.

She settled the vest onto her torso. It fit snugly, and already she felt more durable. And... her thoughts seemed to work faster. That part must've been her imagination. The game couldn't actually make her smarter no matter how many points she assigned to *Intelligence*. But she was happy to pretend, enjoying the buzz that felt like a couple cups of morning coffee.

"Thank you," she said. "It's perfect. And as for those requests you were missing, over the next few days, I'd like you to work on armor for your fellow tribe members. Start with those tribe members with the lowest health and natural armor. Work your way up as you are able."

He gave her a little salute. "Will do."

"As for the rest of you, you're doing great. Continue on."

***

Devon crept through the forest, following the signs of Greel's passage. He'd been clever, pushing aside brush rather than breaking it and jumping from root to root to avoid creating a packed trail near the encampment. But after maybe five minutes of walking, not only had Devon increased her Tracking skill to 4, but she'd also stepped out onto something of a well-used trail. She crouched down and examined the earth, trying to determine whether there were footprints made by more than one person, but even with her *Darkvision*, which had reached 10—tier 2!—she couldn't yet make out anything but trampled soil.

She loosened her machete in its sheath and crept forward, ears perked for sounds from the night. Now that she was away from the encampment, the birdsong had grown louder, and animals—no doubt, many of them snakes—rustled in the undergrowth. The air smelled like the garden section of a home improvement store. Cool against her skin, it was comfortable, but she sensed it would feel cold if she stopped moving for very long.

She reached a section of trail where the area of packed earth grew from just a couple paces across to around five feet. The trail narrowed again on the other side, leaving no real explanation for the opening. She carefully searched the edges of the small clearing, but spotted nothing, until...

There it was. A bundle had been stashed beneath a cluster of large leaves. Greel kept a bedroll and a rucksack out here. She pawed through the rucksack hoping for weapons, but it held nothing but rations and spare clothing. Too bad. She shoved everything back under the foliage and continued on.

A couple minutes later, a low growl rose from the jungle beside her.

Devon leaped back and yanked her blade from the sheath. She held the machete before her face, dropped into a combat crouch, and searched the darkness beyond the trail.

Brush exploded into motion as a massive creature jumped out, claws bared and glinting, a roar rumbling in its throat. It landed on the trail, dagger-like fangs glistening in the faint light. The sabertoothed cat's eyes shone in the darkness. Its tail flicked back and forth, rattling the foliage as it crouched before her.

Shit.

"Nice... kitty?" She said, noticing just then that scales rather than fur covered the beast. So technically not a cat after all. It responded with a growl and swiped at her. Claws glanced off her vest.

"All right, then. We don't need to be friends."

The sabertoothed cat-lizard-thing was at least four times her size. Devon looked down at her machete and shook her head. This wasn't going to be easy. She circled around to get her body onto the open trail where she could move. As she did, the faint moonlight painted her shadow on the packed earth.

Right! *Shadow Puppet.* Time to see with the ability could do.

She focused on her shadow and willed it to elongate. Almost as if flexing another limb, she felt the darkness move in response. The shadow stretched out long, extending beneath the sabertoothed beast, and—defying the laws of physics—stood up tall on the far side of the monster.

Unfortunately, the sabertooth didn't seem to notice. Its tail swished as it crouched to pounce.

Devon raised her blade and got ready to dodge. She gritted her teeth and stared at the shadow, willing the beast to take notice.

And, as if responding to her desire, the shadow leaped forward. She felt its motion as an extension of her body, as if someone had taken hold of her arm and moved it for her. Her shadow-self stomped on the sabertooth's tail.

To Devon's abundant shock, the beast growled and spun, swatting at the shadow. Claws slashed across darkness, and distantly, Devon felt her shadow wither. Energy began to leak from the casting. This wasn't going to last.

Indecision froze her in her tracks. Should she use the distraction and try, despite her better instincts, to take the beast down? Or should she run while she had the chance?

Devon had never gained a lot by running.

With a shout, she jumped forward and landed astraddle the scaled beast. A memory flashed to life, of riding on the bog serpent's head in what felt like another lifetime, Owen calling her a cowgirl. The sabertooth bucked and writhed, reptilian yowls rising from its throat as it struggled to dislodge her. The machete glanced off scales, unable to penetrate. Devon grabbed a finely scaled ear, held it tightly with one hand and sliced through it. The creature roared.

Her shadow looked at her and shrugged as if to ask what the hell *that* was supposed to do.

"If you have a better idea..." she muttered.

But by the time she finished the sentence, her shadow dissolved, all power having leaked from the casting. She glanced at her mana. The added *Cunning* from her vest had increased her pool to 40, though just 20 remained now. She cast *Shadow Puppet* again, forcing her awareness to embrace both her shadow-self and her wildly-tossed body. Her shadow jumped forward and grabbed hold of the sabertoothed-thing's hind leg, weighing the beast down, though not by much.

The beast snarled and reared and almost threw her. She clung with all her strength. It wasn't going to be enough.

Think, Devon.

As soon as she got the idea to distract the sabertoothed-thing with something like a globe of darkness, her shadow rushed forward and enveloped the beast's head. It stuffed arms down the monster's nostrils, and when the beast opened its mouth, the shadow shoved in a leg. Devon cringed. Not exactly what she'd imagined, but it seemed to be working. Now blind and suffocating, the monster thrashed, bolted, and rammed headfirst into a tree. It slumped over, dazed, and stopped flailing long enough for Devon to take aim at its throat. She slashed with the machete, slipping it between the scales and into the soft flesh beneath. The sabertooth gave a rattling cough then went still.

You have gained a special attribute point: +1 Bravery.
You have gained a special attribute point: +1 Cunning.
You have gained mastery in Shadow Puppet - Tier 1: 10%.

Breathing heavily, Devon stood. Her shadow stood with her, no longer acting, but merely following her moves. Ever so slowly, it curled down to lie flat against the earth, melting away into the ordinary darkness cast by the moonlight and her body. Swallowing, Devon crouched and began skinning the beast to activate looting. The monster disintegrated into components.

You have received: Sabertooth Meat x 2
You have received: Sabertooth Scale x 10
You have received: Ivory Fangs x 2 (unidentified)

More unidentified items. Judging by every other game she'd played, that meant that the fangs had some sort of magical ability associated with them.

How to identify items, just another thing on my growing list of crap to figure out...

Devon glanced at her experience bar. The kill had put her a good chunk through level 5, but she still had some distance before her next ding. Oh well.

Stretching, she stepped back onto the trail and checked the game clock. She'd been moving for a couple hours, including the fight. No wonder Greel needed a bedroll for whatever he came out here to do. She doubted he made it back before dawn very often. She sheathed her machete and continued forward, senses alert for more threats. After maybe another half hour of walking, she heard voices ahead and immediately dropped to a crouch. She traveled the final fifty yards over the course of ten minutes, carefully placing each foot.

Once in sight of the clearing where the voices were coming from, she slipped into the foliage, wincing when a single stick cracked. Fortunately, they didn't seem to notice. She peered through the leaves and spotted three shadowy figures. Greel was unmistakable, his hunched shoulders as much a fixture on him as his sneer. The other two were burly men, clad in clothes more suited for the wilderness than she and her followers were in their thin cloth. She couldn't make out what the men were saying, but the tension in the air was obvious. Words were hissed, and occasionally, one of the thugs would shake a fist.

She listened as hard as she could, hoping that she'd gain some sort of skill point by concentrating on the sounds. But before a notification popped up, she gasped as one of the big men pulled back his fist and prepared to strike.

"Now wait," Greel said, reaching for his hip... and the rusty knife he no longer had.

The fist connected. Greel spun but, remarkably, kept his feet.

"Wait," the other of the thugs said. "Rough him up, but don't kill him. We need information on the woman who took over."

Another wet sound cut the air as a fist connected, but incredibly, Greel was *still* standing. To Devon's shock, he kicked, connecting with one of the men's knees and sending him down.

"You little weasel!" The other yelled, snatching Greel by the tunic and lifting.

Devon clenched her jaw. She might not like Greel—and the feeling was mutual—but he was one of her tribe. These men clearly were not. Standing up, she drew her blade.

Chapter Twenty

DEVON PEERED HARD at the men, activating her *Combat Assessment* skill.

Hired Thug
Against just this guy, you might have a chance if you land a lucky blow or the lawyer helps out.

Hired Thug
You want to fight both of them? Not sure why you're even considering it.
Then again, you did take down that ogre...

You have gained a skill point: +1 Combat Assessment.

"All right, you made your point, game," she whispered. Not good odds. She doubted she could count on Greel's help, but her special attributes and Deceiver ability had to count for something, right?

Greel still hung in the air, grasping at the thug's wrists and uselessly kicking his feet. Devon glanced overhead, judging the angle of the moonlight. She'd need to advance a few paces into the clearing before she'd have a shadow. What then? She remembered the spell description for *Shadow Puppet*; it had claimed that her puppets would have different properties depending on what sort of light was used in their casting. During her fight with the sabertooth, her shadow had made physical contact with the monster, but it hadn't inflicted much—if any—damage. Shadows drawn by the moonlight must be physically weak. But it had been quick, almost liquid. And that had been quite a trick, cramming itself into the beast's... facial orifices. Yuck.

Regardless, the suffocation thing was cool. Maybe it would work again.

Devon shoved brush aside and sprinted forward until her shadow appeared on the ground before her. Quickly, she groped for her shimmering awareness of her mana pool and poured magical energy into the shadow, giving the figure life. When she gave the shadow a mental nudge, it arrowed across the clearing. Her creation streamed up the body of the man who held Greel in his grip and enveloped the man's head. The thug let out a muffled cry, dropped Greel into an astonished heap on the ground, and started clawing at the darkness enclosing his face.

The man's fingers tore the vitality from her shadow. Her spell lasted just a breath longer before disintegrating into nothingness. The thug gasped, sucking precious air into his lungs. She peered hard, assessing the damage. His health had only dropped by 10% or so.

Her gaze shot to the other fighter, just now struggling back to his feet after Greel had kicked his knee out. His health was down by a quarter.

Devon's eyebrows raised. Given that Greel had knocked off that much health with a single kick, either he was extremely lucky, or he was... good?

"Greel, get over here!" she called in her most commanding voice. As the lawyer ran toward her, she emptied the last of her mana into another *Shadow Puppet* and sent it darting toward the far side of the clearing.

As her shadow melted into the forest, Devon focused her concentration. Gritting her teeth, she willed her creation to grab a few twigs. It took all her shadow's strength to snap them.

But it was enough. One of the fighters pivoted toward the sound.

"We've got more coming," he growled.

The man with the hurt knee took a couple limping steps toward the thicket. The other thug faced them. His hand now gleamed in the moonlight, armored with brass knuckles. Devon grimaced at the thought of that fist connecting.

"You traitor, Greel," the brass-knuckled man said. "The boss will hear about this."

Greel stood beside Devon's shoulder, a conflicted expression on his face. He didn't like her. The question was, did he like these other guys even less?

"Your boss won't hear anything if they don't make it back to report," she said.

"Good point."

"Where did you learn how to fight?"

Greel shrugged. "You'd be surprised how many people think it's fun to rough up a lawyer. Has given me lots of practice over the years."

Brass Knuckles squinted in their direction, trying to make out details in the dark.

"What's your combat strength?" Devon hissed as she raised her machete.

The lawyer snorted. "Remember that knife you took from me?"

Right. Well, she wasn't about to give him her blade.

The pair of thugs stood back to back, circling slowly. Devon compelled her shadow to break another twig. That distraction wasn't going to last much longer.

"How fast can you run?" She pitched her voice low, hoping the fighters couldn't make it out.

"As it happens, running away from disadvantageous situations is another lawyer skill."

Devon gestured with her chin. "We need to separate them, take them down one at a time. Try sprinting across the clearing to lure one but keep out of reach."

Greel snorted. "I thought I'd let them catch me."

She ignored the remark. "If one chases you, I'll try to take him out. Circle back."

"Yeah, fine." Greel burst into motion. Devon blinked in surprise. He was fast for someone with such a stiff appearance.

As he dashed past the pair of fighters, Brass Knuckles grunted. "Little weasel. He's trying to join the others."

The big man gave chase, Hurt Knee limping behind. As his heavy footfalls shook the spongy ground, Devon's shadow dove beneath the fighter's feet. At her mental command, the shadow substance consolidated. Devon jerked with the shock as the man's toe caught on her phantom. The fighter crashed down hard, breath leaving his lungs in a whoosh. Her shadow slithered away, damaged but still alive.

Brass Knuckles groaned, disoriented. Devon gripped her machete, ready to dash forward, but pulled up short when Greel suddenly yelped, cut hard to the side, and sprinted toward Hurt

Knee. The lawyer planted a foot and launched a flying kick that took the fighter in the side. Devon winced when she heard ribs crack. The man's health plummeted as he and Greel went down in a tangle.

Devon sprinted forward, her Tribal Sandals pounding the wet ground and boosting her speed. She grabbed Greel's hand and dragged him free as his opponent rolled and tried to snatch him. Greel scrambled to his feet and ran with her. The pair slid to a stop at the far side of the clearing.

Both fighters were climbing to their feet, Hurt Knee below half health, Brass Knuckles down to maybe 80%.

"Are you with the tribe now, Greel?" she asked. "No more lies."

"I admit to playing many sides. But I always follow my self-interest when choosing my allegiance. Right now, that's with you."

Devon stabbed a hand into a bag and grabbed one of the ivory fangs. She shoved it into his grip. "It's not a rusty knife..."

He held it awkwardly. "Piercing weapon. I'm not—"

"Would you rather fight barehanded?"

He shook his head and adjusted his grip. Circling slowly, he walked like an arthritis sufferer. Devon never would've guessed he could let loose with moves like that flying kick. There was an advantage in having an ally like that if she could find a way to trust him.

Greel closed the distance as the thugs advanced, more cautious than before. Devon brought her shadow into action. The dark form darted with unnatural quickness, raining light blows on Brass Knuckles to distract him. With a strangled yell, the man waved his hands in the air. Unfazed by her puppet, Greel sprinted forward and landed a glancing blow on the exposed skin of the man's forearm.

The man shrieked.

Devon grimaced as the flesh suddenly pulled back from the scratch, opening a gaping fissure on his arm. The edges of the gash scaled over, turning greenish-white like the flesh of the sabertooth. Greel looked down at the fang with new appreciation.

"Ew," she muttered.

Brass Knuckles freaked. He slapped at his own arm, eyes wide-rimmed.

"Enough of this!" he yelled as he whirled and started running. Devon inhaled. Focused. She tossed her shadow in front of the man to distract him as she sprinted forward, reversed the machete in her grip, and clocked him on the back of the head with the hilt.

He fell to the ground, limp.

The other man staggered backward, hands raised.

"Mercy," he said, dropping to his knees. "I'll pay."

Devon had already closed half the distance between them. She pulled up short as she swung her shadow wide to come at him from the other side.

"We might make an arrangement. I've got some questions I'd like answered."

Greel fixed her with a hard stare. "Don't trust him. He knows what punishments await in Eltera if he tells you anything."

"He can't earn those punishments if he doesn't return to Eltera," Devon said. In the back of her mind, she hoped he might turn coat. She could use more fighters in her tribe.

She caught a look passing between the man and Greel an instant before the thug sprang, landing on his good leg and aiming a fist at her weapon arm.

Greel stood just a step out of his path. Close enough to knock the attack aside. He remained still.

Growling in frustration, Devon sent her shadow forward. The dark figure leaped and collided with the thug, knocking the man just slightly off balance. She stepped aside, raised her blade, and drew it across the man's neck as he stumbled forward. His throat opened, and he raised his hands to clutch it as he fell. He thrashed once and went still.

Devon whirled on Greel, weapon raised. "Traitor. You could've stopped him."

Greel raised one hand and crouched to deposit the fang on the ground. He backed away slowly.

"There's your proof that I mean you no harm. Disarmed, I can't beat you."

He licked his lips. Devon advanced a step. She didn't lower her blade.

"I was afraid I'd nick you if I tried to take him down. You saw what happened..." He gestured at the unconscious man. "As a crude weapon, the fang is beyond my Piercing skill level. The injury that man took wasn't what I intended. More a lucky fumble than anything."

Devon swiped the fang from the ground. She rotated her grip on it in her off-hand. It *did* feel awkward, like it wanted to slip out of her palm. She couldn't envision attacking with it like she could her machete. Maybe he was telling the truth. Maybe not. Eyes narrowed, she shoved the item into her bag.

"And you couldn't just knock him aside?"

"It was a split-second decision," he said.

Devon took a few deep breaths while she considered his claim. There might be truth to it. Even now, she could see the white of bone where the man's flesh had melted away. If she'd accidentally caused that kind of damage, she might have hesitated to get into the thick of melee with an ally involved.

"I'll give you a chance, this time," she said.

She crouched beside the slain man and plucked at his clothing to activate the looting process. He decomposed into a set of items.

You have received: Paper with Scrawled Orders
You have received: Map

It was too dark to examine the paper and map, so she tucked them into her bag. Scooping up a handful of coins, she watched as her inventory gained 3 silver and 2 gold pieces. Devon stalked to the other man. He was starting to stir.

"Have anything to bind him with?"

Greel turned out his pockets but then hurried over and crouched beside the man. He dragged a couple pieces of rope from the thug's pocket. "Seems they were prepared to take a captive. Not sure if these were meant for me or you."

Devon snatched them away and bound the man's wrists tightly. This close, the wound looked even worse. When she checked the man's health bar, she noticed it was falling very slowly. Some sort of poison?

She hobbled his ankles, securing each tightly and then stringing around a foot of rope between them so that he could walk, but not quickly. Finally, she pulled the gleaming metal off his fingers.

You have received: Brass Knuckles
A decent weapon if you're into brawling.
4–9 damage | 12/13 durability

Now that the captive was secure and disarmed, she pulled up the combat log and checked her messages.

*You have slain a Hired Thug. **Experience gain reduced due to powerful assistance.***

You have gained a special attribute point: +1 Cunning.
You have gained mastery in Shadow Puppet – Tier 1: 10%.
You have gained mastery in Incapacitate – Tier 1: 15%.
You have gained esteem with Greel: +150 reputation.

What? The game considered Greel to be powerful assistance? A kill stealing lawyer... so lame! She pulled up her experience bar and saw she *still* wasn't level 6, but even with the reduction, she was close. Finally.

At least the message about her reputation gain with Greel was promising. Maybe she'd be able to trust him eventually.

Devon stared down at their captive. "So, where do we go from here, Greel?"

"For now, we should get back to camp. We have some time before these men are assumed missing. I suggest we use it to prepare for retaliation."

Chapter Twenty-One

DAWN BROKE OVER the encampment as Devon, Greel, and their captive entered the cleared area. The fire from the previous evening had died to low coals, and a tendril of smoke curled into the still air. Devon shaded her eyes and peered toward the new platforms. She smiled to see that her followers had moved Hezbek's hut up top. Seemed the woman was something of a grandmotherly figure to everyone in the tribe.

The others had slept crowded together on the first platform, possibly for warmth, maybe because they felt vulnerable without huts to protect them. In any case, the sound of footsteps brought some of them awake. The hunter, Grey, sat up, as did Bayle, Devon's fighter. She waved at them in greeting.

The captive staggered forward into the weak light. Scars crossed the man's stubble-covered cheeks, and his face had the hard look of a veteran combatant. But the wound on his arm was taking its toll. His health had fallen to 20%, and his eyes were glassy. No doubt he'd only kept marching because he knew he needed to reach a healer to survive the day. Their early progress had been so slow that she'd been forced to untie his hobbles. But he seemed to know the score and hadn't attempted to flee.

Greel cast the man another hate-filled glare. The lawyer had argued against bringing the man back. He was adamant the thug would give no useful information.

To which Devon had responded: "But you will, right?"

That had shut Greel up; the return march had been a largely silent one.

Without warning, the captive collapsed into the dirt. A pointed look at Greel set his eyes rolling. "Yes, fine, I'll go get Hezbek."

Despite the complaint, he left quickly and scampered up the rope ladder. While waiting, Devon pulled out the *Paper with Scrawled Orders* she'd looted. Fortunately, it was written in a language she understood.

We've had disappointing progress reports from our jungle contingent. Travel to Uruquat's Camp and discover the problem. Motivate as necessary. The remaining areas must be searched. Tell the ogre and his eel of an advisor they have twenty days to show results. You are to remain in the area until the time has expired or positive progress has been made.

Devon's shoulders relaxed as she folded the note and tucked it away. Greel's pronouncement about retaliation had put her on edge. Judging by the note, she had at least a little while before the thugs would be noticed as missing. That should give her time to figure out defenses.

She hoped.

As she laid fingers on the map, Hezbek arrived and fell to a crouch beside the wounded man. Devon withdrew her hand from her bag.

She stood silently while the medicine woman assessed the gruesome gash on the man's arm. Hezbek was careful not to touch the wound. After a moment, she sat back on her heels and sighed.

"Well?" Devon asked.

"I haven't seen anything like this before. I'm not sure how to treat it."

"You can try something, though, right?"

Hezbek nodded. "It behaves a bit like a poison. I'll try an antidote while getting his health back up with a potion. That should stabilize him for a while."

"Good enough. We don't really want a full cure right now anyway." She leaned over the captive and spoke loudly. "I haven't yet decided your fate. As things stand, you're a burden. We'll have to feed you and pour potions down your throat just to keep you from dying. But I certainly can't free you. So I sincerely suggest that you make yourself useful."

The man seemed too dazed to respond.

"Let's get him to the shade," she said. She summoned a worker and asked him to help Hezbek with the man. As they moved off, she gestured to Greel, who had started edging toward his tent. She pulled out the orders and the map and held them up.

"Explain."

He gestured to a pair of stumps. "It's been a long night. Can we sit?"

Once they were comfortable, she unfolded the orders. As he read, she watched his face. Nothing in the letter seemed to surprise him.

"I assume you intend to enlighten me."

Greel smoothed his hair and sighed. "As long as you understand that I've pieced this together myself. Officially, our task was to map and explore the area, paying particular note to ruins outside the borders of ancient Ishildar. We were to be rewarded with coin and territory, though not necessarily *this* territory. All this nonsense about founding a kingdom was Uruquat's personal interpretation."

"And the motive of those who sent you?"

"In the distant past, a relic called the Greenscale Pendant was held by the Khevshir vassaldom which bordered Ishildar to the south and east." He raised his eyebrows as if wondering whether she drew the connection. She glanced at the sun and quickly judged that, indeed, they were somewhere southeast of the overgrown ruins. She nodded, and he went on. "Their possession of the pendant was clearly documented, and no record has ever been found of it surfacing elsewhere. Therefore, we can assume that it disappeared somewhere in this region."

"I suppose that's logical," she said.

"This, of course, all happened before the Curse of Fecundity befell the area and caused the jungle to grow over everything. No doubt the search would be much easier otherwise."

"This Greenscale Pendant is one of the five relics that prove dominion over Ishildar, I assume?"

He nodded. "The communities depending on Ishildar were divided into five vassaldoms, each of which was given possession of a relic. Every ruler of Ishildar had to arrange a succession that was agreeable to all five. Following the ruler's death, the heir was temporarily given the relics to transfer ownership."

"I gather something went wrong."

Greel shrugged. "We don't know what caused the process to fail. But somehow, Ishildar was left without leadership. Eventually, without the city to sustain them, the vassal societies migrated or died out."

"Is this Curse of Fecundity related?" Devon asked. Recovering these relics was starting to sound very interesting. And increasingly possible.

"I don't know. So much has been lost. But, I *can* say that the legal document specified that the city must not be inhabited if no acceptable heir was found. There is a particular feature of Carpavan Legalese that allows contracts to be magically binding. I suppose the curse could be the agreement's way of enforcing the stipulations."

Devon laid a hand over her forehead. Magically enforced legal contracts? Emerson's AI had interesting ideas. She stared at Greel, and an inspection window popped up. Despite the 150 reputation she'd gained with him, he still viewed her with below neutral esteem. He might be lying, but the truth probably benefited him here. And anyway, it was an elaborate lie if he was making this up.

She nodded a dismissal to the lawyer, who stiffly headed for his hut. Once he'd ducked inside, she unrolled the map. As she studied the markings, the image floated off the paper and settled into a new window in the interface.

Finally, a proper in-game map. That would be convenient. Rather than peering down at the paper, she tucked it away and instead inspected the interface element. Not only were the notations and markings from the paper map displayed, but also, a small section of Ishildar had been uncovered. Devon smirked as she traced the route she'd followed while fleeing the Stone Guardian. The memory brought up another question. How, exactly, had the medicine woman pulled her from beneath the nose of a massive golem?

In any case, a few markings on the map seemed promising. One location listed an *"Archway leading below ground, collapsed,"* while another mentioned *"Overgrown ruins (unexplored)."* If what Greel had said about the relic was true, those areas seemed like good places to start looking for it.

Aside from the adventuring areas, she noticed a map section marked with *"Limestone, (potential quarry?)"* as well as an *"Ironwood grove."* Both those locations would help with settlement resources. Ironwood wasn't as strong as steel, but it was the next best thing. A skilled woodworker could often craft high-quality ironwood weapons more easily than a blacksmith could learn to forge and temper steel. Her little section of jungle was looking more promising.

Devon glanced at her fatigue bar. Barely half full. She stood and stretched. Time to get serious about assigning professions and finding a permanent home for her tribe.

Chapter Twenty-Two

AFTER DROPPING HER looted *Sabertooth Steaks* into the tribe's food bin and handing Gerrald the stack of *Sabertooth Scales*—he assured her he'd find a use for them—Devon pulled up the settlement interface.

Settlement: Uruquat's Camp
Size: Encampment

Tier 1 Buildings (16/20):
11 x Standard Hut
5 x Raised Platform

Tier 2 Buildings (2/?):
1 x Leader's Abode
1 x Medicine Woman's Hut

Population:
Base Morale: 52%
6 x Worker (unspecialized)
1 x Hunter - Grey
1 x Leatherworker - Gerrald
1 x Carpenter - Prester

1 x Fighter - Bayle

1 x Cook - Tom

1 x Medicine Woman - Hezbek (advanced)

1 x Lawyer - Greel (advanced)

Morale had gone up some, and the platforms now appeared on the list of buildings. She flipped over to another tab that she hadn't noticed before.

Requirements for expansion to Village:
- Advanced NPC: 2/2
- Tier 2 Buildings: 2/2
- Population: 13/20

Well, that sucked in a couple ways. The settlement was already at its cap of Advanced NPCs and Tier 2 buildings but needed seven more members to advance. Seeing as they were in the middle of an unpopulated jungle, that was going to be a problem.

At the very least, she could replace the Leader's Abode with a building that was actually useful, especially since she was still sleeping on Hezbek's floor. She focused on the line item for Buildings (Tier 2), and a new interface appeared showing available options.

Tier 2 Buildings:
  - Crafting workshop:
  A utilitarian building usable by many crafting professions.
  Bonus to: Weaving, Woodworking, Leatherworking, Tailoring, Stone Carving (small).

Requires: Carpentry (Tier 3), 50 x Wood Plank, 6 x Wood Beam

- Forge (basic):

A forge capable of working basic metals.

Required for: Blacksmithing

Requires: Stonemasonry (Tier 2), 60 x Stone Block, 10 x Bucket of Mortar

- Smokehouse:

Preserves raw meat, fruits, and vegetables at many times the rate of a standard campfire. Does not require a specialized worker to operate.

Can process: 40 units of meat, fruit, vegetables, or medicinal herbs per day.

Requires: Stonemasonry (Tier 2), Carpentry (Tier 3), 10 x Stone Block, 2 x Bucket of Mortar, 20 x Wood Plank, 4 x Wood Beam

- Barracks

Sleeping quarters for fighters, increases squad cooperation. Sleeps 6.

Requires: Carpentry (Tier 4), 70 x Wood Plank, 6 x Wood Beam

- Kitchen

Every campfire chef's dream.

Bonus to: Recipe discovery (x3), Tier 2+ recipe output (x2)

> **Requires:** Stonemasonry (Tier 2), Carpentry (Tier 3), 10 x
> Stone Block, 2 x Bucket of Mortar, 60 x Wood Plank, 6 x
> Wood Beam

Devon tapped a finger on her chin. It made sense that the blacksmith profession couldn't work in the crafting workshop because of the risk of fire. And for most of the buildings, she'd need a stonemason. That area of limestone on the map was looking more important. But for now, she looked again at the requirements for the crafting workshop. It seemed the most useful building for their situation.

The workshop would be their next tier 2 building. But first, Prester would have to reach the next skill tier. Ideally, he'd be there by the time they settled in their final location.

She spotted Greel out of the corner of her eye. The man stalked across the camp and slipped into his tent. She strolled over and rustled the door flap.

"Greel?"

"For Veia's sake, what?" he snarled.

"Just a couple quick questions. First, can I borrow some paper and ink?"

The lawyer shoved the items out the door flap without opening it.

"Thanks, I think."

"If it gives you something to do besides bothering me, I'm happy to share."

She rolled her eyes. "Would you mind stepping outside so we can talk? Given the note that thug was carrying, I assume your boss knows where the encampment is."

With a heavy sigh, the lawyer stomped back out of his hut. He pulled up a stump but didn't offer her one. She ignored the snub and crossed her arms over her chest.

"So?" she asked.

"My *boss,* as you call him even though I told you I work for myself, is named Henrik. He's an Eltera City councilman with designs on usurping the governorship of the Western Reaches. After which he plans to install his own regime, of course. That's why his lackeys are so loyal. They expect positions of power after the coup."

"And the Western Reaches includes this area?"

Greel looked at her as if she were the stupidest creature to crawl the earth, but after a moment the expression faded. "Right. Forgot you were starborn. I don't see why you lot are considered so special when you're as ignorant as a bunch of toddlers. Anyway, yes, the Reaches include this basin, the range of peaks you can see to the north, and the hill country surrounding Eltera City. Most of the population lives in the city and hills, obviously, which makes Eltera the regional hub. But if Ishildar could be reclaimed and the Curse of Fecundity lifted... It's not only geography and coast access that makes the location so desirable. Long ago, Ishildar commanded the Reaches because of the magical and martial power its residents gained."

Devon transferred her weight to her other hip and turned her face away from the sun. It was already getting hot out. "How about other expeditions? Did he send different groups to recover the other relics?"

"I have no idea. Probably. And since you asked earlier, I'll be abundantly clear. Henrik knows exactly where we are. If you care for suggestion...?"

Devon almost interrupted to say what she'd already been thinking but reconsidered. She swallowed back her distaste for the man and looked at him with interest.

"Your information has already been extremely helpful. Of course I value your advice."

Greel seemed to sit a bit straighter. "We should relocate as soon as possible. Those platforms might keep the settlement safe from a boar, but if Henrik comes in force…"

Devon widened her eyes as if terrified by the thought. "You're right. Why didn't I think of that?" The words sounded fake in her ears, but the man didn't seem to notice. Instead, he simply nodded and tried—failing spectacularly—not to look smug.

> *You have gained esteem with Greel: +5 Reputation.*
> *You have gained a skill point: +1 Leadership.*

She rolled up the paper and carefully balanced the quill and inkpot in her other hand. "Thanks, Greel, I know you aren't fond of me, but I think we can work well together."

He shrugged. "You're better than the ogre, anyway."

"Then can you do me a favor?" she asked, pushing her luck. "I'm going to set up in the shade. If you send over a worker who hasn't yet taken up a profession, I'll leave you alone for the rest of the day."

With a heavy sigh, he stood and marched into the trees. Devon dragged a pair of stumps to the shade of the canopy. She laid out the paper and waited for the first worker to arrive. She talked to them one by one and wrote down their preferred professions.

After the interviews, she gathered the tribe in the shade of the platforms. The paper in her hand listed out the specialties she'd decided to have the remaining workers take.

1 x Fighter

2 x Lumberjacks (one to retrain as a blacksmith later)

1 x Quarryman

1 x Stonemason

1 x Scout (to retrain as a hunter or fighter later)

One by one, she gave her blessing to her followers. The mood of the group lifted so much the darkness beneath the canopy seemed to fade.

"For now, take your time practicing your new skills. I'll talk to you individually later."

You have gained a skill point: +1 Leadership.

The meeting broke up, but Devon snagged Hezbek and Greel as they started to walk away.

Greel glared. "You said you were done with me for today."

Devon pressed a hand to her forehead. That's right, she had promised. "I just have a quick question for each of you. As advanced citizens, you can each take a second specialty, right?"

The medicine woman nodded, and a guarded look came over her face. "I already have."

Greel snorted. "As have I, though I thought it should be obvious."

"Obvious, how?"

"You aren't very observant, are you?"

A window popped up in her view, showing information on Greel. Before, she'd seen his profession listed as lawyer, but now, a second entry listed him as a Martial Artist - Level 11.

She suppressed a groan. Why hadn't the game shown her the second profession before? Because she hadn't thought to ask? Because she'd needed to see him in combat to unlock the knowledge?

"Maybe I *should* have guessed, but you could have volunteered the information. It would have been nice to know you're such a strong combatant before I assigned one of the workers to be our second guard."

Greel smirked. "Would you really want me as a main defender for the encampment?"

Good point. "No, probably not." She turned to the medicine woman. "And yours, Hezbek?"

The woman was silent for a long time. She walked to a tree and leaned her back against it.

"Many years ago, I was a very different person. A more... aggressive sort. I had a particular skill set that was very effective for adventuring. And even war. It's mostly dormant now, and I prefer to keep it that way."

Things were starting to come together in Devon's mind. "That's how you rescued me from the Stone Guardian."

Hezbek nodded and held out her hand. A ball of crackling light materialized above her palm.

"I was a sorceress. Quite powerful—among those I knew, anyway. Unfortunately, I hurt many people with my magic. The events that prompted my change of heart are a story for another day, but suffice it to say I retired. Years later, I took up medicine as an attempt to atone for the harm I caused."

Devon pulled up Hezbek's inspection window and couldn't help inhaling in surprise. Her second profession was listed as Sorceress - Level 20.

Hezbek's face hardened. "You have my secret, but you must know I won't fight. I won't ask others to follow my pacifist's path. Even though I've changed, I understand that violence is sometimes necessary. I'll leave that choice to others though. Now, I will only save lives."

Devon met the woman's gaze. Her history was far more complicated than Devon would've imagined.

"I won't ask you to do anything you don't wish to," she said. "Will you satisfy my curiosity, though? How exactly did you rescue me from the Stone Guardian?"

"I was in the ruined city on a harebrained exploration for Uruquat. I saw you hit your head. Figured you could use some help. Anyway, the spell was a type of teleportation. It's an advanced technique, and much harder with a passenger. Uruquat was rather upset that I consumed the necessary reagents."

Devon cocked her head, thinking. "You aren't still looking for an apprentice, are you?"

Hezbek smirked. "It might be something I'd consider. Of course, you'd have to be willing to choose Sorcerer as your Base Class." The medicine woman glanced at Greel. "Think carefully, because others could teach you as well. Perhaps you'd be more interested in what they have to offer..."

Greel scoffed. "I'd have to be able to stand your presence first."

Devon sighed and rolled her eyes. "Perhaps we can talk more about it later. For now, I want to check the others. Thank you for your answers."

She hadn't yet reached the clearing when a beeping sound filled the jungle and her interface started flashing.

Right... the alarm. She'd promised Tamara she would take breaks to eat.

With a glance over her shoulder, she slipped between a pair of trees, sat down, and logged out.

***

Devon blinked and stretched as she came to. Overhead, the ceiling fan stirred the air. The light breeze tickled Devon's arms. She climbed off the couch and headed for the kitchen.

The new information from Hezbek and Greel ran through her head. Either one could train her in a base class. Sorcery or martial arts... Which would help her character the most? Or should she hold out until she figured out how normal players were selecting their base classes? The tile in the kitchen was cool against her bare feet, refreshing in the heat of her apartment. Even though E Squared paid her well enough, she'd spent the last six years pinching pennies. Especially when she spent most of her time immersed, it seemed ridiculous to turn on the AC.

Anyway, it couldn't be as hot as Uruquat's encampment on the jungle afternoon.

She smirked at the irony of it.

The cabinet was full of prepackaged convenience foods. She stood on tiptoes and grabbed a box of granola bars then filled a water glass. While she walked to the table, she chewed her lip.

She'd been purposefully ignoring any information on forums or news sites. But now that she had a chance to choose a class, it seemed stupid to ignore information that might help her make the best decision. Especially since she was getting paid to be an in-game overachiever. With a mental gesture, she pulled up a web browser, projected onto her vision by her Entwined implants. Calling up the main site for Relic Online, she navigated over to the forums.

Despite the small player base so far—the company wasn't releasing exact numbers, but a long thread on the forum estimated the player count at under ten thousand—there were pages and pages of forum posts. A quick scan told her that most players had a vastly different experience than hers. Most had started in cities and villages near other players. One similarity, though, was that the quests and events across the world were far more dynamic than any previous game. People couldn't post quest walk-throughs because the content changed from person to person and group to group. There *was* good information on the classes, though. Apparently, when other players hit level 5 and learned their starting attributes, they went through quick tutorials that explained the general strengths of each class. Afterward, a full set of trainers were available to award base class designations.

Devon snorted. Must be nice.

She opened a granola bar and started chowing. At least she could get info on her current choices. She pulled up the subforum for Martial Artists and scanned the first posts. Someone had directly transcribed the text they'd received during the tutorial.

A martial artist is a master of combat, talented in both unarmed strikes and simple weapons. At later levels, they may

*specialize in a specific style learned by traveling to a distant
land and enrolling in schools dedicated to a branch of the arts.*

Farther down, others had posted that damage inflicted was based
largely on a player's *Agility*, though *Strength* played a minor role.
Naturally, defense came from their ability to dodge, with less
emphasis on the armor they wore. The Focus attribute contributed
to the accuracy of their attacks and their mana pool, which powered
some of their more mystical abilities.

She considered that approach. It could work with the Deceiver
class, as far as she could tell. Her shadow could serve as a distraction
or—depending on what she learned about the *Shadow Puppet's*
properties with different light sources—maybe there would be other
dynamics. She'd already gained some proficiency with simple blades
and, thanks to the game's sarcastic sense of humor, a couple points
in unarmed combat earned while falling down.

Devon felt a small twinge of envy when she saw that some of the
players posting in the forum had already reached level 12. She was
supposed to be a star in this game, but she was still stuck at level 5.
She hoped that didn't mean that E Squared would fire her. Anyway,
she wouldn't make forward progress by sitting here worrying about
it.

She backed out of the MA forum and opened the discussion on
the Sorcerer.

Now this was interesting. It looked like the size of a sorcerer's
mana pool was based on *Charisma*, and their spell effectiveness
came from *Intelligence*. Hit points, as with every other class, were a
combination of *Constitution* and, to a lesser extent, *Strength*. With
either of the class choices, she'd have to decide whether to invest in

those stats simply to increase her health or whether to focus on offense.

The Sorcerer class seemed like an awesome fit for her starting attributes. Then again, her highest and lowest attributes were currently just 11 points apart. As the game went on, that minor difference could easily be erased as she spent points to customize her build. It seemed the bigger question was whether she should take another class that relied mostly on mana. If she was spending her pool to cast Deceiver spells, what use would it be to have the Sorcerer abilities?

Taking a class whose attributes would boost her mana might be worth it in of itself. It seemed a sure bet that a Sorcerer would ultimately have a bigger pool than a Martial Artist. Even after recently gaining a couple *Cunning* points, she still had just 50 mana, and she could never be sure when the game would award her new special attribute points.

Of course, she didn't know whether all Deceiver abilities would require mana, and maybe she'd find Sorcerer spells to be really useful in some situations.

Plus, there was one thing about Sorcery that had given her an idea. She just needed to do a little in-game research.

She finished the last bites of the granola bar and brushed the crumbs into her hand. After finishing her water, she set the cup in the sink. On the way to the couch, she thought of one more thing. With a sigh, she opened the website again. In the search bar, she subvocalized, "How do I reroll my character?" If she made a mistake with her class choice, it would be nice to know she could start over.

The question sent her directly to a subsection of the FAQ:

Currently, only one avatar per player is allowed. Characters may not be deleted. After the initial launch phase, E Squared expects the player load to be more evenly distributed across the world. At that point, players may create a second character. Thank you for your patience while we assure that the experience in the starting locations remains smooth and uncrowded.

Well, that answered that. Whatever she chose, she was stuck with it. But seeing as there were plenty of players who were much higher level than her, she just needed to get on with it. As she flopped onto the couch, she checked her messages. There was a recent question from Emerson, and his icon looked like he was still online.

Hey, Devon, just checking in. How has the pain response been? Seems like the problem is isolated to you, but that doesn't make it any less of a problem.

"I haven't noticed. Haven't been badly hurt." She hesitated. Seemed like there was something else she wanted to ask him, a question about the implants that had come up while she'd been having tacos. But for the life of her, she couldn't remember what it was. After a few seconds spent wracking her brain, she finally shook her head and finished her message.

"I'll let you know... Not that I plan to go break a leg for research purposes."

He sent back a laughing emoji. *Thanks,* he said. *Please do stay in touch.*

Chapter Twenty-Three

WHEN DEVON LOGGED in, it was already mid-afternoon in the jungle. Tribe members were practicing their new professions. The lumberjacks hacked at the jungle, stripping low branches from trees and reducing those to firewood. Her new fighter struck at another tree, working up his unarmed combat skill. Now that Hezbek's hut was up on a platform, the medicine woman sat on the rough-hewn planks outside her door, humming while she mixed ingredients inside an earthen bowl. Near the spot Devon had logged out, the captive was sleeping on the jungle floor. Hezbek's potion would probably keep him unconscious for at least a day, but her tribe had taken no chances. His wrists and ankles were bound and lashed to different trees.

She tapped her foot. Devon really hated making irreversible character decisions. There was one more thing she wanted to investigate before deciding between Sorcerer and Martial Artist. Stepping deeper into the jungle, she dug through her bag and pulled out one of the ivory fangs. The item sat awkwardly in her palm no matter how she adjusted her grip. After a few practice swings, she tried to aim a strike at a nearby tree trunk.

The fang's point skittered off the bark, slipped from her hand, and nearly nicked her exposed wrist as it spun through the air.

Devon winced. Too close. As she gingerly crouched to pick up the item, she checked her combat log.

> *You strike at the tree and fumble your weapon. (Skill check failed, Ivory Fang requires 65 points in One-handed Piercing. Your current score: 1)*
> *Be glad it wasn't a critical failure, genius.*

65? Ugh! Back when she'd fought with the rusty knife, it had been just as easy to pierce as slash. But the machete just wasn't good at stabbing. Unless she got another weapon, she wouldn't be skilling into the fang anytime soon. Maybe the skill requirements would go down once she figured out how to identify items or found a weaponsmith capable of working the fang into a less crude weapon. Anyway, she certainly wouldn't finish the day as a martial arts master wielding a pair of magical daggers that killed with just a scratch. She tucked the fang back into her bag.

With a deep breath, she glanced up at Hezbek. Time to get over her fear of being wrong... It was just a game, right? Snatching hold of the nearest rope ladder, she scampered up and crossed a bridge to Hezbek's platform. She took a cross-legged seat before the woman.

"Got time to talk?"

The woman sat her concoction aside. "I was hoping to catch you alone, actually. I'm guessing by our captive that you've learned something about why Uruquat came here. Who gave him the assignment, perhaps?"

That's right. Devon had forgotten about the quest.

"I have learned a lot," she said. "Much of the information came from Greel, actually."

Hezbek's scattering of teeth showed when she grinned. "I'd hoped that was the case."

Quest complete: Who are the Puppet Masters?
You receive 5600 experience!

Congratulations, you have reached level 6!
You have gained 4 attribute points.

Finally, another level. Devon grinned.

"So what did you find out?" Hezbek asked.

"In short, a city councilman named Henrik wants to collect five relics which will give him ownership over Ishildar and all the power the city commands. Uruquat led you out here to search for one of the relics, the Greenscale Pendant. Of course, we have a problem now that Uruquat is gone. Henrik wants results, and we have twenty days before they come to try to extract them."

"I see..." Hezbek fiddled with the bowl beside her. "And where were we supposed to be searching for this relic?"

"It was held by a vassal society in this region. Looking at the map, I have a few guesses, but a lot of the area is still completely unexplored."

"Well that narrows it down. I think?"

Devon snorted. "Yeah... just a hundred square miles of jungle to search. Anyway, I'm making plans to relocate the encampment somewhere that Henrik doesn't expect. Hopefully with better natural defenses."

"And you're thinking of going after this relic yourself?"

Devon held her silence for a moment, feeling the dappled sunlight on her arms. Part of her still imagined joining up with the rest of the population. But what if she could find this relic? What if she could track down the other four...? She'd told these people she wanted to build them a kingdom. Reawakening Ishildar seemed like an awfully good start. "You know, I think I *would* like to find the relic."

"Well then, perhaps we should make it official..."

Hezbek is offering you a quest: Find the Greenscale Pendant.
It's gotta be out here somewhere...
Reward: A Greenscale Pendant, obviously.
Accept? Y/N

Devon accepted the quest. Soon, she'd talk to Greel to see if he had input on where to start searching. As if reading her thoughts, Hezbek cocked her head. "You know, I never liked him that much, but it seems Greel could be one of our biggest assets in the search. It would probably behoove you to get on his good side."

Hezbek is offering you a quest: Deal with Greel.
You really don't want the level 11 Martial Artist in your tribe to hate you, do you?
Objective: Gain 100 reputation with Greel.
Reward: Congratulations, you get to spend more time with the man. Aren't you lucky?
Accept? Y/N

Devon rolled her eyes at the quest text. But the game was right, she needed to do it, so she accepted the quest.

"There was another thing I wanted to talk about," she said.

A knowing look came into Hezbek's eyes. "And?"

"I want you to teach me."

"Do you really want to be a Sorcerer?"

As Hezbek spoke, a prompt appeared.

Will you select Sorcerer as your base class?

WARNING: this choice is permanent.

Accept? Y/N

Devon took a deep breath. "I've thought about it, and yes, I want to be a sorceress."

The jungle around her chimed, followed by notifications.

Congratulations, you have a new class: Sorcerer.

You may now learn your first spells.

Devon quickly pulled up her stat sheet.

Character: Devon (click to set a different character name)

Level: 6

Base Class: Sorcerer

Specialization: Unassigned

Unique Class: Deceiver

Health: 145/145

Mana: 263/263

Fatigue: 5%

Nice! Her mana had gone from 50 to 263! She checked her attributes window:

Attributes:
Constitution: 13
Strength: 10
Agility: 15
Charisma: 21
Intelligence: 21
Focus: 12
Endurance: 11

Special Attributes:
Bravery: 5
Cunning: 4

Available Points: 8

Her attention hovered over the unspent points. Where should they go?

"I suppose you'd like your first spells," Hezbek said with a smirk.

Devon dispelled her interface. She could think about attribute points later. "Can you show me how to create that glowing ball?"

"You mean, *Glowing Orb*? You want to know how to create light? I figured you'd start by *Flamestriking* enemies or something."

Devon smiled. "Well, that too. The orb was the reason I decided to become a sorceress though."

Hezbek looked at her like she was crazy, but Devon just shrugged.

You have learned a new spell: Glowing Orb – Tier 1.
A ball of lightning materializes in your hand. Unfortunately, you can't hurt anyone with it, but the spell could be useful if you forget a torch or something. Requires some concentration to maintain.
Cost: 10 mana
Requirements: Sorcerer

You have learned a new spell: Flamestrike – Tier 1.
A pillar of fire immolates your enemy for 12-17 base damage (scales with Intelligence).
Cost: 20 mana
Requirements: Sorcerer

Devon grinned as the knowledge sank into her mind.

Chapter Twenty-Four

BEFORE HEADING OUT in search of a new settlement site—and hopefully, some good experience—Devon handed out assignments. She told the lumberjacks to keep clearing trees, but to consult with Prester about which trees would be best for turning into smooth boards. She spoke with the hunter, Grey, about cautiously returning to the stream and laying traps for turtles. She couldn't be certain that the sabertooth she'd killed had been the only one nearby, but a quick glance at their resources showed shrinking food supplies. They needed to do more to supplement the stores. On the way to and from the stream, Grey could also keep an eye out for sloths to club. Meanwhile, the fighters would continue clearing local wildlife, salvaging meat and leather where possible. She upgraded Bayle to the other machete and handed down the rusty knife to the new recruit, Falwon.

That left the stonemason, the quarryman, and the scout. The first two were older men with muscles earned by lives of hard labor, whereas the scout, Hazel, was a lithe woman in her twenties. She'd walked gracefully *before* specializing as a scout, but now her movements were almost liquid. Even at level 1, she'd be able to slip through the jungle without making a noise or disturbing the wildlife. Which was good, because Devon needed her help to uncover more of the map.

"Okay, here's the deal," she said to the trio. "We're leaving this afternoon to investigate an area marked as a potential stone quarry. I need you to pack bedrolls because we want to take our time."

As they hurried to gather supplies, the cook, Tom, sidled over. "I assume you'll need rations for your little expedition," he said with a hopeful tone.

Devon's stomach growled at the thought. It was the first sign of hunger she'd felt since joining the tribe and having her food intake automatically deducted every day. She hoped it wasn't a sign that she'd have to start paying attention to that again. More likely, the game was reminding her that when she was away from the encampment, she'd need to bring food.

"I could try to hunt on the way, but I'd hate to subject these poor people to more charred snake meat."

Tom blushed as he handed over a linen-wrapped package. "I was saving these until you'd be able to dine with us. But it seems a good time for you to take them."

You have received: 4 x Pepperleaf-spiced Sabertooth Steaks
These smell delicious!
Grants: +3 Speed, +1 Constitution
Duration: 24 hours

Wow, that was quite a buff for tier 1 food.

She sniffed the package, and her mouth started watering. They smelled absolutely divine. "You weren't kidding about your potential. I imagine even Eltera City gourmands would be envious of these. I'll have a hard time waiting until dinner time."

Tom's ears turned flaming red as he shuffled at the praise. "It's the least I could do, Your Gloriousness."

Back to that again. Well, she *had* told them to call her whatever they wished.

Her small party had returned, bedrolls tied to the bottom of simple rucksacks. The stonemason, Bern, held a mallet and chisel from the encampment supplies, while the mason—Deld, the man who'd been gored by the boar—carried a pickax.

"If you don't mind, we thought these might be useful," the quarryman explained.

Devon nodded. It was good her followers could take initiative. If all she did was manage her tribe, those players back in the starting hubs would get even farther ahead. At the thought, she glanced at the jungle and focused on her map interface, pulling the mini-map forward into an overlay at the corner of her vision. The site of the potential quarry lay roughly north and a little east. If they moved quickly, they might make it before dark.

She handed Hazel the map plus Greel's quill and ink. Her choice to requisition them probably wouldn't go over well with the lawyer, but at least her quest would give her incentive to earn back any lost esteem.

"Can you rove ahead of us and map areas to either side of the explored region?" Devon asked.

The scout furrowed her brow while she considered. "As long as you don't mind if it's rough at first. My cartography skill is still developing."

Devon opened the woman's inspection window.

Hazel: Level 1 - Scout
Health: 34/34

Skills:
Stealth: 20
Cartography: 2
Sense Heading: 15
Detect Freshwater: 5
Forage: 5

Devon nodded in appreciation. The profession had more utility than she'd expected. Hazel could help the tribe find a town site with access to a spring and territory for foraging fruits and vegetables to supplement Grey's hunting.

"I know you will improve quickly," Devon said. "And don't worry if your first attempts show lack of practice."

Hazel nodded and stood straight. "Thanks for giving me the chance."

"Everyone ready?" Devon asked, checking that her weapon and inventory sack were secure on her belt.

Her followers nodded, and the group started for the north edge of the encampment.

Hazel slipped into the undergrowth first, and within a few heartbeats, she was completely invisible. Good. At least that was one follower Devon wouldn't have to worry about when it came to wildlife attacks. She motioned for the other two to stay behind her as she started hacking a path to the north. While she swung her machete and pressed through the tangled foliage, she pulled up her stat sheet. She took a deep breath and shoved 2 points into *Intelligence*, 4 into *Charisma*, and 2 into *Constitution*.

Next, she pulled up the base character sheet to see the effects on her mana pool.

Character: Devon (click to set a different character name)

Level: 6

Base Class: Sorcerer

Specialization: Unassigned

Unique Class: Deceiver

Health: 145/159

Mana: 263/299

Fatigue: 9%

Already, she felt much more powerful. Her health had increased from 145 to 159, and her mana from 263 to 299. Both pools began to fill to their new capacity, pulsing lightly with each point of regeneration.

A downed tree cut across the path at around elbow height, the wood slowly rotting and smelling like sawdust and insects. She tried stooping to hack her way through the tangle of moss and undergrowth beneath but changed her mind at the sight of a nest of finger-sized spiderlings. She jumped back as a few of them hissed and spat yellow droplets into the air. The spray barely missed her arm.

"Maybe I should learn to love the taste of Jungle Antidote - Minor," she muttered. Speaking of, she hadn't brought along any potions, which seemed stupid. But she didn't want to go back now.

Swinging her machete, she detoured around the fallen tree. She wanted to gain some good experience, but without a spell that could affect a wide area, a nest of poison-spitting spiderlings wasn't the way to do it. Fortunately, the insects didn't give chase. They were content to defend their small home.

As she rounded the mass of the fallen tree and headed back for her planned trail, Devon pulled up information on her new *Glowing Orb* spell. Unlike the Deceiver ability, she could see each of the upgrades that lay ahead.

Spell: Glowing Orb – Tier 1
Cost: 10 mana
A ball of lightning materializes in your hand. Unfortunately, you can't hurt anyone with it, but the spell could be useful if you forget a torch or something. Requires some concentration to maintain.

Spell: Glowing Orb – Tier 2
Cost: 22 mana
You can attach the Glowing Orb to another object in order to regain use of your hand. Requires more concentration to maintain.

Spell: Glowing Orb – Tier 3
Cost: 30 mana
You may create up to three separate orbs, and you can attach each to a different object or surface. You must really like this spell.

Spell: Glowing Orb – Tier 4:
Cost: 42 mana
You can create up to six orbs at once! (why?)

Devon smirked as she whacked at another vine. The foliage fell limp to the ground. She wondered where Veia got her sense of humor. Emerson didn't seem like the sarcastic type.

Holding her hand in front of her, she focused on the steps Hezbek had taught her and blinked as a ball of light flashed to life. It fizzed against her palm, but otherwise had no weight. A notification told her she'd gained 1% mastery in tier 1 of the spell.

Behind her, Deld and Bern gasped. Devon smirked. The spell description didn't add how impressed your level 1 followers would be by your sudden ability to materialize light.

She noticed that her mana bar had indeed dropped some, but the cost was low compared to the size of her pool now. She held her arm out to the side and looked down. Very little direct sun reached the ground beneath the canopy, which kind of made her *Shadow Puppet* ability useless in the deep jungle. Not a problem now... She wondered what kind of propertics her shadow would have when created by lightning.

Distracted by watching her shadow, she swung absently at a large group of vines dangling in front of her face.

The vines hissed.

Devon stumbled back, slamming into her followers and falling onto her butt. Her machete went flying. She quickly scrambled to her feet and shoved the men back as a diamond-shaped head the size of a microwave rose from the ground. A muscular body dangled from a branch at least twenty feet in the air. Heavy coils wrapped

CARRIE SUMMERS

the massive limb. The python's glowing red eyes burned into her, and its forked tongue licked the air as it tensed for a strike.

What is this, karma for my tree viper murdering spree?

"Stay back!" she yelled. Devon bent her knees and looked at her hand. She groaned when she saw the orb had been extinguished. The description had mentioned maintaining a bit of concentration...

Fumbling, she struggled to orient while searching for her fallen weapon. The snake wove back and forth, looking for an opening. Devon jumped from foot to foot, ducking to make herself a difficult target.

She spotted her machete glinting dully in a mat of dead leaves just ahead. With a sharp intake of breath, she dove for it, managed to catch the hilt, and came up from her roll with her weapon in the guard position.

She launched a *Flamestrike*, squinting as a column of fire erupted from the forest floor and enveloped the snake.

The flames vanished.

The snake continued to weave as if nothing had happened.

Devon peered at the monster until a health bar came up. She might have shaved off 1%. If that. A quick glance at the combat messages at the edge of her vision showed that the snake had resisted. Easily.

Damn.

The snake struck, reptilian scent washing over her as she dodged to the side and sprinted across the small cleared area where the beast hung. Fumbling, Devon started the summoning motions for *Glowing Orb*. She wished she'd practiced more before leaving the encampment. Her fingers were awkward, the motions clumsy as the snake twisted in the air to orient on her again.

Finally, light bloomed in her hand, sparks from her orb reflected from the reptile's burning eyes.

She shook her head. "Not so sure this is going to turn out well," she muttered.

Dashing to the side to keep the snake off guard, she focused on her shadow and dumped mana into conjuring a puppet. The dark figure rose from the ground, fuzzy at the edges like the ball of lightning she held. She felt along her connection to her creation. The figure seemed to fizz against her awareness much like the lightning crackling in her hand. The snake arched its head and body, tensing for another strike.

Flexing her awareness of the shadow, she commanded it to attack. Her creation flowed across the small space, and when the dark form contacted the python, it passed straight through.

The air crackled and snapped, and sparks traveled the length of the reptile's body. The beast was paralyzed.

Devon grinned.

And then the feedback smacked her.

Electricity surged through her body, the initial shock followed by burning along her nerves like an army of fire ants. She squealed through gritted teeth. Damn this pain sensitivity! She squinted at the python. The snake had lost maybe 15% of its health. Her eyeballs ached as she swiveled them toward her own health bar and saw a 5% reduction.

The pain was short-lived, at least. But as she took a shaky breath and forced her legs to keep moving, she felt her connection with the shadow die out.

Her off hand was empty. Kind of hard to concentrate on channeling a spell when you felt like you'd put your finger in a light socket. She backpedaled as the snake started to move again.

"Can one of you climb?" Devon yelled to her followers. "Tear down branches if you can. I need sunlight."

Her followers were shadows in the foliage, having backed off. Sticks began to crack as one or both of the men started wading through the undergrowth.

Devon glanced toward the reptile just in time to dodge a heavy swing of the monster's body. As the scaly flesh slid past her, she lashed out with her machete.

The blade glanced off without displacing so much as the scale.

"Shit," she muttered. She kicked at the muscular beast, but it was like trying to damage a tree. The rebound sent her stumbling. Groaning in dismay at the idea, she cast another *Glowing Orb*, and wincing, raised her *Shadow Puppet*.

As the snake turned, once again lining up for an attack, Devon gritted her teeth and send her shadow onto the beast.

The shock pounded her, stiffening her body, setting fire to her limbs. Light flashed behind her eyes as sparks arced over the snake's body. Moments later, it was over, leaving her dazed and gagging. She bent over her stomach and retching. The shadow was already gone, vanished when her orb did.

Her health was down 20%.

The snake was down to half.

Devon tried to summon the courage for another lightning shadow attack, but she couldn't bring herself to do it. Better to die and wake up in Hezbek's cot than go through that again. Instead, she circled, swinging halfway around the clearing so the snake was forced to twist awkwardly. Setting the ball of her foot into the muddy ground for purchase, she sheathed her machete and jumped.

She snatched hold of the snake like a climbing rope in elementary school gym class. But thicker. And this rope smelled like dead skin and decaying wood. She wrapped her legs around it, held on tight, and started shimmying up the beast's body. The snake flailed like a vertical jump rope, but Devon clung with every ounce of strength she had.

It tried to bite but couldn't bend far enough. Slowly, the beast began to coil up. Above her, a loop formed and started descending, ready to slip around her shoulders and crush the life from her.

Devon started bouncing like she was trying to unhook the rope from the gymnasium ceiling. Each time she dropped her weight onto the snake, the coil loosened a small amount. Still, between yanks, the python wound tighter.

Finally, she heard a groan followed by a loud crack. Above, the branch bent and broke with a bone-jarring snap. Devon and the truck-sized snake came crashing to the ground. She jumped free just before the heavy body smashed her flat. The beast took another 10% damage. She growled in frustration. She'd never win at this rate, not unless she could handle electrocuting herself a couple more times.

Beside her, another branch crashed down, sending twigs flying. She leaped aside and looked up to see her followers high in the trees. Another limb detached, knocked free by Bern's quarry mallet, and plummeted for her.

Should have mentioned not *to drop the branches on my head.*

She ran, planting a foot on the dazed snake's skull, and leaped. The heavy branch crashed down behind her. While she was in midair, another branch snapped.

A bright beam of sunlight lanced down, bathing Devon in its golden glow.

She kicked out and smacked a tree trunk with her foot to stop her forward progress. As she landed, she caught sight of her shadow in a pool of sunlight. All harsh edges and finely-cut lines, the shadow rose from the ground at her command. The snake raised its head, eyes squinting against the glare.

On instinct, Devon formed her shadow-creation into a spear. She hurled it into the snake's eye, sharp black edges slicing through with no effort. The snake hissed and recoiled, and its health bar dropped to 20%. Moments later, the shadow shattered.

Devon staggered at the sudden knockback. At least it didn't hurt.

Her mana was getting low. Just a couple casts left. She stomped forward, summoned another dark form, and speared the python as the beast turned to flee. The lance glanced off the beast's spine but still scored a 10% hit before shattering and setting her stumbling again.

The snake slithered toward the undergrowth. Fast. She watched in desperation as the front half of its body vanished into the thicket.

She was *not* going to lose this XP. Still stumbling from the knockback of her shattered shadow, she sprinted a few clumsy steps before getting her balance. Feet pounding the earth, she sprinted for the snake, stepped on its tail, and ran along its back, crashing through brush. When she neared its head, she reversed her grip on her machete and clubbed it hard with the hilt.

The python went limp. Planting a foot on top of its skull, Devon crouched and plunged her machete through the eye socket she'd pierced with her shadow.

Coup de grace: kick them while they're down, why don't you...?
You have slain a Corrupted Python.

Quickly, she scanned her combat notifications. A couple things caught her attention.

Your Shadow Puppet shocks A Corrupted Python for 542 damage. (+100% chance to hit, +200% damage due to Bravery score of 5)
Your Shadow Puppet shocks YOU for 23 damage. Nice going...

You have gained mastery in Shadow Puppet – Tier 1: 10%
You have gained mastery in Glowing Orb – Tier 1: 2%
You have gained mastery in Incapacitate – Tier 1: 5%

Devon sank to a crouch to catch her breath and slid the tip of her machete across the snake's skin. The body disintegrated into loot. She glanced at the items, and her brows drew together. The *Gigantic Snakeskin* wasn't a surprise, but the *5 x Snake Meat, Tainted* was unexpected. Why tainted? In any case, she left those items on the forest floor and picked up the final piece of loot.

You have received: Stomach Contents (open to examine).

Devon grimaced. Did she really want to do this?

With a deep breath, she held up the white and red mass and touched the point of her knife to it. The stomach burst open, goo flowing down her hand. She fell backward from the cloud of stench and wiped her hand in the mud. The slime soaked into the ground, leaving a small, grime-covered object. Devon dug through her bag until she found her *Everfull Waterskin* and poured lukewarm liquid over the thing until it was clean. Finally, she picked it up with her thumb and forefinger and inspected it.

You have received: Strange Bauble of Carved Bone - unidentified

She blinked. It looked just like the bauble she'd looted from Uruquat, only the first one hadn't come from inside a stomach. Thankfully. She dropped it into her bag as a test. Indeed, the baubles were the same. Or similar enough that the game stacked them in a single slot.

Deld had made it out of the tree, and he stepped up beside her.

"That snake... It was like the boar."

"How so?"

"Red eyes and ten times normal size... During our first week in the jungle, Uruquat claimed to have slain a similar beast, a red-eyed parrot the size of a small child. He saved a bone charm that he'd cut from the bird's innards—looked a lot like that trinket you just stuffed in your sack."

"That is strange."

"I hope this isn't going to become a bigger problem for us," Deld said.

A quest popup appeared.

Deld is offering you a quest: What's Wrong with the Wildlife?

Seems strange to have run across two rabid, glowing-red-eyed, oversized beasts in the same area of jungle. Everything else around here seems pretty normal as far as cursed ruins of lost civilizations go. Your settlement would probably be safer if you tracked down the source of the problem and dealt with it.

Objective: Find the source of the Strange Baubles of Carved Bone.

Reward: Unknown

Accept? Y/N

Devon shrugged. Sure, why not. Before standing, she tried to stuff the *Gigantic Snakeskin* into her bag. No luck. But not a huge loss. The snakeskin vest Gerrald had made was a nice gesture, but eventually, she'd meet other players. A full snakeskin suit would be awfully 1980s hair band.

After a few minutes rest to recover hitpoints and mana, Devon checked with her followers to make sure they were ready. Before leaving the scene of the fight, she stopped in the small pool of sunlight and summoned another *Glowing Orb*. She stood on the edge of the golden pool and held her arm out so that two shadows spread from her feet, each cast by a different source. She focused on them, one after another, and raised a pair of dark figures from the ground.

Devon nodded. Just as she'd hoped.

Chapter Twenty-Five

THE SUN NEARED the horizon, making it harder and harder to see without darkvision on the jungle floor. Devon's fatigue bar was nearing three-quarters full, and her feet felt leaden. For the last hour or two, she'd been casting *Glowing Orb* over and over. Each time, she held it in her hand until her mana refilled from the cast, then dismissed it and cast the spell again. Tactfully, her followers had made no comments about this behavior. Her efforts had earned her a whopping 89% mastery in *Glowing Orb* – Tier 1.

As the jungle began to brighten ahead, suggesting some sort of clearing, Devon glanced at her mini-map. It looked like the quarry was close. As if confirming the suspicion, Hazel slipped from the undergrowth like she'd materialized from thin air. Devon jumped in surprise and lost control of her *Glowing Orb*. She sighed. Gotta keep practicing. Or maybe try putting some points into the *Focus* attribute. As Hazel stepped closer, the map in the corner of Devon's vision flashed to indicate new information. The scout's explorations had revealed an area three times as wide as the narrow path Devon and her little party had followed.

Devon greeted the woman with a handshake. "That's a lot of ground to cover. You're fast."

Hazel gave a little bow. "And my cartography improved quite a bit. The map should be at least 50% accurate."

Devon suppressed a groan. She wasn't sure whether 50% accuracy was better than no knowledge at all. In a few spots, Hazel had made notes about more ruins and caves—could be interesting to check out. But maybe it would be better to have the woman go back over the area as she gained skill before Devon mounted a dungeon-crawl expedition.

As Hazel greeted the two men, raindrops began to spatter on the canopy, knocking aside leaves and continuing their fall onto the group. Devon sighed and wished for a cloak. At least the rain wasn't frigid like it could be in a cooler region.

She gestured to the lighter area of trees that should lead to the potential quarry. "Did you check out the limestone, Hazel? I'm hoping for caves."

Hazel nodded as she squinted into the sky. "Yes, thank Veia. Big enough to keep us dry. Let's go."

Devon was no mason or quarry worker, but to her untrained eye, the massive fists of limestone that punched through the jungle did indeed look promising. Hazed by the falling rain and dusk-darkened light, the stones loomed to four or five times her height, and a knot of rock behind the first set was even taller. An area of flat stone slabs and rubble separated the group from the outcroppings, even from a distance the dark holes pocking the area around the base of the escarpments looked like caves. Hazel led the way as the party dashed across the flat area to reach the nearest opening. They ducked beneath the overhang and sighed with relief.

The floor of the cavern was glassy smooth, polished by trickling water over the years. Though not large, the cave was deep enough for them to fit comfortably and stretch out bedrolls, though the men had to stoop to move about. All in all, it was a cozy niche, and once everyone had laid out their bedding, Devon settled in to grind out the rest of her mastery in *Glowing Orb*.

The closer she got to the next tier, the sparser her mastery updates became. But with 3% remaining, she decided to blow through her mana to try to reach the next spell. She was beginning to regret it until the last cast gained her the final percentage point, and she got the notification for access to *Glowing Orb – Tier 2*. She waited patiently while her mana filled back up to the 12 points she needed, then cast the spell again.

The little ball of lightning still fizzed in her hand, but now it seemed to dance. It wasn't quite so stuck. Carefully, she placed the glowing ball against the wall of the cave, willed it to stick, then ever so slowly pulled her hand away.

The orb remained, and she grinned. Most level 1 sorcerers probably complained about having such a "stupid spell." But sitting in the comfortable glow of her conjured light source, she had to disagree.

The others seemed to enjoy the light as well, and on a whim, Devon moved it to the floor in the center of the cave, sort of like a campfire. Faint smiles appeared on her followers' faces.

Thinking of the age-old ritual of sharing food around a campfire, she reached into her bag and pulled out the steaks. She unwrapped the linen and handed out the slabs of meat. She had to admit it felt a little strange holding a one-pound steak in her hand rather than on a plate, but with the first bite, she forgot all about it. Even cold, *Pepperleaf-spiced Sabertooth Flesh* was the best thing she'd ever eaten. Her followers fell to eating with gusto, rolling their eyes with pleasure.

The rain fell in a calming rhythm, a curtain of wet beyond the mouth of the cave.

"Does it rain often?" she asked. With all the growth in the jungle, she was surprised it had been dry as long as it had.

"I was beginning to think you were our good luck charm when it came to weather," Deld said. "We hadn't had a streak of sunshine like the one you brought since we arrived."

Between bites, Bern set his steak on his knee and looked at the *Glowing Orb* with faint concern. "By the way, Your Gloriousness... I don't mean to question, but that thing's not going to shock us is it? My mother always told me to stay out of the watering hole when the thunderstorms were on the loose."

Devon smiled and ran her hand through the orb. "It's harmless."

But his question did get her thinking. Though it hadn't rained since she'd entered the game, the ground was still slick and muddy. Could that explain why the shock from her shadow had lashed back at her? Ground currents? She chewed her lip. Maybe. But she didn't really want to test the theory.

She finished her steak and lay back on her elbows. It was nice to have gained level 6 earlier in the day. A quick look at her experience bar showed her she had 6,452 of the 39,600 she needed for level 7. As she stared at the numbers, a small tooltip appeared.

Experience gain set to 60% of normal due to dual class advancement.

Devon's head flopped back. Great...

That was a bummer, though she supposed it was probably balanced. She did have spells from two classes, plus an oversized mana pool. Still, pretty annoying.

236

As she rolled onto her side to watch the flickering of the orb, the quarryman, Bern, started telling Hazel about their encounter with the python. He built it up, creating suspense about the dark jungle and their slow march and the rustles in the undergrowth. His flair for the dramatic gave Devon an idea. As he spoke, she sat up and focused on her shadow. She pressed mana into the cast, but kept her shadow low to the ground, slipping it around behind Bern and toward the mouth of the cave. Catching the eyes of Hazel and Deld, she pressed her finger to her lips. As Bern described them walking into the small clearing owned by the python, Devon molded her shadow into a snake. The darkness slithered across the floor and rose up behind Bern. A diamond-shaped head hovered in the air behind the big man's shoulder. Devon imagined her shadow hissing, and to her shock, a loud *SSSSS* emanated from her creation.

Bern whipped his head around, shouted, and scrambled across the cavern.

Devon quickly dissolved her casting and joined in Deld's and Hazel's laughter. After a moment, Bern's booming belly laugh shook the cavern.

A notification popped up.

You have learned a new spell: Ventriloquist – Tier 1.
Your illusions can make a variety of noises at medium volume. This includes voices and many mundane sounds such as doors closing, swords being drawn, and so forth. Sounds that you can personally make have a higher chance of success.
Cost: 10 mana
Requirements: Deceiver class

Devon smiled as she dismissed the notification. Yeah, it might be nice to know what spells and abilities she would gain as a Deceiver, but it was also fun to discover them. She lay back down and pillowed her head on her arm as Hazel started telling a story about the time Uruquat freaked out when a tree viper slithered into camp. The others joined in, adding to the tale.

Devon sank into the comfort of their companionship, enjoying their laughter and their stories. Her eyelids grew heavy and sleep washed over her.

***

A rumbling brought her bolt upright, shaking her head in confusion. She'd never fallen asleep in a game before—unless she counted the forced loss of consciousness while fleeing the Stone Guardian.

Apparently, it was just another feature of Relic Online.

The orb had gone out, no doubt fizzled when she'd fallen asleep. Outside, weak light painted the area around the outcroppings. The storm must have moved off, leaving light cloud cover. The front edge of the cave still dripped, but it didn't seem like any rain was still falling.

She stiffened when another rumble came from outside.

Moments later, a frustrated shout split the night.

Devon scrambled to the front of the cave. What the hell?

She peered across the open area, her darkvision augmenting the faint glow of the cloud-veiled moon. There, past the open area of bare stone, a mule-drawn wagon cut a shadow from the jungle behind. Around eight figures clustered around the vehicle, one tugging on the mules' halters.

"Come on ye damn beasts. Pull!"

The animals tossed their heads and strained against their harnesses, but the wagon scarcely rocked. Devon shook her head in amazement. What kind of idiots would try to take a wagon through this jungle? She slipped out of the cave and edged through the rubble, staying low to avoid being seen. It appeared that one of the wagon's wheels had gotten mired in some particularly deep and sticky mud. No doubt, the heap of canvas-covered cargo in the wagon bed only made the mules' task harder.

Devon slipped closer still and noticed that the figures were shorter and stockier then she'd first gathered. Full beards bushed out over their chests, and they wore a mixture of chain mail and heavy leather.

Dwarves. Other than the ogre patriarch formerly known as Uruquat, they were the first non-human race she'd seen.

Two of the dwarves held torches high above the scene. In the glow, Devon tried to make out what might be covered by that tarp, but it was lashed down tight. She considered offering help but decided to watch and wait a little longer. An attempt to inspect them with *Combat Assessment* returned a noncommittal statement about the idiocy of attacking eight dwarves by herself.

"I told you we shouldn't have left the mountains," one of the men said. By the comparatively short length of his beard, Devon guessed him to be one of the younger members of the group.

A woman—beardless, thank goodness— responded. "And what would we do, get poorer and poorer until we starved? With all the starborn coming to Eltera and taking up mining, our old trading partners don't need the iron and weapons we used to provide."

Devon perked up. Weapons? That could be awesome for the village, but it could be very bad if these dwarves had sharp steel and reason to be angry. One of them, a dwarf wearing dark chain mail, detached from the crowd and started stomping her way. Devon shrank back, hoping he'd turn aside, but he continued straight for her. Crap. She looked around for better cover but saw nothing. On instinct, she glanced down at her feet and the faint shadow drawn by the moon. Casting *Shadow Puppet*, she drew the darkness up around her.

> **You have learned a new spell:** Fade – Tier 1.
> *You seem to melt into the shadows, gaining +20 to your Hide skill (scales up with Cunning).*
> *Your surroundings must make sense for this spell to succeed. (If you turn into a shadow on a bare, sunbaked landscape, you're going to be pretty obvious)*
> **Cost:** 20 mana

The man kept coming, but he didn't seem to notice her. He stopped with his belt buckle just a couple feet away from her face.

The dwarf started to unbutton his fly. Seriously? The NPCs in this game took leaks?

Enough with the stealth. Devon jumped away to avoid a shower she had no desire to experience. The dwarf yelped and stumbled back, going down in a clatter of armor and weaponry. A nice looking warhammer clanged against a rock. Near the wagon, weapons hissed as the dwarves drew their steel.

Devon raised her hands. "Wait! Sorry, I didn't mean to startle you. I mean you no harm. I heard your shouts and hoped I could help you with..."

She gestured toward the wagon as she backed away from the sprawled dwarf. Her spine went rigid as she heard the unmistakable click of a crossbow being readied.

"Just give the word, Dorden," a female said. She raised the bow and pointed the bolt straight at Devon's forehead.

***

Rocks clattered as Devon's followers spilled from the cave. She cringed. She'd hoped to avoid getting them wrapped up in this mess.

Pasting on her most winning smile, she hoped her 25 *Charisma* was good for more than growing her mana pool. "We're just explorers, much like you seem to be."

The dwarf on the ground growled and rose to his feet, warhammer clutched in his fist. "By the stones, I think this lass is a filthy starborn."

"I—yes, but I overheard you speaking. I'm not like those..." She wrinkled her face in disgust, remembering that most dwarves had decent darkvision and could probably see her expression. "...those foul Eltera City starborn. I'm not interested in moving in on people's livelihoods. I only want to make my way out here. My friends and I are working to establish a settlement." She gestured toward the huddle of NPCs outside the cave.

"Friends, huh?" one of the torch-wielding dwarves spat. He started toward Devon's followers, weapon still drawn. "Anyone who befriends the starborn deserves to share their fate."

"Halt!" Devon shouted. "We've done nothing to harm you, and I don't want this to come to blows. But these people are my tribe, and yes, my friends. I won't hesitate to defend them. So I urge you to stop. Right. There."

She summoned her fearsome *Glowing Orb*.

The dwarf with the warhammer took a step back. He probably thought she was preparing to hurl a lightning bolt. She gave him a menacing stare to reinforce the idea.

The torch-bearing dwarf stopped in his tracks.

"Now, could we please start over? Let's at least discuss things before we start a fight that none of us wants."

The dwarves near the wagon shifted, none seeming ready to speak. After a moment, the close dwarf lowered his warhammer. "Convince me why we shouldn't just dispatch with you and take whatever items you might have. It's been a hard journey, and this terrain is ferocious, but we've got no choice but to keep going if our clan wants to survive."

Devon drew a deep breath and extinguished her orb. She lowered her arms and showed her palms in a conciliatory gesture. After a moment, she smiled again. That's how politicians did it, right? Smile no matter what?

"To start, I'd like to offer our help in getting your wagon out of that quagmire," she said. "Though I'd venture it would be easier in the morning. These rocks have plenty of caverns. What do you say we join forces at sunup?"

The dwarf, apparently the leader, glanced back at his clan. A woman who had the softer figure of advancing age shrugged. "I don't see the harm, Dorden. We won't get free of the mud tonight, in any case."

"How do I know this isn't some ploy for ye to ambush us in our sleep?" Dorden asked.

"The truth is, I don't like my odds regardless of whether half of you are asleep," Devon said. Maybe it wasn't a good idea to show weakness, but this group would soon see that her three followers weren't combat trained. No matter how good a player she was, she wouldn't fare well against eight armed and armored dwarves.

Dorden stroked his beard and then grunted. "Fair."

"And perhaps..." Devon said as more ideas crowded into her head, "perhaps we could talk about other ways we might work together for mutual benefit."

Chapter Twenty-Six

DEVON KEPT WATCH the rest of the night. Her fatigue bar had been newly refreshed by the sleep she did get, and she wanted to be able to protect her tribe members if things turned south.

The dwarves seemed similarly cautious. After a while, it got a little awkward when she kept accidentally making eye contact with the sentry outside their cave.

To distract herself, she stared into the darkness in hopes her *Darkvision* skill would improve. But it seemed she'd advanced too far to gain skill on a moonlit night. Probably needed to get underground to keep gaining skill.

By the time a watery dawn broke over the jungle, her knees ached from crouching. She stood eagerly and shook the stiffness from her legs. The dwarves had left a guard on the wagon, and as the rest of her party emptied from the cavern, the young woman crossed the rubble to join them. Devon glanced back into the cave and decided not to wake her followers. It had been a long march to reach the limestone outcrops, and she had a full day planned. Now that they'd confirmed the quarry location, they could start searching in earnest for a new settlement location. Stone was the heaviest resource to transport, so they'd want to build nearby.

She smoothed her hair—might as well keep working the charisma angle—and walked toward the dwarves, hands in her pockets.

Many of them did a poor job disguising their surprise at seeing her tattered clothing and simple machete. No doubt they were a little embarrassed for considering her such a threat the night before.

Well, she might be a relative newb still, but it wasn't *her* wagon stuck in the middle of the jungle. Now that it was day, she got a better look at the trail they'd hacked through the forest. It wove between towering trees and curved away toward the mountains.

She stopped about ten paces away from their group. "My offer still stands. We'll help you get unstuck, no strings attached."

Dorden lowered his brow and looked at her in confusion. "Are ye saying we won't need strings to pull her free?"

Devon sighed. "Sorry, just a starborn saying. I mean, we'll help you without needing something in return. It would be best, I think, to unload the cargo until the wheel is free."

The dwarves bristled at this and muttered among themselves. Devon overheard the words "cutpurse" and "thief."

She stopped herself from rolling her eyes. It was sort of stupid to get annoyed with NPC's, even if they didn't *seem* like computer-controlled characters. Regardless, she needed to stay on their good side if she hoped to make allies of them.

She put on what she hoped was a trustworthy expression and stepped closer to the group. None reached for their weapons, which was some progress. As she drew within a couple paces, one of the women muttered to a male beside her. "She's got herself a fancy vest. Looks right nice."

At least the *Charisma* stat seemed to function. That was the only explanation Devon had for compliments on the garment.

"We're honest people, I swear it," she said. "Of course, I hope we'll benefit from lending you a hand, but we won't do it by stealing."

Dorden met her gaze, tugging on his voluminous beard. "Fair enough," he said. "You're right about the unloading. We're only hesitating because what's in that wagon is all we have left."

"Where are you heading, if I might ask?" Devon asked. The sun crested the treetops and shone into her eyes. She squinted and shaded them as she looked at the wagon.

"The coast. Figure maybe we can find trading partners with access to shipping routes. The Western Reaches..." Beneath the overhang of his mustache, it almost looked as if his lip was trembling. Devon had never seen a dwarf cry, but it seemed she might today. After a moment, he swallowed and continued. "The Western Reaches aren't friendly to our kind anymore. We should have prepared, established better networks with the human settlements so that when the starborn came with their thirst for resources and their willingness to sell hard-earned ore... I can't stop thinking that if we'd just tried a little harder, we wouldn't be in this position."

Devon pulled up her map, but she couldn't see the coastline. Judging by the scale, that meant the ocean was at least thirty or forty miles away. "You won't miss the mountains?"

Dorden snorted, or maybe he was sniffing back tears. "Of course. The mines and the crags are our home. By the time we reach the shore, we won't even be able to see the peaks. But it was leave or starve. My clan has to eat."

Yeah. Devon understood their plight. Since leaving her mother's home at sixteen, she'd moved to plenty of shitty apartments because they were close to jobs she hated. Like the dwarf said, she had to eat.

She scanned the group, noting the armor and well-crafted weaponry. "Looks to me like you'd be able to hunt for food."

Dorden patted his warhammer. "Oh, we can fight, all right. That's one thing about the mountains. Plenty of attacks by goblins and the occasional cave troll to keep your combat reflexes sharp. Problem is, we lack... finesse, you might say. Tend to smash our adversaries just a bit too flat to harvest usable steaks."

This was her opening. "My group can supply food and medicine." As she spoke the words, she wondered if they were actually true. Grey had been keeping up with the tribe's needs more or less, but add the appetites of seven dwarves... Well, if nothing else, Devon could help with the hunting in the short term.

"I'm listening," Dorden said.

"We'll trade for iron, or even better, finished weapons. Plus anything else you have in surplus."

Dorden narrowed his eyes and looked over her shoulder. Devon's followers had stepped from the cave and now stood blinking in the morning sunlight. "You and these three? No offense intended, but ye hardly seem to be thriving out here."

"There are more of us. My tribe's camp is a couple hours walk from here."

"I see. So why are ye out here?"

"We're searching for a new site for a village. We have plans to expand and build a fine community in the area."

Devon hadn't missed noting that the dwarves' number would put the tribe's population at 21. One more than what they needed to level up the settlement. She didn't want to push the issue though. This seemed like a bad time to get hasty.

Dorden grunted and continued to tug at his beard.

"We have plans to be here for a long time," she continued. "With no intention of discriminating against non-starborn when it comes to trade deals. As it happens, I'm the only starborn in the tribe."

Behind their leader, the other dwarves were looking at the surroundings with a mixture of skepticism and hope. A few eyes lingered on the distant crags beyond the ruins of Ishildar.

She gestured at her friends. "My tribe and your clan could be allies in a changing world. By cooperating, I think we'd be stronger than either of our groups is alone."

The dwarf patriarch grunted, arms folded over his chest. He nodded slowly. "Where we settle next is not a decision to be made hastily. I admit, putting down roots here would let us keep contact with those who—foolishly, in my opinion—remained in the mountains. But we aren't cut out for jungle living."

Devon shook her head. "No, me neither. But for now, it's the choice I've been given."

"Well, in any case, we'll accept your help with the wagon. Getting her free will give us some time to think."

"I'll talk to my people," Devon said. "We'll be over there in a minute to help you unload."

***

Devon's followers looked up at her expectantly as she approached. And strangely, the men started blinking with their jaws slightly agape. Devon looked over her shoulder to see if she'd missed something. Behind her, the group of dwarves were grumbling as they started unfastening the tarp that covered the wagon's cargo. Nothing surprising there. Devon smoothed her clothes and ran a hand through her hair. Did she have a hunk of it sticking up or something?

"I've been meaning to ask you, Your Gloriousness," Hazel said. "Do you put anything on your skin at night?"

The woman wanted skin care advice? What the hell? A heartbeat later, it dawned on her. She'd put four points into *Charisma* the day before, but her features had been hidden in the dimness beneath the canopy. Devon groaned inwardly. Was she going to have to deal with this kind of stuff indefinitely? A cloak with a hood to shadow her face was sounding nice. In any case, hopefully her followers would get used to her smoking hotness.

"Here's the deal," she said, waiting for the men to put themselves together enough to meet her eyes. "Deld, Bern and I are going to help the dwarves get the wagon unstuck. I'm hoping it will lead to an alliance, so be nice. Hazel, I'd like you to scout the area this morning. After lunchtime, be ready to show me potential sites for our new village—look for defendable terrain, fresh water, and resources. We'll plan to head back to camp in the late afternoon with a solid start on our new empire." She added a sarcastic twist to her words because of how far they'd have to go to make that sort of claim, but her followers were too awed by her charismatic presence to get the joke. They simply nodded and dashed to work. Devon shrugged and strolled over the stony rubble to help out with the wagon.

Chapter Twenty-Seven

"AND, HEAVE!"

With a series of creaks and groans followed by a loud squelching sound, the wagon came free and lurched onto solid ground. The dwarves cheered. Devon released her grip on the wagon bed and took a seat on a small boulder.

The dwarves' possessions were strewn about the area: bedrolls and canvas tents, casks of ale and barrels of food, and—most importantly to Devon's eye—a glittering array of weaponry and armor laid out near a sizable row of iron ingots.

The sun hung high in the sky, and a glance at her real-world clock showed that it was getting late back home. Really late. But she needed to see this in-game day through.

Mopping her brow, she strolled over and admired the weapons. Dorden stepped up beside her. "Interested in anything in particular?"

"I only have a bit of coin with me, and anything we could barter is back at our camp."

"Why don't you tell me what most interests you, and we'll see what we can do."

A trade interface appeared in front of her face. Devon wasn't sure how to move the items into the window, but quickly found that when she focused on a nearby battle axe, an icon appeared for it. She pushed that away with a mental gesture. The dwarves had plenty of greatswords and two-handed axes and massive warhammers, but neither Devon nor any of her followers had the strength or combat prowess to wield such heavy weapons yet. On the far edge of the line, though, a few smaller blades glinted blue-gray against the stone. She focused on a pair of items that appeared in the interface as:

Item: Fine Steel Dagger
Crafted by a skilled hand, this blade is among the best of its type.
7-10 Damage | 49/49 Durability

Item: Superior Steel Knife
As far as knives go, you can't do much better.
5-9 Damage | 55/55 Durability

"How much for these?"

Dorden sucked his teeth. "High-quality steel there. I can't take less than 4 gold, 50 silver."

Devon shook her head. "I'm afraid I don't have that much. Best I could do is 2 gold, 90 silver."

He sighed. "I like ye lass, but I've got a clan to care for. Can't just give away our wares. Can you do 3 gold, 50?"

Devon had almost that much, but she didn't want to spend it. Especially since the game had given her an intrinsic aptitude in bartering. That had to be worth something. "Then I'll have to buy just one of the blades, I'm afraid. We haven't had a lot of opportunity to earn coin out here."

A low rumble came from Dorden's throat. "Truly sorry I can't accept your offer, lass, but I'm thinking... I would consider letting one of the blades go on credit, provided I had your word you'd compensate us fairly with food once we're settled."

Devon's surprised jerk accidentally shut the trade window. "Are you saying you agree to the alliance?"

The dwarf nodded. "I've been talking with my clan. We've decided to give it a shot. We'll stay here as long as you and I can work out a proper arrangement to trade our goods and labor for food and..." He shrugged almost as if embarrassed. "And a sense of community. We left a lot behind in the mountains and it'd be nice to know we had friends where we stopped. As you probably know, dwarves are fiercely loyal. We don't feel right walking about with all this sharp steel and no allies to protect."

Devon stretched out her hand. The dwarf's large, callused palm swallowed it up.

"Consider it a deal," she said. They finished up the trade, gaining Devon a skill point in *Bartering*. She grinned as she pulled the steel dagger out of her bag. The hilt settled easily into her palm—already it felt more comfortable than the machete. Plus, she could start working on that *One-handed Piercing* skill.

"When Hazel returns, we plan to inspect a couple sites where we can lay down foundations for the settlement. Care to join? It would be nice if we were close."

"I'd greatly enjoy that, lass."

***

The first site Hazel had found had a nearby spring and good access to fruit-bearing trees, but it didn't offer much in the way of natural defense. The second option, however, put a grin on Devon's face the moment she stepped into the glade.

Unlike the rest of the jungle, the trees here grew sparsely. Dappled sun glinted off a stream that burbled through the center of the proposed site, but the real treat was at the back edge of the area where a rib of stone erupted from the jungle floor. The cliff face was semicircular, wrapping the glade in sheltering arms. On the inside perimeter, a rudimentary stone ramp provided access to potential lookout points up top, but the other aspects—according to Hazel who had scouted the entire base of the escarpment—would be very difficult to climb. The cliff would provide a sturdy backrest for the village without placing anyone in danger from being attacked by assailants on the high ground. It was a slightly longer journey from the quarry, but closer to some of the ruins marked on the map. And with dense trees surrounding the area, Henrik's people would have to either be very persistent or very lucky to find them.

Devon looked to Dorden who had both fists around his beard as he contemplated. "What do you think?"

A slow smile cracked the dwarf's face. "And here I thought all the rock around this area was limestone. Fine for building, rubbish for extracting ores. But that there is fine granite. I can almost smell the glimmer of gold and iron down in that cliff's belly."

Devon raised an eyebrow. She wasn't sure she wanted an open mine right inside the village, but they could talk about that later. Besides, where there was one outcrop, there were likely more. "We can site the boundaries of our respective camps later, don't you think?"

The dwarf nodded. "I don't expect to have problems. I've got to say, this looks like home to me."

Hazel was nearly bouncing with pride, and Devon took the time to congratulate the woman. They turned back toward the future quarry to tell the others. Just as the jagged top of the quarry's stone showed between the trees, a snort shook the bushes. A boar leaped out, normal-sized without red eyes. Dorden yelled and brandished his hammer.

"Keep his attention," Devon said. "But see if you can avoid bludgeoning it to inedibility."

The dwarf laughed as he shouted in the wild pig's face. The beast snorted again and attacked in a sweeping motion with its tusks. The boar's head glanced off iron plates fastened over the dwarf's thighs.

Devon couldn't help grinning. It had been a long time since she'd fought with a tank holding a monster's attention. She circled around behind the squealing hog and leaped, plunging her new dagger into the back of its neck. The boar squealed as blood spurted, but it didn't drop. Dorden delivered a kick to the thing's head, knocking it to the side. The beast's neck cracked, but it didn't seem broken. Its health fell to 30%. Spotting an opening, Devon leaped in and dragged the razor edge of her new weapon across the hog's throat. The beast fell over dead, and she knelt to activate looting.

"Looks like we've earned ourselves a pig roast tonight," she said.

The corpse decomposed into a *Hog Carcass* and a *Boar Pelt – Fair*.

"Want the pelt?" Devon asked.

He shook his head. "All I want is the grub."

Devon didn't even try to fit the carcass into her bag. She could scarcely lift it. After staggering forward under its weight, she handed off the meat with relief. Dorden snorted in amusement as he carried it back to the quarry with one arm.

As they joined the others, Devon glanced at her clock. It was mid-afternoon in game, but almost dawn in St. George, Utah. Devon couldn't stay online any longer. Distantly, she felt the fatigue and hunger of her neglected body. She made arrangements with the dwarves and her followers. Deld and Bern could start quarrying stone and preparing mortar right away. Meanwhile, Hazel would lead half the dwarves on a straight march back to the camp where they would invite everyone to follow them back to the quarry for a bonfire and celebration. Devon made sure to give Hazel instructions for Tom, the cook. Whatever magic he might be able to work on the roast pig would be greatly appreciated. Tonight, the tribe could sleep in the caves. It wouldn't be as comfortable as their huts and cots, but now that they'd identified their future home, the site where she would grow their settlement into a community, and maybe even a society... She didn't see any reason to remain in the small circle hacked from the jungle by Uruquat.

She left instructions for them to start ferrying personal possessions and camp supplies to the new site, under guard of the fighters and dwarves. By the time Henrik's people arrived, if they did manage to find her new camp, they'd meet stiff resistance to any attempts to mess with her tribe.

Satisfied, Devon trudged back toward one of the caves. The others seem to understand that her starborn nature meant she needed to vanish from the world from time to time. Either that or they didn't want to offend her by asking. In any case, she slumped onto her bedroll and stared at the ceiling, listening to the laughter from outside as humans and dwarves set about their tasks. With a sigh of contentedness, she logged out.

Chapter Twenty-Eight

EZRAXIS PERCHED ON a spire of cracked black stone. She gripped the rock with her talons. Chips broke off under the pressure of her iron-hard claws. Around her, hot wind blew across a shattered landscape, gathering sulfurous fumes from steaming vents and black smoke where the earth itself burned.

She spread wings that cast a tremendous shadow over the tower's base. The designs on her ribs and forearms, etched by her own claws and empowered by the blood of her enemies, glowed a fierce red when she shrieked.

Beneath her, sycophants wailed and groveled, their twisted forms suffering with the need to please her and the knowledge they could never do enough. Imps and wraiths and animal-like werebeasts crowded the base of the pillar. Hellhounds patrolled the fringes of the group, assuring that none of the beasts could flee without consequences.

The beings scuttling across hard stone and wind-scoured sand would either fight for the glory of Zaa and his general, Ezraxis, or they would be made sacrifice, their blood given to the cause instead.

Her god's voice entered through her spine, coursed through her bones, and filled her body with ecstasy.

Yes, he said. *You have pleased me today.*

Chapter Twenty-Nine

EMERSON WOVE A course between saguaro cacti and weathered granite boulders. He wasn't much of a nature guy, but the message he'd received from Devon had tipped him over the edge. He'd needed to get out of his condo for a while.

She'd sent the message around five in the morning, right after she'd logged out, he assumed. The text had been simple.

Newsflash: pain is still a major issue. I can't be the only one.

The problem was, now she wasn't. He had a similar report from her old guildmate, Owen. As far as Emerson knew, the pair had had no contact since starting in Relic Online. He hadn't monitored their in-game messages, hadn't monitored anything about their game progress for fear he might start tweaking the AI's heuristics. But given what Devon had said about not wanting to hook up with her guildmates anytime soon, not to mention the distance between their starting locations, he seriously doubted there'd been communication.

Which brought up the question: out of going on thirty thousand subscribers to the game, why were two of his handpicked team experiencing the same problem? He'd started them in the sandboxed areas of the world to give Veia a challenge. Eventually, the rest of the player base would migrate away from the directed content, and Emerson wanted to know that the game experience would hold up. But why would a starting location make a difference in pain sensitivity? The lack of newbie quests and class tutorials shouldn't cause the pain responses to wig out. So what was the deal?

He stopped in the shade of a larger cactus. Though it was only midmorning, the Arizona heat was starting to build. Like an idiot, he'd forgotten water. Mini-Veia had even tried to remind him, but lately he'd been tuning her out.

He was now running the general AI in parallel with the previous smarthome software, hoping Veia would get a clue by watching the so-called expert. It still wasn't working, and Emerson would soon have to give up unless he came up with some sort of insight. Unfortunately, he hadn't been sleeping well, which compromised his ability to problem solve.

Was his insomnia due to worry about Devon and Owen? Excitement and anxiety about the launch? By all reports, the game looked like it was going to be a runaway success. Management was happy with how things were going.

That is, if he could solve the load issue. They were currently capped at fifteen thousand active users. Counting for downtime, that meant roughly thirty or thirty-five thousand subscribers. Not enough. And still, as far as he knew, nobody seemed to give a shit about performance on Penelope's side of the content engine.

Emerson crouched down and picked up a rock. With a sidearm toss, he sent it skittering across the desert floor. A little rodent squeaked and sprinted from the shadow of a skeletal bush.

That was probably the root of his poor sleep. Frustration bleeding into dreams. Lately, he'd been thrown into nightmare landscapes where he teetered on the brink of deadly falls or where crazed beasts tore off his limbs.

He shuddered as emotions from last night's parade of nightmares surfaced. With a deep breath of desert air, he shook his head and headed back to the bus that would take him home.

No, not home. Maybe it was time to pay a visit to the customer support group.

Chapter Thirty

THE PIG ROAST had apparently gone well. When Devon returned, almost a day and a half later in the game, some of her tribe members still looked hungover from the dwarven ale.

A sort of cargo train had been organized, and most of the camp's supplies and possessions were already piling up at the new village site. All they needed from Devon was the final say on where the huts should go. While the others had ferried supplies, Bern had quarried ten stone blocks even with his hangover, and Deld was busy baking shards of stone in a pit near the new camp to create lime for the mortar.

The dwarves had set up camp at the mouth of the glade, providing protection for Devon's tribe. A few dozen paces away, Devon marked out private locations for each of the huts on the jungle floor. Uruquat's little iron chest was nestled among the heaps of stuff. Since she still didn't have a way to open it, she set it down near the spot she planned for Hezbek's hut. Eventually, either she or one of her followers would gain the lockpicking skill. Until then, Hezbek would keep it safe.

Most of the platforms from the old camp had been disassembled already, their planks salvaged for new construction. Some would be reused for a defensive wall and lookout towers. But another project took precedence. Prester had reached skill tier 3 in carpentry, and he was practically frothing at the mouth with eagerness to get started on the crafting workshop, so she gave her blessing to a central location for the building.

The prisoner had been stuffed into a small alcove at the base of the cliff. He'd gone without healing potions long enough to wake up and make the march from the old camp to the new, but Hezbek had been forced to dose him again to keep him from dying, so he now slept with wrists and ankles once again bound. Devon glanced at his wound, which was largely unchanged, shrugged, and moved on. According to the medicine woman, he'd continued to stonewall the tribe's questions when he was awake. They were going to have to stop feeding him between potions, see if that might motivate him.

After running through additional oversight tasks like checking with Grey on the food supply and sending Hazel out to widen her survey of the surroundings, she took a seat beside the gurgling brook. It felt strange to have accomplished enough organization that there was nothing left to do for a while. She could actually focus on her character. It would be nice to grind out a couple levels. She stood and stretched. On the way toward the mouth of the little glade, she spotted Greel and realized there was one other task she wanted to accomplish today.

He glared and stomped forward with a sullen expression when she waved him over. "Yes?" he asked, sounding like an annoyed teenager.

Devon gritted her teeth. The man really had a way of making people dislike him. Nonetheless, she needed him.

"I have something for you," she said.

Greel narrowed his eyes. "Am I supposed to jump up and down with joy?"

"Well, I'd hoped..." She pulled the *Superior Steel Knife* out of her bag and held it out.

Greel hesitated, one eyebrow lowered as if wondering what the catch was. After a moment, he reached out a tentative hand.

"It's yours," she said. "I hope it's an adequate replacement for your beloved rusty knife."

Greel swallowed and seemed to struggle with what to say. Finally, he nodded.

"Thank you," he mumbled.

"Maybe you'll decide to lend your combat strength to the village defense," she commented.

Greel snorted. "We have a ways to go before you can put me on guard duty with the rest of these incompetents. But it is a nice knife."

You have gained esteem with Greel: +120 Reputation.

You have completed a quest: Deal with Greel.
Congratulations! You have a new ally, as long as you don't do something else to anger him.

Finally. She inspected him just before he moved out of range and saw that she was now 5 points above neutral with him. So, not BFF-level esteem. But at least he didn't hate her anymore.

That finished, she hiked up her belt and straightened her snakeskin vest. Time to hunt.

***

For the next few play sessions, Devon moved in wide circles around the new camp, hunting wildlife and practicing her skills. During the week, she asked Hezbek for a little primer on herbalism and was able to start supplementing the medicine cabinet with ingredients at the same time that she brought back meat for the cookpot. She stuck with monsters lower level than herself, enough of a challenge to grant decent experience, but easy enough that she wouldn't get hurt—at least not badly. The last two experiences with the pain setting had been enough to put her off for a while. Every fight, she tried to use a variety of skills—especially dagger strikes that raised her piercing skill. Partway through the week, she reached level 7. She put a point into *Endurance* so her fatigue wouldn't build so fast, another into *Focus* in hopes it would help her keep concentration on her *Glowing Orbs*, and two into *Intelligence*. Her character sheet looked like this afterward:

Character: Devon (click to set a different character name)

Level: 7

Base Class: Sorcerer

Specialization: Unassigned

Unique Class: Deceiver

Health: 168/168

Mana: 304/304

Fatigue: 36%

She clicked over to the attributes section to verify the new values:

Attributes:

Constitution: 15

Strength: 10

Agility: 15

Charisma: 25

Intelligence: 25

Focus: 13

Endurance: 12

Special Attributes:

Bravery: 5

Cunning: 4

Available Points: 0

Finally, she checked out her skills window:

Skills:

Unarmed Combat: 3

One-handed Slashing - Tier 2: 12

One-handed Piercing - Tier 2: 10

Darkvision - Tier 2: 10

Tracking: 4

Stealth: 2

Combat Assessment: 4

Sprint: 1

Leadership: 8

Bartering: 6

Special Skills:

Improvisation: 3

Her slashing and piercing had reached Tier 2—which unfortunately meant that the skill gain had slowed way down. She was still *really* far from using the ivory fangs. But at least it was progress. Finally, she checked her abilities and saw that *Flamestrike - Tier 1* was at 92% mastery, and *Shadow Puppet - Tier 1* was at 68%.

When she was in the village during meals, she sat around the campfire with her followers and the Stoneshoulder Clan, as she learned they were called. Tom's cooking raised everyone's morale, as did the new digs. The canopy cut the worst of the heat and even helped block some rain, but it wasn't so thick as to be oppressive.

Sometimes, Devon wondered if the glade and the cliff behind it had been sculpted from the landscape just for her tribe. Then she got to wondering how much attention the AI was paying her, and she started down the rabbit hole of wondering why her experience was so different from what she'd seen on the forums. She thought of Relic Online as a game less and less frequently, and when she did, it was a little disappointing, like a spell had been broken. So aside from her alarms for eating and sleeping and the occasional glimpse of the real-world sunshine, she stayed in game and enjoyed it.

Shadow Puppets raised in the sun and moonlight were awesome in combat, giving her the chance to challenge herself with multi-mob encounters, even if she avoided those where she might get hit hard. But as for the lightning shadow, she wasn't ready to test her theory on wet versus dry ground. Anyway, between her *Flamestrike* spell, her dagger, and her *Shadow Puppets,* she'd started to feel like a one-woman war machine. Even if her hopes for summoning a horde of shadows by using sorcerer spells that created different types of light never worked out as she'd hoped, she could see that her class combo was more than a little overpowered. Especially when used cleverly.

When she dinged 8, she decided to wait to spend more attribute points until she'd tried a few more challenging encounters. Hezbek taught her the *Freeze* spell, which encased mobs in ice. As a celebration, she gathered the tribe. She cast *Shadow Puppets* and molded them into fantastic shapes before freezing them, leaving a garden of ice sculptures that were soon chipped apart and used to chill ale. Soon after encamping, the dwarves had made it a priority to set up their brewing casks. Some sort of dwarven magic made the ale crafting process go much faster than Devon would have expected, and the nightly campfires had no shortage of grog.

Toward the end of her week of leveling, Gerrald presented her with a new pair of trousers.

You have received: Boar Hide Leggings
These are definitely more fashionable than the snakeskin vest. Well done.
+1 Agility +2 Charisma | 30 Armor | 25/25 Durability

Of course, the added *Charisma* combined with a pair of tight leather pants earned her another few days of stares until her followers once again got used to her shocking good looks. But the bonuses were worth it. She almost wanted to strut.

All in all, it was one of the best weeks of Devon's life.

Unfortunately, on the day the final roof was raised on the crafting workshop, prompting the dwarves to crack an extra cask of ale, the shit hit the fan.

Chapter Thirty-One

DEVON HEARD SHOUTING from the edge of the camp. She gave a quick nod of apology to Prester who was showing her a couple features of the crafting workshop and dashed toward the edge of the glade. Two small groups staggered into the filtered light of the camp. Devon's pulse sped when she saw Deld shuffling forward, clutching his shoulder. Bern walked on one side of the stonemason while Bayle followed a step or two behind. A couple dozen paces behind the trio of humans, Dorden struggled forward, arm around Heldi, his mate and the dwarf who had threatened Devon with her crossbow back on the night of their meeting.

Devon gasped as the pair drew closer. Heldi was doubled over her gut, hands clutching the shaft of an arrow. The front of her chainmail shirt was soaked with blood. Devon caught Dorden's eye, searching for an explanation. The patriarch stared back, grim-faced.

Devon whirled. "Fetch Hezbek! Tell her to bring healing potions!"

The groups staggered to a stop at the informal boundary between camps. Devon sprinted over, shaking her head in shock. "What happened? Ambush? Who shot you?"

Bayle's face was ashen, almost as if she'd been struck. But she had no visible wounds. Dorden simply looked at Devon and growled. Devon blinked, confused, while the dwarf turned toward his camp and bellowed. "Thunnold! Get out here! Heldi's hurt."

Hezbek arrived, clothing flapping, satchel clinking. She quickly glanced at the two injuries, pulled a pair of potions out of her satchel, and tossed one of the clay pots to Devon. She gestured with her eyes for Devon to take care of Deld while she ran to help Heldi, who was clearly in worse shape.

Devon unstoppered the pot and placed it against the Deld's lips. The man swallowed and grimaced at the taste. Moments later, he began to sway. His hand dropped from his shoulder, giving Devon a peek at the wound before the skin began to knit. As best she could tell, an arrowhead had nicked the outside of the muscle, passing through without becoming lodged. Deld slumped against Bern who picked the man up and started trudging for Deld's hut.

"Going to lay him down," he said. Bayle followed behind, eyes darting. Devon watched them go, confused by the fighter's behavior, before turning her attention to the dwarves.

Hezbek had already administered a potion, and Heldi's color was better. The medicine woman examined the arrow lodged in the dwarf's belly.

"I'm going to cut the head off and pull it out the way it went in," she said. The dwarf woman was already unconscious, head lolling. Her body slumped forward like a ragdoll as Dorden went down on a knee and laid her across his thigh. Hezbek pulled out a small blade and sliced through the arrow shaft, then grabbed the fletching and yanked it free. Heldi moaned, and a bit of blood welled.

"She'll need more healing once she sleeps off the effects of this one," Hezbek said.

Dorden growled, and for some reason glared in the direction of the tribe's camp. "Will she live?"

Hezbek nodded as she smoothed the dwarf woman's hair. "I believe so, but it will take time."

"Dorden, what happened?" Devon said.

The dwarf simply looked at her and shook his head. "We'll talk of this later. Perhaps once I'm sure that my mate will survive."

***

She found Bayle and Bern inside Deld's hut. The stonemason was resting peacefully now, his wound scabbed over and hardly noticeable. Bern stood protectively over the man while Bayle crouched in the corner, fingers tapping her knee.

"Will you please explain what happened?" Devon asked as she laid a hand on Deld's shin, assuring herself the man was okay.

Bayle and Bern shared a glance. "I'll do it," the woman said. The big man nodded and stalked to the door. He peered out, then let the door flap fall and took a seat on the floor.

The fighter took a deep breath before speaking. "Everything went as normal for most of the day, your—Devon. The dwarves brought me along for guard duty at the quarry, and Dorden had loaned me a short bow for practice."

Devon nodded. The dwarves had been helping Bayle and Falwon, the camp's fighters, increase their skills.

"All right, then what happened?"

"Well, while Bern was freeing a stone block, he exposed a vein of moss agate."

Bern nodded. "It caused the block to fracture wrong. Cost me a couple hours of work."

"A vein? The dwarves said limestone wasn't good for—"

"Not for the metals they usually seek, but agate is one of the gem types that occurs in it." Bern shrugged. "Or so Dorden said."

"You should've seen the dwarves' faces," Bayle said, picking up the tale again. "Their eyes were wider than the tops of ale casks. They said jewel crafters and enchanters would pay a hefty price for agate. Especially moss agate, which is known for its nature-based magical properties."

Devon had an idea where this was going. "They didn't try to take it from you, did they?"

Bern pointed to Deld's rucksack. "We have samples in there. No, they didn't try to take anything. Dorden was mumbling about asking your permission to work the vein and divide the profits, but that's all I heard. Until..." He glanced at Deld.

"Go on," Devon said.

Bayle swallowed. "We left the quarry early because we thought you'd want to know about the discovery. We were about halfway back when Deld yelped and grabbed his shoulder. It was confusing for a minute, until I saw the blood and recognized it as an arrow wound. Or... a crossbow bolt."

Devon blinked in shock.

Bern swallowed. "It was so unexpected, we didn't know how to react at first. All three of us turned to look. The dwarves were behind us on the trail. Heldi uses a crossbow, you know."

"Did she look like she'd done it?"

Bayle grabbed fistfuls of her hair. "That's the thing, I'm not sure. Everything happened so fast. Deld definitely got hit, and I didn't know what to do. I drew on Heldi just in case, but I didn't intend anything else."

Devon swallowed. This was not good. "Did you look at the crossbow? Did it have a bolt loaded?"

"I—yes, actually. I think so. I was pretty sure the shot came from her. Still am... I think. What other explanation is there?"

"So you drew on her, and then?"

"Dorden pulled out that hammer of his and stepped closer, and I started shaking. I was terrified, to be honest. They're both better fighters than me. Together, they'd crush me. I knew I had to protect Deld and Bern. But I swear, I didn't shoot her on purpose. I was trying to talk to them to figure out what had happened, and my fingers slipped. I felt the string twang. Saw the arrow sink into her gut."

Bayle dropped her head into her hands. Bern crossed the small room and laid a hand on her shoulder. After a moment, she swallowed and collected herself. She raised her head and continued.

"Dorden was red in the face, looking between Heldi and me. Somehow, I don't know what trick he used, but Bern managed to talk him down. Heldi was already bleeding bad, and Bern mentioned seeing to the injuries before anyone died unnecessarily." She took a shaky breath. "So that's it. I'm sorry, Devon."

Devon chewed her lip. The situation sounded to her like a series of mistakes. She didn't think the dwarves would turn on them like that, not before at least *asking* for the agate. The truth was, Devon would be more than happy to split any proceeds. But she'd heard plenty of tales about dwarven thirst for riches. She couldn't completely deny that they had motive.

"Remind me again, how far away was this?"

"About halfway to the quarry," Bern said.

Devon nodded. "I need you to take me there. Before this goes any further, there's one piece of information we have to track down. We need to find the arrow or crossbow bolt that struck Deld."

Bern stood. "I'm ready to go as soon as you need me."

Devon stepped outside and waved down Hezbek as the medicine woman returned from the dwarf encampment. Hezbek blinked nervously as she hurried over. "Something's got the dwarves riled."

"Indeed. And possibly with good reason. I'm working on it, but I need to track down some information. How long until Heldi wakes?"

"She'll come around briefly in about a day," Hezbek said. "But I'll need to dose her with another potion right away. It will be two or three days before she's fully recovered."

Devon nodded. "Do what you can to keep the peace. Tell Dorden I promise to make this right. But be careful... Find Greel and tell him to keep an eye on the dwarves. Hopefully he can manage that."

The medicine woman looked like she wanted to ask more questions, but she simply nodded and headed deeper into the camp. With Bern following behind, Devon searched the glade until she spotted Hazel. The little scout was whittling with a kitchen knife, carving a crude figure. Devon made a mental note to offer the woodworking trade to the woman someday.

"Are you rested enough to head out?" she asked.

Hazel jumped to her feet and self-consciously dropped her hands to her side. "Of course, Your Gloriousness."

"Good. I may need your tracking skill. We'll follow Bern. Keep alert for threats."

Chapter Thirty-Two

THE TRAIL BETWEEN the camp and quarry was a few feet wide with leaves and grass trampled into the mud. It seemed like regular passage kept trails through the jungle cleared, which was nice. Even nicer, the paths that didn't get used quickly became overgrown. Devon had been worried that Henrik's people would be able to follow their route from Uruquat's original camp to the new glade, but already, she'd noticed that the trail between the old camp and the quarry was nearly invisible.

In any case, the cleared track should help her find the missing arrow without too much trouble.

When they arrived at the scene of the altercation, she realized she hadn't needed Bern to guide her. The site was clearly marked by sticky blood that spattered the leaf litter. Devon brushed a strand of hair from her forehead then pinched the bridge of her nose. "Okay, let's find this arrow."

With the tip of her dagger, she started pushing back the brush at the edge of the trail, looking beneath leaves. Judging by the angle of the shot, the bolt or arrow wouldn't have landed far from the trail. After a few minutes searching, she pulled out her old machete and started hacking away the undergrowth.

"Something's bothering me, Your Gloriousness," Bern said. He was standing in the middle the trail, head cocked.

"What's that?"

"Well... Bayle dropped her bow after she accidentally shot Heldi. I wasn't thinking because I was so worried for Deld and Heldi, but I'm pretty sure she didn't retrieve it before we left the area."

"But it's not here..." Devon said. A cold feeling was building in her gut. As she took a deep breath to return to the search, Hazel stood from the thicket. "Found it!" she chirped, holding up a long-shafted arrow.

Devon nodded. That was definitely not a crossbow bolt.

Immediately, memories surged. How many times had she run across a room full of monsters, too many for her to take on alone, and started using the game mechanics against the mobs? In almost every MMO in existence, you could often pit enemies against one another by causing them to mistakenly damage each other. It worked particularly well against monsters of low intelligence or— like in the case of Devon's alliance with the Stoneshoulder Clan— when the mobs were grouped into different races or factions.

It wasn't hard to envision how the same thing could have happened here. One or two players, too low-level to take on a band of five dwarves and humans, had spotted the group. One of the players had shot Deld but made it seem as if the strike had come from the dwarves. The plan had almost worked, too. If Dorden had attacked Bayle and Bern, it would have left most of the group injured or dead. Afterward, the players would be left to mop up, taking the loot and experience for themselves.

She couldn't be sure that's what had happened, but it seemed likely. Players would definitely have picked up an abandoned short bow, whereas NPCs might not have.

Devon shook her head in frustration. She should have anticipated this moment. Players would find the jungle and the ruins of Ishildar eventually. But she'd let herself get too comfortable with her NPC tribe. And she knew how players thought... They wouldn't see her tribe members as people. Sure, some gamers were reluctant to kill friendly humanoids, if only because they didn't want to lose esteem with certain factions. But given what had happened here, the person or people who planned this ambush didn't care about that. And most of her tribe members would be sitting ducks without the dwarves to defend them.

She took a deep breath. First things first, she needed to warn the camp. Then she had to verify the attackers' identities and figure out where they'd gone.

"Hazel, I want you to find the shooters' trail. Stay close and don't risk yourself. I'll be back in just a few minutes after I escort Bern to safety."

With that, she set off at a trot, the quarryman at her heels.

***

"No one leaves the camp until I return, got it? Tell Hezbek and Greel."

Bern nodded as he slipped down the trail and entered the glade. Devon watched for a minute, listening for any sounds of trouble inside the glade, then spun. She hoped that if players decided to attack the camp while she was gone, the dwarves would come to her tribe's defense. At the very least, their canvas shelters were the first buildings any players would encounter, a fact that would bring the dwarves into the fray regardless. She hated to think of her allies that way, as bait for potential player attacks. But they weren't part of her tribe. Not yet. And with what had happened today, maybe not ever.

After hearing no sounds of conflict, she doubled back toward the quarry. When she reached the scene of the fight, Hazel materialized from the brush. Devon jumped and let out a shaky laugh. At least she didn't have to worry about her scout being easily detected.

"Did you find a trail?"

Hazel nodded. "They followed this path back to the quarry and then set out in a different direction."

"Lead on," Devon said.

Beyond the quarry, the attackers had hacked their way through the jungle much like Devon had done for the last weeks. She doubted they liked it any more than she did. Unfortunately, though, the dense growth hadn't been enough to keep them away. She squeezed the hilt of her dagger. Stupid players.

"This area sucks, dude."

Devon stiffened when she heard the voice filtering through the undergrowth. Soon after, a curl of smoke reached her nose. She motioned Hazel back, and the woman retreated without complaint.

"Yeah, but we came all this way. There's got to be something more interesting than a couple stray dwarves out here."

"Those ruins looked kinda cool."

"Yeah, if you feel like fighting a stone giant. Anyway, let's give it a couple more game days before we bail, eh?"

Devon crept closer and spotted the two figures crouching before a small fire. The bigger of the pair, a warrior judging by his gear, held a stick over the flames. Shapeless meat clung to it.

"There's got to be something in all this jungle. Otherwise, why waste the real estate?" the other player continued. Devon didn't know enough about the classes to be sure, but he had a mace holstered at his side and white vestments beneath a chain shirt. A cleric? Seemed a likely duo to set out together.

The warrior rotated the stick. "Yeah, I guess. Even if the city's over our heads, there's got to be some mini-dungeons around."

Devon stiffened at the thought. She'd been so concerned about her tribe that she hadn't even considered the other problem players presented. She glanced at her quest log and the mission to find the Greenscale Pendant. She hadn't been focusing on the search because she'd assumed she'd get to it eventually. But if players found it first, it totally hosed her plans.

She used *Combat Assessment* and was rewarded with more information than she'd expected. Both players were level 10, two levels higher than her, but without the unique class. She could probably take them out, but she was well enough acquainted with player psychology to know where that would lead. They'd come back for revenge, possibly with friends.

She guessed they were probably bound nearby. Otherwise it would be stupid to venture so far. Thinking about those sorts of logistics reminded her that she had no idea what happened to a player's gear when they died. Her only death had happened at level 1 when she'd been wearing nothing but ratty trousers and a cloth tunic. If nothing else, they might have to come back to retrieve their stuff.

Devon shook her head. She couldn't take them on directly. How about training a horde of angry monsters down on them? With her *Shadow Puppet* and her ability to *Fade*, she could probably get away with it. But again, an exciting fight would only make this area of the world *more* interesting for them. While she crouched there thinking, the warrior lifted the stick out of the flames. As he held it toward the cleric and laughed, Devon recognized the poor creature they were cooking. Who the hell thought it was okay to eat parrots? Assholes!

The warrior tore the meal in two and handed half to his friend. They ate in silence then stood.

"Should we find ourselves a dungeon?"

"Christ, I hope so."

As Devon crept along the path they cut through the jungle, she wracked her brain for ideas. The players were already bored by the area. But if they found any of the ruins she knew were scattered through the old vassaldom, they'd probably change their minds. Somehow, she needed to convince them to give up, but she couldn't do it by fighting. The experience of being in this area had to be obnoxious—apparently more obnoxious than needing to cut their way through jungle every time they moved.

"Hey! Nice! Check it out," the warrior shouted. Devon's heart sank as she crept forward. The pair was standing in front of a darkened passage, an overgrown archway leading into a ruined stone building. Judging by the age-rounded carvings on the outside and the lofty dome, spoiled only by a few ragged holes at the center of the building, it looked like an old temple of some sort. Just the sort of place where an ancient civilization would store a relic. She doubted she was that unlucky, but it sure would suck if that were the case. She needed a plan, quick.

Checking her mini-map, she saw that the building was on the edge of the area she'd most wanted to explore. Hazel had marked quite a few sightings of the corrupted animals nearby. Devon had asked the scout to keep track so that, eventually, she could make progress on the "What's Wrong with the Wildlife" quest.

"Hey, Mark? I gotta log for an hour or two. My mom just messaged me... homework."

The warrior snorted. "Lame."

"I know, right? But she'll take away my subscription if I don't do it."

"Yeah, I know. Let's just clear the first room and logout in there, sound good?"

"What about respawn?"

The warrior shrugged. "The game seems smarter than that, but we could handle it anyway, right? Just more XP."

"Yeah, good point."

The pair moved closer to the entrance and peered inside. Muttering something under his breath, the cleric conjured a light that hung just above his shoulder. The pair stepped into the darkness.

Wild chittering erupted from within the temple, followed by a wet thunk.

"Holy shit, dude! That is one massive arachnid."

"Sweet. Now kill it. Those red eyes are creepy."

More thuds and grunts and chittering followed.

"Heal, please," the warrior whined. Devon slipped closer and peered through the entrance. The cleric's light source washed the stone walls with a silvery glow. Shadows moved wildly as an absolutely giant spider skittered across the room and struck at the warrior again.

"Yikes," Devon muttered. It was definitely one of the corrupted beasts. The spider was leaking green blood from half a dozen wounds, and one leg lay twitching on the ground. Devon looked down at her shadow, sharp-edged in the sunlight where the temple poked through the trees. She didn't want the warrior and cleric to receive the same quest she was on from the spider's stomach contents. Could she steal the kill using only her *Shadow Puppet* while managing to stay hidden? They definitely couldn't know there was a player around.

She shook her head. A bad gamble. She'd just have to hope the quest loot didn't drop. Fists clenched, she watched as the warrior opened the spider's abdomen with a huge swipe of his broadsword. Ichor sprayed, coating the players. With an enraged roar, the warrior struck again and again, chopping at the corpse even though it was clear the arachnid was dead.

The cleric wiped slime off his sleeve. "Overkill much? Dude, you're going to ruin the loot."

The warrior sighed and gave the corpse a last jab. "Sorry man. Hate spiders."

He crouched beside the remains and activated the decomposition with a poke of his sword. "Shit, yeah, you're right. We've got a mangled spider stomach, shredded carapace, and disgusting goo."

The cleric sighed and sat down. "I'm sure there'll be more. At least we finally found something fun to do. Logging now... I'll text you after homework, K?"

"Sounds good," the warrior said as he peered through the next door. "See you then."

The cleric vanished from sight, and a few seconds later, the warrior sat and logged as well. Devon stood. One or two hours in the real world. Two and a half to five in-game. Not much time to think of something, but it would have to do.

Chapter Thirty-Three

A PLAN STARTED to come together in Devon's mind, but she needed to get back to the camp to put it into action. As she jogged back, she marked time on the game clock. Hazel trotted along behind her, apparently unfazed by all the running back and forth. When they reached the quarry, Devon stopped and planted her hands on her knees to catch her breath. Her fatigue climbed more slowly after the point she'd invested in Endurance, but she could still stand to work on it.

"Mind waiting just past the entrance to the trail they cut?" she asked the scout. "I don't want it getting overgrown while I'm gone."

Hazel nodded and hurried back to the path as Devon set out again, bound for the village. When she reached the border of the glade, she shook her head in dismay. Relations seemed to have gone from strained to worse. A pair of dwarf guards that usually patrolled the outer edge of the dwarven camp, watching for oversized wildlife, now stood stone-faced on the unofficial border between camps. Their short swords were sheathed, but their hands hovered close to the hilts. Meanwhile, Greel stalked the perimeter of the tribe's camp, looking nonchalant. But Devon was sure he had that steel knife tucked into some hidden pocket or another. She gritted her teeth and ran to Hezbek's hut. The medicine woman greeted her with a worried expression.

"Can you teach me any new spells?" Devon asked. She didn't think so, but it was worth a shot.

Hezbek's brow furrowed. "Now?" She shook her head slowly. "You'll soon be ready to levitate, but you need a little more experience first."

Crap. Floating around wasn't going to help her. "Nothing else? What if I power level?"

"Power... what?" Hezbek shook her head again. "In any case, no, it won't be for a while yet."

Devon had worried that would be her answer. Stepping farther into the hut, she took the mortar and pestle from Hezbek, set them down, and took hold of the woman's hands. Hezbek's skin had the thin crinkling quality that Devon associated with the elderly. Guilt was a cold ball in her stomach. She hated to ask the medicine woman to stray from the path she'd chosen for her so-called retirement.

"Would you do something for me, Hezbek? I will never ask you to harm someone, and I'm not asking that for that now. But I *am* hoping to scare them a little."

A look of confusion was followed by a narrowing of Hezbek's eyes. "So that's why you wanted more training. You need me to cast a spell that you haven't learned yet."

Devon swallowed and nodded. "A couple of them, maybe. But I swear it's to protect the tribe. I don't think you'll regret it if you help me."

"Perhaps you could explain..."

"I will, but it will take a while, and we don't have much time. Can you trust me?"

Hezbek slowly withdrew her hands. "Of course, child. I'll do as you ask."

"Thank you," Devon said, straightening. "I'll explain on the way. We need to hurry. Bring water—it's a bit of a journey."

Hezbek licked her lips. "Now, wait. Are we going somewhere? I have a patient..."

Right. Heldi.

"Can Dorden administer the potions?"

"I suppose so."

"I'll go talk to him."

The dwarf stared her down, arms crossed. He wouldn't let Devon into the hut where Heldi lay sleeping, so she met him in the open air in the center of their camp. She felt dwarven eyes on her and knew they wouldn't hesitate to attack if Dorden gave the nod.

Devon swallowed. "The agate is yours to mine and sell as long as it doesn't disturb quarry operations. Do you remember the saying...? No strings attached."

Dorden said nothing. He continued to stare at her with open distrust.

"Listen," she said, "I know you didn't shoot Deld. And I realize that Bayle *did* send an arrow into your mate's belly. But it was an accident. She's inexperienced, and her fingers slipped. I found the arrow that nicked Deld—proof that it didn't come from Heldi's crossbow—but surely you can see how the situation might have been confusing. Still, my tribe is at the greatest fault for this terrible accident. I hope the mining rights can serve as recompense, along with my vow to take care of those responsible for the situation."

He still looked skeptical, but his face was beginning to soften. She knew dwarves were stubborn and plowed on in hopes enough talking would sway him. "I won't ask for forgiveness until Heldi is fully restored. Even then, you can leave and settle elsewhere, and we won't touch that agate vein." She took a deep breath, not eager to speak the next words. "But I need to take Hezbek with me to deal with this threat."

The medicine woman, fortunately, chose that moment to arrive. She extended a pair of clay pots toward the dwarf leader. "As soon as she stirs, give her one. It'll put her back to sleep, and I think it will complete the healing. If she wakes a second time before I return, give her the other to be safe."

After a moment, Dorden reached out and took the pots.

"Do we have a truce for now?" Devon asked.

Dorden agreed with a grunt and a nod.

***

Outside the temple, birdsong filled the forest. Leaves rustled as small animals moved through the undergrowth. Devon approached cautiously and leaned her ear toward the entrance, listening for voices.

The players hadn't yet returned. She waved Hezbek forward, and they entered the first room together.

"If they arrive early, you know what to do, right?" Devon asked.

The medicine woman nodded. Devon really hoped the players didn't log back in before she was ready, but it was nice to have a plan just in case.

As Hezbek stepped to the edge of the room and put her back against the wall, Devon cast a *Glowing Orb,* then reached through the door into the next room and placed it on the wall. Electric-blue light filled the chamber, glowing off the thick cobwebs in the corners. Devon grimaced. She didn't like spiders any more than that warrior. But she didn't have time to be choosy. Drawing her dagger, she stepped into the room.

The webs erupted with life as five dog-sized spiders uncurled and clambered down the walls. They rushed across the floor toward her, eyes glittering.

Devon took a step back and swung with her dagger, catching one of the spiders along its right side. Her strike severed four legs, and the arachnid fell over sideways. It squirmed on the floor, alive but neutralized.

Just as she started to get cocky, another spider leaped. It latched onto her forearm and bit down, fangs puncturing her skin.

"Ouch!" she yelled, shaking the thing off. The wound ached. At the edges of her vision, she saw red. Damn, she hated the pain response in this game. She kicked as another spider lunged, knocking it aside but doing no damage.

A wave of nausea hit her. The scene wavered. Shit, poison.

Clenching her teeth, Devon circled around the wall of the room and cast *Flamestrike*. A burning pillar lanced through the ceiling and sizzled one of the spiders. It shrieked, shriveling as it drew its legs close. The smell of singed hair filled the room.

A poison tick sent another wave of nausea through her. Her health dropped to 75%. Devon backed away, the spiders following her like a pack of dogs. She swung wildly with the dagger and they nimbly dodged back. One spat, and yellow venom splattered on her cheek. Her health dropped to 70%. At the edge of her awareness, she felt the restriction on *Flamestrike* ease. The spell had a five-second cooldown, and during that time, she found she just couldn't put her mind through the necessary steps to cast it. Now, though, she took another step back and called down fire. Another spider squealed and died. The poison ticked again, knocking her down to 65% health. As she staggered, one of the spiders lashed out with a leg, slicing her across the shin. She gagged at the pain and limped back.

The sudden eruption of chittering and hissing and clicking feet told her she'd taken one step too far into the next room, the temple's main chamber. She cast a panicked glance over her shoulder and saw another dozen pairs of eyes glittering in the light of her *Glowing Orb*. *Flamestrike* was ready again, and she knocked the life from one of the last two spiders in the room with her then leaped over the other.

She looked at the advancing horde and shook her head. She was going to die here. Might as well try everything she could. Besides, the major point of taking the Sorcerer class was to create new and interesting light sources to exploit her Deceiver abilities. It was a useless choice unless she actually tried to use the combos.

Jaw clenched, she willed her *Shadow Puppet* to rise from the ground. Edges crackling like black electricity, the dark figure rose. Devon kicked at the lone spider near her, sending its sliding away, then gritted her teeth and forced her shadow to dart into the other room.

Sparks erupted from her puppet, cascading over the herd of spiders. Arachnids screeched and died, falling in concentric circles from the locus where her shadow stood with arms spread wide.

She watched the wave of electricity approach, cringed, stared at her health bar as she braced for the pain. The spider in front of her squeaked but kept coming. Pain lapped up her legs.

It stopped before reaching her knees. In the other room, her shadow fizzled. She sighed in relief as she stabbed the nearby spider through the eyes. It died and slid off her blade.

"Devon," Hezbek called as another wave of poison shook her. Devon's health was down to 40% as she turned to look at the woman. Hezbek pulled a pot from her rucksack and tossed it over.

You have received: Jungle Antidote - Minor

The spiders in the other room were advancing, but slowly. Most of them dragged paralyzed limbs and deadened abdomens. Grimacing, Devon uncorked the pot and poured the liquid down her throat. The taste was as foul as *Jungle Healing Potion - Minor* but disgusting in a different way. Immediately, her vision cleared.

None of the remaining spiders were fast enough to harm her. Devon grabbed the *Glowing Orb* off the wall and waded into the writhing mass. One by one, she put the things out of their misery. For a moment, the temple was silent until a loud chime shook the walls.

Congratulations! You have reached level 9!
You have gained 4 attribute points.

You have gained mastery in Glowing Orb - Tier 2: 1%
You have gained mastery in Shadow Puppet – Tier 1: 3%

"You can come in now," she said as she caught her breath.

As Hezbek shuffled forward, Devon searched the perimeter of the temple's main chamber. Cobwebs hung in curtains from the ceilings and covered much of the architecture. In a little alcove, there was a stone hatch that probably led to some sort of catacombs. Yet another thing that would interest the players. She gathered some rubble and strewed it over the top of the hatch just in case they made it this far. As she looked back over the rooms filled with nearly twenty spider corpses, she wondered whether she should loot them. Better to leave the bodies, but it was hard to pass up the chance. Still, she doubted she'd get much besides random spider parts. Better to have the plan succeed.

Hezbek crept somewhat tentatively into the final chamber. "It's been a long time since I was that close to battle. You fought well."

Devon smiled. "Then let's finish what we came here to do."

Hezbek straightened, looking very serious. But the gleam in her eyes made Devon wonder if the older woman was enjoying the adventure more than she let on.

"Don't we need to group up?" the woman said.

Devon laughed. "You're right. It's my own plan, and I forgot that part." She hadn't known it was possible to group with an NPC, but she was glad, seeing as Hezbek's part wouldn't work on conscious players unless they were part of a group.

The invite popped up in her interface, asking if she would like to group with Hezbek. When Devon accepted, the group interface sprang up, showing her Hezbek's health and mana. Pretty standard.

"All right. This has got to happen fast. We can't give them time to pay a lot of attention to me."

"I remember," Hezbek said with a faint smile that suggested she didn't really need the review.

"Okay then," Devon said as she stepped into a beam of sunlight that fell through the temple's vault. She brought her sun-cast

Shadow Puppet to life, then formed it into a set of narrow blades that she wedged into cracks in the stone ceiling at the temple's main entrance. Next, she cast *Fade* on herself and sat back to wait.

The players entered in a flash of light, first the cleric, then the warrior. As soon as they stood, Devon cast *Freeze* on her shadow, encasing the thin blades in ice. She quickly followed with a *Flamestrike* targeting the roof.

"Freeze-thaw cycle. Thank you, high school geology," she muttered as the tunnel entrance collapsed, blocks loosened just enough by the expansion of ice in the cracks. The players yelled and backed away from the falling stone and dust just as Hezbek ran into the room.

The players whirled, the warrior drawing his sword.

"Oh no!" Hezbek yelled, "Escape has been cut off! The spider lord comes! Wait, who are you—"

"Uh, who are you?" The warrior asked, lowering his blade slightly.

Hezbek glanced over her shoulder as if terrified of something in the main chamber. "I am a medicine woman of the Uruquat tribe. My companion and I have come to cleanse these halls."

"Dude, she's an NPC." The cleric said, his eyes on the spider corpses.

Hezbek backed away from the temple's main chamber. "The spider lord will soon appear. Our acts have summoned his wrath. Will you join us in battle?"

The warrior grinned. "Sweet, an event. And we showed up just in time for the boss fight. Hell yeah, we'll join."

Moments later, two names appeared in the group list. Hezbek backed against the rubble of the entrance as Devon took over the plan. She cast another *Shadow Puppet*, bringing it to life in the temple's main chamber. Stretching its substance thin, she formed it into the shape of a house-sized spider. With her *Ventriloquist* ability, she made the thing shriek.

"Holy shit," the warrior mumbled as he raised his sword.

While the players were distracted, Hezbek had begun casting. Devon heard a thunderclap as her stomach suddenly flew into her throat.

Her feet landed on bare stone, and high-altitude sun lanced her eyes. Devon blinked away tears as the glow of the teleport spell faded. The party was standing on a trail on a high peak overlooking rolling farmland that had to be the Eltera hill country.

"No!" Hezbek cried, clutching at her hair. "Not again! He's found us unworthy and banished us. Will we ever defeat the spider lord?"

The woman was doing a remarkably good acting job, if a little melodramatic. Devon cast *Fade* again, stepping into the shadow of a rock outcropping. So far, it seemed the players were so bewildered by the situation they weren't paying attention to her. She used *Ventriloquism* and caused a low growl to rise from a cleft in the stone behind the players.

Hezbek's eyes widened. "Oh no, is that a... cave troll?"

As the players turned, the medicine woman jumped into action. Her hands began to glow, and she dashed forward and clapped the players on the shoulders, resetting their bind points to this location.

Devon almost laughed at how well this was going, but she focused on her ventriloquist act, turning the growl into a roar.

"There's no choice, we have to run!" Hezbek yelled, turning and dashing the other direction as she kicked the players out of the group. Devon sprinted after her, and they rounded a bend in the trail as Hezbek worked through the motions of another teleport spell. A breath later, Devon's stomach turned over as the spell took hold. She opened her eyes to the dappled shade in the camp.

Then, she started laughing.

Chapter Thirty-Four

"JUST LIKE THE old days," Devon muttered as she crawled out of bed. Bright sun leaked around the edges of her blackout shades, and she squinted as she pulled the string to open the blinds.

Back when the market for items in Avatharn had been so hot that she hadn't even needed her day job at the Fort to help pay the bills, she and her guildmates had spent most nights gaming and at least half the days sleeping it off. But once she'd started her shifts in the Wild West, she'd gotten used to seeing the sunshine again. It was nice to be awake when the rest of the world was. But lately, she'd had to stay up late dealing with problems in the game.

She pulled on a pair of yoga pants and switched out her jammie shirt for a tank top before shuffling to the kitchen. As she got the coffee started, she peered into the cabinets in search of breakfast. Her stocks were running low. She yawned, wondering if she should just order grocery delivery. Lots of people found the notion of physically going shopping for food to be kind of quaint, but Devon usually dragged herself down to the store. It had started during her months of scraping by. The practice made it easier to buy discount fruits and veggies without getting a bunch of moldy crap delivered. Now, shopping was one of her only excuses to get out of the apartment.

She poured a bowl of cereal, added milk, and took her coffee to a small table beside a window with a view onto the concrete balcony of the apartment complex. While she ate, she opened her messages. The first was from Tamara.

Hey, where are you? I came by around ten... Ended up with more day-old bagels than I could eat. Knocked for like five minutes, but finally decided you weren't answering. Busy, huh? Did you take up mountain biking without me? Anyway, drop a line.

Devon rubbed her eyes. She wasn't usually a sound sleeper. Seemed strange that she'd slept through five minutes of knocking. Maybe Tamara had caught her during one of those deep sleep cycles she'd read about. She sent back a note.

"Sorry, I'm out of town for the mountain bike world cup... Actually, I was sleeping. You don't have one of those polite little girlie knocks, do you? PS. We should grab tacos again soon."

Next, there was a note from Emerson.

Hi, Devon. Can you call me when you get a chance? Prefer to talk in real time rather than text. I'm getting my implants adjusted, reach me here instead:

At the end of the message, he'd dropped in a link for an old-fashioned video conference.

Devon grimaced. Video chat? Maybe after she'd had a chance to wake up.

As she slurped the milk out of the cereal bowl, she couldn't help laughing about the "event" they put on for the players last night. Even though she tried to restrain herself, she finally caved and pulled up the forums. Under a subsection for the Western Reaches and Eltera City, there was a new thread labeled: Jungle event, OMG so lame!!

She snorted as she read the rant from someone with the handle "The_Kr4cken". The message was loaded with expletives and choice descriptions such as "nothing worth killing" and "stupid ass event that TPs you halfway back to Eltera" and "wasted two days of play time."

The other player, SenorFrog on the forums, had responded with a similar description.

Just to further dissuade players, Devon made a post as an anonymous user:

Same!!! OMG! Devs on crack or something??

She laughed as she closed the forum window. After a quick shower and change of clothes, she stopped in front of the mirror. She tried combing her hair one way and frowned then grabbed it into a ponytail, pulling out a couple of strands to hang near her face. With a quick look at her profile, she realized what she was doing. Worrying about her hair because she had to call some guy in Arizona...

"So stupid," she muttered. For good measure, she took her hair back out of the ponytail and messed it up a little bit, tangled strands piling over her shoulders. With a sigh, she grabbed her old tablet and flopped on the couch. She entered Emerson's contact into the video chat program.

"Oh, hey!" Emerson answered with what seemed like forced casualness.

"Hey, what's up? What's going on with your implants? I haven't used this program since I got mine."

He shrugged, and a guilty look came over his face. "Actually, nothing. It's... I didn't really want to talk over the Entwined hardware. I don't think there are privacy issues, but... you know. Better to be safe."

Devon didn't like the sound of this. She blinked as her brows drew together. "Is there a problem? I was hoping you had a solution to the pain thing."

He shook his head quickly. "No, nothing like that. But the pain thing... I still haven't been getting any answers, and it's frustrating. It definitely shouldn't be happening. I guess I wanted to let you know that it's okay if you take a couple weeks off while I sort out a solution. I'll cover for you."

"Cover for me? As in E Squared—that would be my employer, as you recall—wouldn't know I was on vacation? Isn't that some kind of fraud?"

"I was just thinking there'd be no need to draw attention to you taking a little break. If the issue did come up, I'd take all the blame. I am... Well, my equity in the company has set me up all right. Worst case, if something went wrong, I could cover your salary..." He trailed off, clearly realizing that he was straying into creepy territory again.

Devon raised a brow.

"No obligation, of course," he said, cheeks red with embarrassment.

Devon sighed. The poor guy really wasn't all that great socially. But that had its own charm, and he did seem to be trying to look out for her.

"You don't think there's anything dangerous, do you?"

He bit down on his lower lip while he considered his words. "No... It just bothers me. At the very least, I expected to recruit you for something fun, not torture. I mean it about the time off. I totally understand if you want to hang tight until it's resolved."

"Thanks, Emerson. I'll keep it in mind."

His mention of the pain had brought back unpleasant memories of the fight with the spiders in the temple. The swarm had surprised her enough that her adrenaline had masked some of the pain. But he was right, she wouldn't exactly call the combat experience fun— when she got hit anyway.

Fortunately, she didn't get hit very often. And the truth was, there was so much else going on, she couldn't afford to take time out. A couple weeks without playing would be more than a month in game. In that time, players would probably show up and attack her tribe, and quite likely, someone would find the relic.

No way was she going to stay logged out and let all that happen.

"Well, let me know," Emerson said after a moment of awkward silence. "I feel responsible since I recruited you and all."

"Thanks," she said. "I will. Anything else you need? Otherwise, I should get to the store. Running out of Cheetos and Jolt Cola."

He blushed again. "No, that's it. Thanks for getting back to me."

"Not a problem." She reached for the disconnect button but hesitated when Emerson looked like he was going to say something else. After a second though, he nodded, and the connection dropped.

Chapter Thirty-Five

WHEN DEVON LOGGED back in, around a full day had passed in the game. It was midmorning, and even though the tribe members were going about their work, an uncomfortable silence hung over the glade. She understood why when she approached the dwarf camp. Sentries still stood on the border, Dorden among them. Heldi was up and about, but she seemed weak. Devon spotted her sitting on a moss-covered stone near one of the canvas shelters.

"Nice morning, eh, Dorden?" she asked as she walked up.

Hard eyes turned her way. "I suppose," he said flatly.

"Thank you for maintaining the truce. I see Heldi is feeling better."

He shrugged. "There'd be nothing left of your tribe if she hadn't recovered," he growled.

Devon kept her face still. The little dude wasn't going to let go of this grudge easily, was he? She stepped closer, arms at her sides in what she hoped was a non-threatening manner.

"The arrow shot was a mistake," she said, chin raised. "You realize that, right?"

Dorden's eyes narrowed. "I'm not so sure. I've done quite a lot of thinking the past few days. Why did Bayle draw on my wife in the first place?"

"She was reacting to Deld's injury. The shot came from their backs, and the only people behind them were you two. You can see how she could be confused, right?"

"That's just it. That first arrow... I know Heldi didn't shoot it, but there *is* another archer in your tribe." His eyes flicked to Grey, who was setting turtle traps in the small stream that gurgled through the camp.

"Grey?" She narrowly avoided laughing. How could she explain that he was a total hippy?

"See, it occurs to me that some of your band might think they'd be better off with some of our weapons. Makes me wonder if your hunter there tried to land an arrow in one of our backs but missed and hit one of his own."

Devon shook her head, raising her hands to try to cut off this line of conversation. "It wasn't Grey. I found the culprits. There were a pair of starborn in the jungle."

"Starborn, huh? And where are these aggressors now?"

She thinned her lips. "They've been sent away."

Dorden crossed his arms over his chest. While they'd been talking, a few more of their fighters had stepped closer, matching glowers on their faces. Devon was starting to feel decidedly outnumbered.

"Surely ye must have some proof of this claim, then? Because it seems rather convenient to blame it on starborn then explain that they've been sent away."

Devon blinked. Proof? She assumed she'd be able to explain everything once the threat had been eliminated, but apparently, she hadn't counted on dwarven stubbornness or the amount of thinking Dorden had been free to do while his wife was unconscious.

"I didn't—I suppose I wasn't considering I'd need to prove anything to you. I was pretty focused on protecting our shared home."

Dorden snorted. "Your home, ye mean. We're just hired guards camping at the edge."

"Your Gloriousness?" Hazel appeared out of a nearby tangle of brush.

"Yes?"

"If it's proof they need, I may have it."

Dorden glanced at her with thinly concealed interest. Maybe Devon had misjudged, and it wasn't stubbornness so much as the desire to be certain he was doing no harm to his clan by trusting her.

The small scout nodded and hurried forward, digging in her belt pouch. She pulled out a small strip of leather with a bronze design fixed to the end.

"What's that?" Devon asked. She held out her hand and accepted the item.

You have received: Seal of Eltera.

"Seal of Eltera?" she muttered. "I don't know what this is."

Hazel shrugged. "I plucked it off the warrior's belt. You see, I've never met a starborn before, except you, Your Gloriousness. I've been practicing my *Stealth* and wanted to test it."

Devon forced a smile. It was better proof than the whole handful of nothing she had to show Dorden, but she wasn't sure whether the object would prove there'd been starborn here.

A low growl rumbled in Dorden's throat. After a moment, he nodded. "Ye may not know what that is, but I do. The governor's seal." He shook his head. "That little bronze emblem is the bane of my clan. The governor in Eltera issues those things to every new starborn in the city. Gives them favored trade status. While craftsmen like me and my clan line up outside the city gates with our wagons just hoping for entry, starborn traipse through without a glance and dump their ore and loot for coppers. So I suppose I believe ye, lass. And unfortunately, if the starborn are here, I'll also be saying my goodbyes."

Devon gripped the item tight, then dropped it on the ground. "Listen, Dorden. I understand your desire to move on. It might seem that forging on toward the coast will take you farther from Eltera and the starborn masses. But the truth is, more and more starborn will be coming to this world. You can't fight that. No matter where you go, you'll find them. But I'm doing what I can to keep them from coming here. At least until we prepare. I've talked about founding a community, a city, a kingdom even. And it will start right here. I assure you if you stay, your clan will never go hungry, and you'll never receive poor treatment for lack of being starborn.

"I can't force you to do anything, but I can say with complete honesty that I believe your best chance to survive in this changing world is to stay here. Join my tribe, and you'll be as valued as any members."

Faint grumbling rose from the dwarves, and Devon wasn't sure what she'd said wrong. Maybe they just needed a minute to come to terms with reality. Heldi rose, somewhat unsteadily, from her seat on the rock and walked up beside her husband. The proud dwarf woman set her jaw and met Devon's gaze. "We've been known as the Stoneshoulder Clan for generations. How can we forsake our ancestors by suddenly calling ourselves the tribe of... Kumquat was it?"

Devon resisted the urge to smack herself on the forehead. She should have thought more carefully about her words.

"Please accept my apologies. I didn't mean that at all. In fact, I don't know why we've clung to the name of a dead ogre. What would you say to continuing to think of yourselves as a clan, but as joining a larger organization, too?"

She activated her settlement interface and focused on the name. The text highlighted, and she replaced it.

"Hereby, I'd like to call our settlement Stonehaven in honor of your clan and as a statement about the sort of place it should be. All citizens will be part of the Stonehaven League. But you will still be an independent clan. I will never take that from you."

"So if we join your... settlement, does that make you the leader?" Dorden asked. She could see the emotional storm on his face. The clan patriarch wanted to do what was best for his people, but surely it must be a blow to give up his leadership.

"Ultimately, someone must bear the responsibility for final decisions. I will take that responsibility and burden, but I have never made decisions alone. And I don't want to start now. Would you join Hezbek as the first two members of my city council?"

Dorden's chest rose and fell while he considered. After a long moment, he glanced at his wife. She nodded, a small motion.

"For the good of my clan, I accept this arrangement," Dorden said. He stuck out his hand and they shook.

***

It turned out Dorden was an advanced NPC, so he couldn't be added to the settlement right away. Instead, Devon added the other dwarves one by one until she reached the population requirement for transitioning from an encampment to village. When she did, the buildings took on a subtle glow for a moment, and then a low chime filled the air.

Congratulations! Stonehaven is now a village.

Devon looked at Dorden. "Stonehaven is now able to accept another advanced citizen. Will you join?"

With a grin, the dwarf patriarch accepted. He clapped Devon on the back, causing her to stagger forward. The dwarf laughed. "Flimsy humans," he said. "Can't imagine what my forefathers would think of me joining up with the likes of you."

Despite his words, a grin showed beneath his beard.

"Huh? Can you look up when you speak? It's hard to hear you from way down there," Devon said with a wink.

The dwarf laughed and stomped off toward the cook fire where Tom was busy concocting some sort of meal.

Devon opened the settlement interface.

Settlement: Stonehaven
Size: Village

Tier 1 Buildings - 17/50 (0 upgraded):
11 x Standard Hut
6 x Canvas Shelter

Tier 2 Buildings (2/5):
1 x Medicine Woman's Hut
1 x Crafting Workshop

On the tab for advancement, she checked what she'd need for the next level:

Requirements for expansion to Hamlet:
- Advanced NPC: 3/7
- Tier 2 Buildings: 2/6
- Tier 3 Buildings: 0/3
- Population: 21/100

Having just scraped together the 20 citizens necessary for a village, the 100 needed for a Hamlet seemed nearly impossible. But that was a problem for later. Right now, they needed to make sure their village survived which meant fortifying the perimeter, strengthening the defenses, and preparing for onslaught.

She joined the others at the campfire, humans and dwarves laughing and gently ribbing Tom about how long it was taking to get a meal ready. She pulled Prester and Deld aside.

"Now that we're a proper village," she said, "we need to start building like one. Are both of you ready to work?"

The men grinned, nodding.

"Deld, I'd like you to start working on a forge. Our new villagers have quite a few ingots that could be worked into useful items, and I have a feeling we'll soon need to repair weapons and armor."

"And me, Your Gloriousness?" Prester asked.

"We'll need some more advanced buildings soon, but before we start construction, we have safety to consider. I see that we can now upgrade our tier 1 structures—do you have any ideas for that?"

"Well yes indeed," he said, touching his brow. "I propose we replace the huts with timber buildings—that would provide better protection from the weather and animals, and if we ever did have attackers within the village..." A look of concern passed over his face.

"I doubt it will come to that. An attack breaching the outer defenses isn't likely. But yes, real wood buildings would keep our village safer. What about fortifications? Do you have access to any plans for defensive walls or guard towers?"

Prester chewed his lip as he thought. "I do know how to build a guard tower. It came with my tier 3 plans. As for the wall... I think I might be able to improvise something."

Devon nodded. "Keep me appraised on your resources. I know the lumberjacks have been working consistently, and Bern's been toiling away at the quarry."

"I definitely have enough to start," Deld said. "With no major surprises, I imagine the supply will keep up. Seem correct, Prester?"

The carpenter nodded.

"Speaking of the quarry... Will you keep making the trip with Bern?" she asked.

Deld nodded. "Fairly often. He asks for my opinion on what size blocks to cut. And I still need chips for the mortar."

"I'd like you to start varying the path you take to and from. I realize that will slow your progress a bit, but the trail we've created nearly led a pair of starborn to Stonehaven. We were lucky they followed it in the other direction."

The stonemason nodded, a grim look on his face. "A wise choice, Your Gloriousness."

"Now go ahead and get some stew. It looks like Tom has finally declared his concoction edible."

Chapter Thirty-Six

LATER THAT AFTERNOON, Devon pulled Dorden aside as they were walking toward a meeting she'd called in the center of the village.

"A couple quick questions for you, if you don't mind," she said.

"What is it, lass?"

"I believe our ultimate security depends on exploring the surroundings. In particular, we need to find the source of the corruption that's transforming the wildlife. And more importantly, we need to find a particular relic."

"All right," the dwarf said. "When I agreed to follow ye, I knew I was choosing to respect your judgment. If ye believe that this exploration is the best course, I won't question ye."

"Thank you, my friend. I'd hoped to get some advice from you on the implications of this plan."

He couldn't hide the prideful straightening of his spine at her words. "I'll do my best to advise ye, lass."

"You see, in order to assure there's enough food to go around, I've been supplementing my hunter's contribution with some hunts of my own. But I need to stop focusing on slaughtering wildlife to work on the other goals. Alone, Grey can't keep up. I've asked Hazel, our scout, to add what she can by foraging. Still, I'm worried it won't be enough."

"Hmm," the dwarf said. His bushy eyebrows trembled as he worked over the notion that there might not be enough food. She'd heard the way to a dwarf's heart started with his stomach and hoped she hadn't just undermined the trust between them.

"Our village can support four more advanced citizens," she said. "I'm not opposed to teaching one of my lumberjacks to hunt game between chopping trees. But I thought maybe one of your clan would find it an honor to be raised to an advanced level. Provided they can keep from ruining the meat."

Dorden stopped in his tracks about thirty paces from where the rest of the villagers were congregating. "If you're serious...?"

"Of course."

"Heldi has long wanted to learn the hunter's craft. She's always felt it was wasteful the way we fought without salvaging food from the spoils."

Devon smiled. "Consider it done then, I'll speak to her as soon as she's feeling better."

"She might feel better sooner if you spoke to her right after the meeting..."

Devon smirked. "Fair enough. As for my other question... The fight ahead may be difficult. I hope that no one will suffer mortal wounds—I'll gladly take those blows if I'm able, seeing as I have the starborn ability to be resurrected. Even so, I'm worried some of you will get hurt. Hezbek can provide healing potions, but the recovery time is so long. I can't imagine, given all the fighting your clan has done, that you've been forced to lie unconscious every time you get healed."

"Ha!" Dorden exclaimed. "Thank Veia ye finally asked. I didn't want to demand, ye know, but it is a rather annoying situation."

"Then there's a way around it?"

"Of course. Ye either need a priest who draws upon Veia's blessing to grant the healing boon, or ye can get that blessing elsewhere."

"And none of you are a priest, I assume?"

Dorden snorted. "A bit too eager for skull-crushing, these lot are."

"Then how do we receive this blessing?"

"With potions, ye gotta get them consecrated. But to do that, ye need a temple to Veia. Or at the very least, a shrine."

"A shrine to Veia?"

Dorden nodded.

"And do you know how I might get one of these shrines?"

"Aren't ye the one supposed to be making construction decisions for our little settlement?" he teased.

Right. She should have thought of that. Devon opened the settlement interface and scanned through the list of available buildings. The tier 2 offerings hadn't changed, though it seemed that the forge could be upgraded to work with rare metals and the barracks could have an addition to sleep eight. She clicked on tier 3. Aha, there it was, tucked between *Inner Keep* and *Stables*.

- Shrine to Veia.

   Bestows Veia's blessing. Blessings vary based on offerings supplied and the items or persons receiving the boon.
   Requires: Stonemasonry (Tier 2), 3 x Stone Blocks, Settlement leader sworn to Veia.

That seemed easy. By the time Deld was done with the forge, he'd probably have the skill to build it. Too bad it used up a Tier 3 building slot, but it would be worth it to have potions work on her followers without putting them to sleep. Plus, it seemed there could be other blessings.

"I'll order it built as soon as we have the materials and expertise," she said. "With good fortune, none of your clan will have to sleep off one of Hezbek's potions again."

"Unless the consecration process improves the taste, they may still want to," he said with a laugh.

When they reached the gathering of villagers, Dorden stepped into the huddle and turned to face her. Devon climbed onto a boulder to help her voice be heard over the group.

"Greetings, my friends," she said. "I'll keep this short because we have much work to do. Today, every fighter in this camp will begin exploring the area. We'll organize parties of two and three to move together through the jungle and finally uncover the secrets that lie out there. Dorden and I will work with you to set up a guard rotation at the village perimeter and quarry, but the protection will be thin. To achieve our aims, we must be bold. For the time being, there will be only one guard in each place so that we have the resources to tame this jungle. I'm appointing Greel—" The man jerked, startled. His eyes narrowed. "—as the official record keeper. Please report the results of your explorations and especially any sightings of red-eyed beasts. Fight if attacked but avoid combat otherwise. We want no unnecessary injuries. Within five days, I want there to be no remaining mysteries in this jungle. We'll meet every evening to discuss our finds."

After she gave the signal for the group to disperse, Greel came stomping toward her, snarling.

"So I'm the clerk now? The secretary?"

Devon shook her head. "You're the only person with the brains to keep it all straight. I can't be here all the time. I need you to help me keep track of our efforts. And... I need your knife in camp. I can't stand leaving just a single guard, and while I don't wish to post you as a fighter—I get the sense you'd rather not have your skills be known—I'll feel better knowing you're here."

The man gave a beleaguered sigh. "Fine."

He started to walk away.

"Greel," she said, "keep my people safe."

"Yeah, yeah."

***

For the next few mornings, Devon joined the rest of the village fighters for a breakfast of something Tom called *Stonehaven Scramble*. Grey had found a bank downriver where some sort of mud-dwelling reptile laid daily clutches of eggs. Devon wasn't so hot on eating alligator eggs or whatever they were, but the taste made up for it.

The taste and the buff. The morning meal gave everyone a +3 to their *Constitution* as well as a point in *Strength*. The strength didn't do much for her, but she could almost see the added power in her followers' weapon arms. And when she ventured out with Bayle to clear another handful of temples and random ruins, she noticed the difference in the fighter's damage.

Unfortunately, clearing random ruins didn't seem to be doing much but slowly uncovering the last major area on the map. The closer they moved to the center of the unexplored region, the more corrupted animals she and her followers encountered. So that was progress, but it was frustratingly slow. Over the course of the exploration, Devon finally leveled *Flamestrike* to tier 2, increasing the single target damage and adding splash damage to nearby enemies. The other high point came when Devon dinged 10. Hezbek taught her the Levitate spell, which she filed away as something to experiment with later.

On the fifth day, she and Bayle returned to camp early. It was just midafternoon, but after hacking through the jungle all morning, massacring a few low-level animals for their meat, they'd found themselves back at Uruquat's original camp. Already, the jungle had swallowed most of the clearing, leaving just the remnants of the Leader's Abode and the skeletons of a couple platforms in place. Except for the map sector assigned to Dorden and Heldi today, there was nowhere left to explore. Well, they could start retracing their steps to clear out catacombs and basements in ruins they'd previously cleared. Devon had figured it unlikely that an ancient relic of central importance to the region would be dumped off in some farmer's basement, so they'd avoided going underground. But it seemed they might have to.

Between his mortar creation and his work on the forge, Deld had reached tier 2 in stonemasonry. He was taking a short break from forge construction to piece together the shrine to Veia on a flat pad of land between the stream and the cliff. It was a tranquil meadow, perfect for contemplation and—Devon hoped—pleasing to the game's goddess AI. Devon lay down in the grass and watched him work after he assured her it would be no bother. She'd begun to drift off when shouts came from the far edge of the camp.

She sprinted through the collection of huts intermixed with wood-walled cabins and gasped at the sight of Dorden and Heldi staggering into camp, an echo of the scene following the player ambush. A gash had been opened on Dorden's forehead, and blood streamed into his eye. His wife's chainmail was torn, and she carried an arm awkwardly against her stomach. When they reached the brook, Dorden fell to his knees and splashed water on his face. Devon noticed that the shield he sometimes carried had been cracked nearly in two.

"What is it? What happened?" she asked as she ran over.

Heldi swayed as she turned. "Well, we found the source of your crazed monsters, at least." The woman fell to a seat beside the stream.

Devon sighed. Another few hours, and the shrine would likely have been completed. "Get Hezbek," she said to a dwarf who had hurried over. "And when the others come in, tell them to stay close. I'll be heading out this evening, alone. No one else should endanger themselves until we can get our healing potions consecrated."

Chapter Thirty-Seven

FINALLY, A CHANCE to put these quests to bed. Devon crept closer to the site where the dwarf pair had run into trouble. Though Dorden had tried to describe what they'd found, Devon wasn't quite prepared for the view. After hacking through the jungle for weeks, the simple sight of so much open air shocked her. Where the other ruins had been overgrown, strangled by foliage, the center of the corruption was all gray stone and tumbledown buildings. Like a circle stamped from the jungle, the streets of the ancient town converged like spokes to a massive central temple. In these outlying areas, red-eyed creatures shambled between crumbling buildings. At the nexus, the temple seemed to pulse with an odd energy. Black and purple currents swirled over the façade, and occasionally flares of light shone through windows and cracks in the old stone.

Devon set foot on a broken cobblestone street, and everything seemed to dim as if a pall hung over the city. Toppled buildings closed in on either side, feeling like jaws ready to clamp down. Shadows moved in rubble-strewn alleys. Ahead, a pack of massive, red-eyed monkeys screamed as they ran through an intersection.

You have discovered: Temple of Sorrow.

Quest updated: What's Wrong with the Wildlife?
Congrats, looks like you found the spot. Now what?

"That's not helpful," she muttered.

Quest updated: What's Wrong with the Wildlife?
*Fine, expunge the force that is corrupting the area's animals.
(Hint: it's probably in the temple building.)
Clear enough for you?*

Devon rolled her eyes and shoved away the notification.

Though the sun hadn't quite set, the streets felt dark. As she crept forward, she waited for the roar of an attacking animal, but it seemed almost like she moved in a bubble of stillness. The area felt like a scene from a classic undead apocalypse movie, except instead of zombies, corrupted jungle creatures watched her from afar. Devon headed for the temple, shoulders tense, hand hovering over her dagger.

She walked for about a half an hour, checking each cross street and feeling more and more like something wasn't right. At an intersection maybe three streets away from the temple courtyard, she stopped short. A pair of boars, looking much like she imagined the beast menacing Uruquat's camp had, stepped into the alley in front of her. It was almost a relief to confront an enemy. Devon drew her dagger and made a quick *Combat Assessment.* Both were level 11, marked as "superior", which she assumed meant they were tougher than an ordinary monster of the same level.

She stepped to the side of the street to put the wall at her back, and with a quick mental twist called a *Flamestrike* down on the closer boar. The beast squealed as its flesh set fire.

That was a relief. At least she'd become strong enough that they didn't resist. With the last light of the sun, she summoned a *Shadow Puppet* and sent it lancing toward the injured boar. The spear pierced the boar's neck and erupted between its shoulder blades before shattering. With a dying squeal, the boar staggered and collapsed. The knockback from the shattered shadow sent her into the wall, but she quickly recovered her balance.

Nice, two hits. Of course, *Flamestrike* gobbled mana. Her pool was down by a quarter and she still had one boar left. Shouldn't be a problem, as long as—

A roar cut off her inner dialog. Where the first boar had fallen, some sort of mutated crocodile thing stepped into the street. Its head was almost as big as a compact car.

Devon focused on the newcomer, using her *Combat Assessment*.

Corrupted Croc - Level 17
What are you, crazy?

"Well, crap," she cursed. She tried *Flamestrike* anyway, tier 1 so she didn't waste mana. It washed over the croc's scales and fizzled.

All right, so this wasn't going to be easy. Not a solo mission, anyway. Time to cut her losses and return once her followers could heal.

She turned to run.

And saw why the streets had been so quiet. The corrupted creatures hadn't been ignoring her. They'd simply fallen in behind her. Filling the alleys and streets between her and the jungle, an army of oversized, red-eyed creatures stood growling. In front, some sort of condor thing with a wingspan wider than a four-lane freeway flapped into the sky. With a shriek, it dove.

Desperate, Devon cast *Freeze* on the bird. It plummeted to the ground and blew a crater in the street. The ice shattered in a glittering explosion of shards.

The bird climbed slowly to its feet, favoring a wing. But it continued to advance.

The condor shrieked again, and the corrupted army charged.

Devon burned through her mana, casting *Flamestrike* as fast as her cooldown allowed. She took down another two beasts before they were on her, ripping her to shreds with talons and beaks and claws.

The pain was like nothing she'd ever experienced. And then it was over.

You gain special attribute points: *+2 Bravery.*
You were slain by a Corrupted Parrot.
Respawning...

Chapter Thirty-Eight

DEVON AND HEZBEK both shrieked when Devon respawned in Hezbek's cot, awakening with an arm and a leg tossed over the woman. Hezbek jerked upright, shoving Devon onto the splintering wood floor of Hezbek's newly built home.

"I—codswallop but you scared me, girl," Hezbek said once she'd collected her wits.

Devon coughed, shaken by her death and the unexpected situation at respawn. "I guess we forgot to reset my bind point." She glanced toward the window where wooden shutters had been closed and latched. Evening light still leaked through the cracks. "You're in bed early."

"When you're my age, child, I might give you license to comment on my sleep habits. But for your information, I'm taking a nap. Or rather, I was."

"Sorry," Devon muttered as she stood.

Hezbek's brows drew together. "Are you all right? I guess you died."

Devon ran a hand through her hair then patted her body. The vest was still on, as were her hide pants. She laid a hand on her hip; the dagger was still there, too. Pulling up her message log, she saw a notification informing her that between levels 10 and 20, her items would suffer durability loss at death. She wondered what happened after level 20 but decided that didn't matter right now.

"I got in a little over my head, I guess you could say."

Hezbek chuckled. "Well, I'd like to hope that won't happen again, but maybe we ought to figure out a new bind location."

"How about at the Shrine to Veia?" Devon's legs shook as she stood. The death—or more precisely, the events leading to it—had rattled her hard. There must've been a hundred mobs lined up against her. How in the hell was she supposed to deal with that?

Well, she'd have to think of something. With a deep breath, she opened the door. The medicine woman grabbed a small pouch of reagents and followed Devon out of her new cabin.

Deld had finished the shrine while Devon had been away. It was a cute little tower of stone, the middle of the three blocks set on end. The top block had a small basin carved from the stone, now filled with rainwater from a shower in the afternoon.

"The construction requirements said I needed to swear myself to Veia," she said. "Any ideas?"

Hezbek shrugged. "Do you believe in her?"

"I... well, in a way, I suppose. I know she creates everything we experience here."

"Then why don't you tell her that?"

Devon swallowed and placed a hand on the shrine. "Your creation is... I'm not sure how you do it, Veia, but this is more than a game for me. You've created something I can believe in."

A yellow glow surrounded the shrine, motes of light falling away from it like fireflies.

Congratulations! Your village now has a Shrine to Veia.

Devon shrugged. That wasn't too hard. She turned to Hezbek and nodded, and the medicine woman pulled out the reagents she needed for binding. After the spell casting was finished, Devon laid down in the grass. She needed some time to think about all this, come back fresh. If she could *handle* coming back after being torn apart like she had been outside the Temple of Sorrow. Emerson's words echoed in her mind as she hovered her awareness over the logout button. *Take a couple weeks off while I work on the pain thing.* Right then, Devon was sorely tempted.

***

It was midnight when Devon dragged a chair from the kitchen table out onto the balcony terrace of her apartment complex. Hearing the noise, a neighbor nudged open their curtain. Curious eyes peered out before the curtain was quickly drawn tight. With its cheap rent and crappy maintenance, the apartment complex wasn't the sort of place where people put down roots. Devon didn't know her neighbors, and most likely, they didn't want to know her. Sitting outside nursing a beer under the desert moon probably made her look pathetically friendless, but Devon didn't really care. She needed time away from her couch to think.

The quest for the relic, the strange purple temple, and the corrupted animals were related. They had to be. Sure, there was a minuscule chance that the quest lines led to different content, meaning she could blow off the corrupted animals quest and still find the Greenscale Pendant without going back into that death trap. But she'd already explored the rest of the area, minus a few basements. Devon knew down in her gamer heart that awesome rewards weren't given for conquering random mini-dungeons with no real danger to the player. The solution to both her main objectives lay in the Temple of Sorrow, but reaching it seemed impossible.

She took another swig of beer, which was rapidly getting warm in her hand. Down in the parking lot, tires crunched as an autocab dropped off a pair of drunken college students. In the distance, she heard the hum of tires over the freeway. And somewhere, far beyond the sprawl of stuccoed homes, a pack of coyotes yipped. She'd been spending so much time in game lately that the sounds of the desert and city seemed like the imaginary world. The chirring of insects and cacophony of jungle birds was more natural than this. That might have bothered some people, but it didn't get to her. Whether the reality she chose to inhabit existed on computer servers somewhere, or whether it lay in this city built atop red soil and frozen lava rock didn't really matter.

What was important was the kind of person she played in that reality. As much as she wanted to take Emerson up on his offer, she simply couldn't abandon Stonehaven to the disasters that would befall it without her. Which meant she had to find a way to do the impossible. She had to make her way through the sprawl of ruins, either by wits or by her blade, and she needed to take down whatever dwelt in that temple. The question was, how?

As unachievable as the quest seemed, she didn't actually believe the game would give her an assignment she couldn't complete. As a level 10 sorcerer, it might be impossible. But she wasn't just a sorcerer. Somehow, her unique class and attributes were key to her mission. Aside from her panic during the fight with the spider swarm, she'd avoided using her lightning shadow. But, thinking back to the effectiveness against both the horde of spiders and the corrupted python that had resisted her *Flamestrike*, she had the uncomfortable feeling that her lightning-based *Shadow Puppets* were her strongest advantage. They worked on a wide area and didn't seem to take damage as easily as her moon- and sun-conjured puppets.

So how could she use them without incapacitating herself whether by pain or by sheer damage?

During the fight with a python, the lightning damage had been unbearable. She'd theorized the wet ground had conducted electricity back to her, and her battle on dry stone with the spider horde seemed to confirm it. But even then, she'd been shocked in the lower legs. Which meant the damage definitely came from the floor.

As the solution came to her, she shook her head. It had been staring her in the face for days, but the pain response had made her too afraid to even mess with her greatest power.

Tomorrow would be different. She stood and dragged her chair back inside. Best to rest up, because she doubted she'd spend much time logged out until the Greenscale Pendant belonged to the Stonehaven League.

Chapter Thirty-Nine

DEVON LOGGED IN to the sound of the stream and the kiss of a light breeze on her skin. Slanted sun rays lit the little meadow around the shine. She laid an affectionate hand on the shrine as she stepped past it and hopped over the brook to begin her day.

She visited Gerrald in the crafting workshop first. The leatherworker grinned when she entered.

"Are you finally ready to replace that snakeskin vest?" he asked. "I've been hoping..."

Devon didn't let her relief show. She had been worried about hurting the man's feelings.

"My skills have advanced to the point I could use an upgrade," she said tactfully. "How has your work on armoring the rest of the tribe been going?"

She'd noticed scattered pieces of leather armor appearing on the villagers. Though she hoped they'd never have to fight, it was nice to know they were better protected.

The man nodded and flipped open a ledger. She squinted at his chicken scratch but couldn't make any sense of it.

"I'm afraid I can't read this script," she said.

Gerrald chuckled. "No, you wouldn't be able to. The guildmasters in Eltera City were concerned about others discovering our trade secrets. They invented a special alphabet for us to use. In any case, I've outfitted around two-thirds of the villagers in armor pieces they have the expertise to wear. I'm happy to continue..." he said, eyeing her now-ragged leggings and vest. They'd taken quite a beating with her death and were now down to about 40% durability.

"Eventually I'd like that, but first, I need a set of the best gear you can make."

"Veia be praised," the man said, stepping to a chest that had been built into the wall during the workshop's construction. Curious, Devon peered in as he lifted the top. An inventory screen representing the chest's contents sprang up in her vision.

Chest:

27 x Heavy Leather

43 x Medium Leather

17 x Light Leather

13 x Leather Strap

10 x Sabertooth Scales

102 x Sinew

10 x Polished Moss Agate

"The agate... Did that come from Dorden?"

Gerrald nodded. "I wasn't supposed to say anything. I haven't yet worked out how to incorporate the stones, but I feel like increased skill will help me understand how to embed them into equipment, which I believe will grant bonuses much like the runes I engrave."

Devon smiled. She'd granted Dorden rights to the agate without expecting anything in return. It seemed, though, that his loyalty now lay with the league as much as his clan.

"I need the most armor value you can add, and as many pieces as you think I have the skill to wear while still moving gracefully. You've done an excellent job with your enchantments. Add what you can there. And when you're finished, I'd like you to do the same for Bayle and Falwon."

The man gave a little salute. "I'll begin this afternoon."

"I'll be sending Dorden your way as well. Most of the dwarves' armor is chain and plate, but many of the pieces are held on with leather straps. Please repair what you can for them."

"As you say, Your Gloriousness," he said in a cheerful voice as he started digging through a tool chest. Devon smiled to herself as she slipped out the door. Even NPCs must get bored grinding out the same low-level items over and over to skill up. She hoped the chance to craft some items of higher difficulty would refresh him enough that he'd be able to finish the townsfolk's armor without losing too much morale.

"How long do you think it will take?"

Gerrald already had a pair of leather shears in one hand, a length of strap in the other. The strap flapped against his face when he raised a hand to scratch his head. "One and a half or two days, I'd say. I swear it will be as fast as someone of my skill can go."

"I don't doubt it," she said. "When you're finished, you'll likely find me at the edge of camp practicing some of my own skills. Otherwise, I'll be resting near the shrine."

***

Devon summoned a *Glowing Orb* and stuck it to a tree. While her mana refilled, she sprinted to the village perimeter and back. When the purple mana bar flashed a last regeneration pulse, she dismissed the *Glowing Orb* and cast it again. Finally, after an hour of creating the balls of light, not only had she leveled her *Sprint* skill up to 8, she finally got the notification for her next tier in the spell.

You have learned a new spell: Glowing Orb - Tier 3
Cost: 15 mana
You may create up to three separate orbs, and you can attach each to a different object or surface. You must really like this spell.

Finally. Before moving to the next phase of her preparations, she pulled up her character sheet. She'd gained 3 levels without spending attribute points, wanting to think about where to assign them after confronting some more challenging situations. The Temple of Sorrow certainly qualified. Staring at the attributes section, she assigned 1 point to *Constitution*—she would have added more if not for the +3 she gained from her daily helping of *Stonehaven Scramble*—3 to *Focus*, 6 to *Charisma*, and 2 to *Intelligence*. The results looked like this:

Character: Devon (click to set a different character name)
Level: 10
Base Class: Sorcerer
Specialization: Unassigned
Unique Class: Deceiver
Health: 223/223
Mana: 375/391
Fatigue: 16%

Her attributes window now showed this:

Attributes:
Constitution: 19
Strength: 11
Agility: 16
Charisma: 33
Intelligence: 26
Focus: 16
Endurance: 12

Special Attributes:
Bravery: 7
Cunning: 4

Available Points: 0

Now, to get fancy.

Devon chose three trees spaced around twenty paces apart. She checked the spell description for Levitate.

Spell: Levitate - Tier 1
Cost: 35 mana
Duration: 5 minutes or loss of concentration
You float a few inches off the ground.
- +10 intimidation against creatures of low intelligence.
- Cushions falls under two stories height, eliminating falling damage.
- Movement speed reduced to 62%.

When she cast the ability the first time, her head swam as gravity gave up some of its hold and other forces pushed upward. She clenched her jaw until she got used to the sensation then focused on the first of the three trees. With a mental twist, she summoned a *Glowing Orb* and attached it to the trunk. Next, she turned to the second tree. When she tried to walk towards it, her feet paddled the empty air. Hmm. That wasn't going to work.

After some experimentation, she found that if she focused on the ground and imagined herself gliding over it, she began to move. It took a few minutes to get the technique dialed, but eventually, she reached the next tree. She cast another *Glowing Orb* and stuck it to the bark. Finally, she focused on the third tree and began the slow process of getting herself there. A third orb appeared on the trunk, and she returned to where she'd started. Her mana had almost refilled by the time she reached the first tree, and she only had to wait a minute or two before dispelling the ball of lightning and replacing it.

"Four down, what, three thousand to go?" she muttered aloud. Man, she hated grinding. But she hated failing quests and losing out to other players much more. She turned toward the next tree.

Seventeen hours and thirty-seven in-game minutes later, Devon received a notification.

You have learned a new spell: Glowing Orb – Tier 4:
Cost: 42 mana
You can create up to six orbs at once! (why?)

In the intervening time, she'd also leveled up her levitation, getting the notification:

You have learned a new spell: Levitate - Tier 2
Cost: 55 mana
Duration: 10 minutes or loss of concentration
You float a couple of feet off the ground.
- +18 intimidation against creatures of low to medium intelligence.
- Cushions falls under four stories height, eliminating falling damage.
- Movement speed reduced to 75%.

Though playing with levitation was now nearly as easy as walking, Devon dispelled the effect while testing her new *Glowing Orb*. She decorated six nearby trees with glowing balls of light and glanced down at the half-dozen resulting shadows. Funneling mana into them, she raised six *Shadow Puppets* from the jungle floor.

Good. She nodded and dispelled everything.

With a yawn, she headed back to the shrine and logged out. Tomorrow, the real fun would begin.

Chapter Forty

CLAD IN HER snazzy replacement armor, Devon took one last glance at the new items on her equipment screen.

Chest: Superior Medium Leather Doublet
Sabertooth-scale reinforcements give this chest piece 150% of the armor value of ordinary medium leather.
+3 Constitution, +1 Bravery | 70 Armor | 50/50 Durability

Legs: Superior Medium Leather Trousers
Sabertooth-scale reinforcements give these pants 150% of the armor value of ordinary medium leather.
+1 Constitution, +2 Charisma | 42 Armor | 50/50 Durability

Hands: Superior Medium Leather Gloves
+1 Agility, +3 Intelligence | 17 Armor | 35/35 Durability

Head: Forest Leather Headband
A deep brown leather band set with stunning moss agates.
+3 Intelligence | 45/45 Durability
Extra: +10 armor versus nature-based physical damage, +20 nature-based magical resistance

Gerrald had also made her boots, but Devon had asked that he give them to Grey. She couldn't bring herself to give up her Tribal Sandals just yet. As for the headband, she couldn't help but wonder whether Gerrald had known he could inset the moss agates when she'd asked for new gear. He'd had a faintly guilty look about him when he'd handed it over, perhaps evidence that he'd cooked up the plan with Dorden ahead of time.

In any case, she was as ready as she could get for the coming battle. She faced her followers.

"Okay, warriors, we're doing this street by street. You *must* stay behind me. Do not come forward until I say, and don't approach closer than a hundred paces or my spells may harm you. If I fall, retreat to Stonehaven. We'll regroup there."

She paused and looked over the group. Bayle and Falwon looked suitably intimidating in their new gear, and the dwarves seemed almost too eager to move in.

"As for your job, you'll be guarding my back against corrupted beasts that circle around. I may need to leave some wounded creatures behind to keep momentum. Put them out of their misery if you can. Got it?"

Her followers nodded. She'd been worried some might argue about hanging back. Fortunately, they seemed to understand the circumstances.

As she stepped back onto the first cobblestones, the strange silence in the city seemed to swallow her up. Devon tapped nervous fingers against her thighs.

"One more thing," she said. "You have consecrated potions. Use them as soon as you get hurt—you should be at full health all the time."

A few of the dwarves grimaced—the consecration process did nothing to improve the smell, and no one had been brave enough to taste the potions yet. Still, she was sure they'd use them if needed. She had her own stack of *5 x Jungle Healing Potion - Mid* and another *5 x Jungle Mana Potion - Mid.* They were the only items in her inventory aside from her *Everfull Waterskin,* an extra portion of *Stonehaven Scramble* and the stupid soulbound pocket lint—not knowing what lay ahead, she hadn't wanted to start the mission with a heavy bag.

Devon cast *Levitate* and rose a couple feet off the ground. She glided toward the first intersection where an alley opened on one side of the street. Swinging around the perimeter of the intersection, she placed six *Glowing Orbs* in a rough circle. The sun hung low in the sky. Combined with the strange pall that darkened the city, the dusky light allowed the glow from her spells to reach her. Devon's shadows radiated in a dark starburst around her.

Still, no creatures approached. The ruins were as still as they'd been during her first foray into the area.

"Fool me once..." she called out. "Not this time."

She peered into the darkness of the alley. Things moved in the recesses of the narrow corridor, darker shadows within the gloom. That hint was all she needed. She cast a tier 2 *Flamestrike,* and as the column of fire geysered in the alley's depths, animals shrieked.

A pack of rats the size of Rottweilers came rushing out of the alley, eyes red, teeth yellow and glistening. Patches of fire still smoldered on their fur where the spell had splashed, and the final beast emerged dragging a charred leg and tail.

Devon poured mana into her shadows and pulled six puppets from the cobblestones. The spells drained more than half her pool, but that was okay. Out of combat regen was quick.

She gritted her teeth to dispel memories of the pain of electrocution. Before she could lose her courage, she commanded her shadows to attack. With a crackling that echoed off the nearby walls, her puppets struck, diving into the mass of rat flesh. Lightning arced from body to body, rolling in a sizzling wave that paralyzed the beasts and set their fur alight. Rats screamed as the shadows drove another pulse of electricity into the horde.

While the rats died, Devon floated above the area of effect, immune to the ground currents.

A final shock sucked the last vitality from her shadows. As her puppets faded away, just one rat remained alive. It tried to flee toward her followers, but she snared it with a *Freeze* spell and called down a *Flamestrike* to finish it off. The rat shuddered and died. Notifications about experience and skill gains started flooding her vision, but Devon waved them away.

"Who's next?" she called.

***

Street by painstaking street, Devon cleared alleyways and crannies until the entire outer ring of the city was empty of monsters. Still, she was nervous to move inward, fearing the corrupted animals would circle around. But there wasn't much choice. She stepped onto the first intersection deeper into the city and hurriedly stuck her *Glowing Orbs* to the walls.

Just as she reached the center of the intersection, a wave of spiders poured over the rooftops. Her shadows rose from the ground. The spiders screamed and died. Too easy. Devon waited until her mana pool was full then started gliding for the next intersection.

The roar came from behind, claws screeching against stone.

"Devon!" Heldi's cry brought Devon whirling around. She dashed to the nearest wall and slammed an orb into place as she searched for the threat.

Between Devon and her group of followers, a corrupted jaguar leaped from atop a building and landed facing the small group of dwarves and humans. Devon slapped another *Glowing Orb* onto a wall as she swept forward. The massive cat, large as a stegosaurus skeleton, prowled forward. It jerked as a crossbow bolt pierced its chest. Tail switching, the jaguar snarled and seemed to focus on Heldi and her crossbow.

Devon cast *Freeze* on the beast and pressed forward. She cursed once she got close. Unfortunately, the cat was too near to her followers for a lightning attack.

"Back off!" she yelled as the jaguar shattered its icy prison. It clawed the ground, spinning out as it tried to pounce on Devon's friends.

Devon threw a desperate *Fade* spell over her followers, hoping to clear their aggro. Shadows rose from the ground, fuzzing their shapes and blending them with the background. The cat slowed but didn't stop.

She brought down a *Flamestrike,* burning the animal's fur, but the beast still advanced, searching for the prey it had been so determined to eviscerate. Clenching her jaw, Devon focused on the shadow beneath her feet. She raised a *Shadow Puppet* and sent it high up a wall, gliding toward her followers. Exceedingly careful not to let it touch anyone, she brought the shadow down to street level and molded it into Heldi's approximate shape. She cast *Ventriloquist* with her best imitation of a dwarvish yelp and sent the shadow Heldi scurrying down a side street and out of sight.

The cat shook its head as if disoriented, then turned its attention back to Devon.

> **You learned a new spell:** Simulacrum
> *You may manifest a rough approximation of a person or NPC. Colors, motion, and voices are rough but passable. Your creation is unlikely to fool a creature of mid to high intelligence.*
> **Cost:** 40 mana
> **Duration:** 2 minutes

"Not now!" she hissed, brushing away the notification.

The jaguar leaped. It hung in the air above her, blocking the setting sun.

"Oh lord this is going to hurt," she muttered, scrambling to the side. As she escaped the jaguar's shadow, the idea struck her. She slammed mana into her shadow to summon a sun-cast *Shadow Puppet*, forming it into a black spike erupting from the ground. The jaguar came down hard, and the spear plunged through the animal's chest, opening a hole in its back before shattering.

Devon flew back, gliding at least a hundred paces from the knockback as the animal died.

She just hung there in the air for a moment, so tired. That had been too close, her mana sinking to 30%.

With a few deep breaths, she watched her pool refill in five-second pulses. It had only reached 65% when she heard the next wave of attackers. She slid to the wall and started casting a *Glowing Orb* as the hissing approached.

Hissing and... ribbets?

Groaning, Devon rummaged through her inventory and came up with a mana potion. She downed it in one disgusting gulp and hurried to finish hanging her orbs.

"Come and get me!" she yelled.

***

The final corrupted tree frog sizzled as she finished it off with a tier 1 *Flamestrike*. Devon dropped to a seat in the middle of the cobblestones on the final street outside the Temple of Sorrow, exhausted. If more monsters came now, she wasn't sure she could even climb to her feet, much less concentrate hard enough to float in the air while commanding a half-dozen electric executioners. As she dragged out her last mana potion—just in case—a notification popped into her vision.

> **Quest update:** What's Wrong with the Wildlife?
> *You've cleansed the corrupted animals! Well done. Now about the source...*
>
> ***You have gained a special attribute point:*** *+1 Bravery.*
> ***You have gained special attribute points:*** *+3 Cunning.*
>
> ***Congratulations! You have reached Level 11!***
> *You have 4 new attribute points.*

Devon flopped back onto the street, relieved. She couldn't even be bothered to spend her attribute points.

From the previous intersection, the closest she'd allowed her followers to approach, Bayle called out, "You okay?"

She nodded and waved them back toward the edge of the ruins. "We're done here. Let's pull back."

"What about the.... Don't you think there's something going on in the glowing building?" Dorden shouted, clearly trying to remain tactful.

Devon slowly clambered to her feet. "It can wait. I don't know about you guys, but I'm hungry."

Chapter Forty-One

"YOU SURE YOU don't want a full night's sleep?" Dorden asked. The dwarf sat with the rest of her followers in a circle around the large fire they'd built to keep out the jungle night.

Devon shook her head. "Nothing like a power nap to knock down the fatigue score." She'd conked out almost as soon as she'd taken a seat beside the tipi of wood Bayle had been building in preparation to light the campfire. By the time she'd awakened, the moon had traveled halfway across the sky. After scarfing the *Stonehaven Scramble* from her inventory, she felt almost as good as new.

She bent and straightened her legs one by one to work the stiffness from her knees. "If I'm not back by dawn, head to the village. It may take me a few attempts to deal with whatever's in there." She gestured toward the temple.

"You mean, you may lose your life," Heldi said quietly.

Devon nodded. The notion of her death clearly didn't sit easily among her followers. As far as she knew, they had only one life. It seemed like that was part of the game design, a living, breathing world where a player's actions permanently changed the realm. It would never have worked without something like Veia creating the content, because even the simplest quests couldn't be reused. A mission to kill the bandits harassing some small town in the middle of nowhere would eliminate those bandits for good, and a new threat would have to come around to replace them.

Maybe the long hours of playing were making her overly emotional—or maybe she'd taken the "settlement leader sworn to Veia" thing too seriously. Either way, she felt a strange wave of appreciation and affection for the game's AI.

Devon laid a hand on Heldi's shoulder to reassure her. "If I die, rest assured I will return to the village and try again. I'll ask for your help if I think it will aid the mission. We *will* retrieve the Greenscale Pendant if it's in that building, or if it's not, we'll eliminate whatever force is endangering our village by corrupting these creatures."

As Devon slipped away, the village fighters settled back into a somber discussion. She hoped they'd get some sleep tonight though doubted it would come easily.

The Temple of Sorrow stood alone on a city block paved with massive slate flagstones. This close, the walls seemed to hum and vibrate to a beat that matched the undulations of purple and black across its walls. The front entrance was a dark hole in the building, offering no clues to what lay inside. Devon gripped her dagger tight as she cast a *Glowing Orb* and stepped beneath the archway and into the temple's entrance corridor.

Immediately, the oppressive sense that had filled the town intensified, squeezing her from all sides. She felt as if a presence oozed through her pores, filling her with despair. Gritting her teeth, she shook off the sensation and raised the orb higher, its blue glow crackling off ancient stone walls. She strode forward, footsteps clicking against the floor slates.

As she stepped into a T-intersection where the entrance corridor dead-ended, she looked back. Devon's heart slammed her ribs.

Behind her, a long hallway stretched into darkness. There was no entrance archway, no moonlit city. No escape.

"Guess that answers the question of retreat..." She turned to the right, determined to use her old dungeon-crawling trick of always exploring the rightmost passage so that she usually needed to make only left turns to find her way back out. As she started forward, the light from her orb seemed to dim. Darkness pressed down like the weight of the ocean on a drowning person. She took a deep breath to assure herself the air was clear and focused on her orb. The light bloomed as the darkness retreated.

You resist the Fear spell. (+110% chance due to Bravery score of 8)

Maybe Relic Online would never stop surprising her. When she'd been feared in other games, the software had just taken control of her body and forced her to run. Here, she had no doubt she'd have *felt* the dread if her Bravery score hadn't helped her resist. Hugging her ribs with her elbows, she shuffled forward. She shouldn't think about that sort of thing, not right now.

The corridors seemed to go on forever. At every branch or intersection, she turned right if the passage allowed. No beasts leaped out to challenge her, and no more spells attempted to twist her mind. All she knew were these endless, twisting tunnels.

Devon walked for an in-game hour before stopping. From the outside, the temple wasn't nearly big enough to hold such a large maze. That either meant she'd entered some kind of pocket dimension, or there was some sort of illusion at work. Could she have gone in circles? Maybe. The scenery didn't change. Just gray stone walls and more gray stone walls.

With her dagger, Devon tried to make a scratch on the wall, but the blade wouldn't bite. She pried at a crack between stone blocks but couldn't free a piece of mortar. She could start dropping items to mark her progress, Hansel and Gretel-style, if she hadn't emptied her bag before beginning this little adventure.

Frustrated, Devon looked through her pitiful collection of items anyway. She could dribble a trail of water on the floor from her *Everfull Waterskin*, but chances were it would dry too quickly. Earlier, she'd chugged almost all of her potions, tossing away the clay pots in her haste to get back to the fight. That left just a couple health potions and her soulbound pocket lint. She hadn't inspected it in a while, and when she hovered her attention over it, an item inspection window popped up.

Item: A Truly Enormous Ball of Pocket Lint
Have you ever heard of Chekov's Gun? Look it up.

When, exactly, had her ordinary pocket lint become "an enormous ball?" And what the hell was Chekov's Gun?

Devon pulled out the item. The ball of fluff was truly immense, filling both her hands. Though she knew what would happen, she set it on the floor and tried to take her hands away.

To her shock, the lint remained.

Somewhere, in the giant server room where Emerson's AI concocted its evil plans, Devon imagined Veia was laughing.

Standing, she pulled a little tuft of lint from the ball and dropped it on the floor. She walked ten paces and did it again.

And again.

***

About twenty minutes later, Devon arrived back at her first piece of dropped lint. She sighed and leaned against the wall.

"Well, I guess that answers that," she said aloud.

Now what?

There was clearly some sort of trick involved, a hidden door or an illusion or both... The problem was, she didn't have any sort of detection abilities.

But she did have her own two hands.

Starting out again, she ran fingers along the wall as she walked. The blocks were cool and ever so slightly damp. She hadn't gone far when she paused, noticing a piece of lint that had strayed closer to one wall than the others she'd dropped. As she watched, the little ball of fluff rocked then slid another inch, moved by some unseen breeze. Devon dropped to her knees before the opposite wall and started searching for the source.

There. Down near the floor, the shadows seemed to fold wrong. She'd seen a similar effect when she'd cast her *Fade* spell on the dwarves.

Now that she understood what she was seeing, the hidden catch was obvious. She flipped it with the toe of her sandal, and the faint breeze became a cool wave of air as the door shifted aside.

The space beyond the door was pitch-black. Even when Devon stuck her arm through the door and fixed a *Glowing Orb* to the wall, the feeble pool of light faded after just a few feet.

Air currents wafted over her skin, plucking at the stray strands of hair that had fallen over her face. Her first footstep into the chamber echoed off distant walls.

She swallowed and summoned another orb, holding it high as she tiptoed forward. Small clouds of dust puffed from beneath her sandals with each step over the pitted stone.

At first, she mistook the noise at the far side of the chamber for an echo of the faint rustling sounds she created while moving. But when it grew to a louder grating, much like the door had made when it slid aside, Devon took hasty steps back and slapped the new orb against the wall while she started conjuring another.

More stone grated, crystals crunching. Dust rose from cracks between the massive blocks of the floor as they began to vibrate.

Shadows stretched from her feet, but in the darkness of whatever grand hallway this must be, they seemed stunted and weak. She pressed mana into the first shadow and raised a puppet anyway. Moments later, her creation wavered beside her. Its presence pressed against her mind, fizzing with energy.

The sensation bolstered her courage as much as anything could. Devon sidestepped, preparing to fix three more orbs to the walls.

Ruddy light bloomed on the far side of the chamber, a pair of flame-red eyes hanging high above the floor. Devon's guts turned to ice as she realized how massive the hall and its inhabitant really were.

Her hands shook as she summoned the rest of her *Glowing Orbs* and *Shadow Puppets*. Finally, she cast *Levitate* and felt her feet leave the floor.

The thing on the far side of the chamber stomped forward, sending stone chips flying. With a shaky breath, Devon used her *Combat Assessment*.

Child of the Stone Guardians - Level 16 Superior
Good luck, sucker!

"Uh, thanks, I think?" she said.

She called down a *Flamestrike* on the immense creature, momentarily outlining it in fire. A smaller version of the Guardian that had introduced her to Relic Online, the golem was still massive. The column of flame crawled over its stony flesh, leaving behind patches of black. Unfortunately, the attack only shaved off a percentage or two of health.

Well, she didn't take the sorcerer base class for its offense. All she'd really cared about was the mana and the chance to exploit *Shadow Puppet* by creating more sources of light than she'd normally encounter.

With a shout, she sent her shadow minions in. Electricity leaped from their bodies, arcing over the stone monster and... fizzling?

She yanked up her combat log.

Child of the Stone Guardians is IMMUNE to lightning damage.
Your Shadow Puppet takes 168 points of damage from contact with its enemy!
Child of the Stone Guardians is IMMUNE to lightning damage.
Your Shadow Puppet takes 193 points of damage from contact with its enemy!

The messages repeated over and over, ending with six notifications when her puppets had died.

Well, shit.

The golem took a few more ground-shaking steps toward her. Devon's jaw began to ache as nausea swelled at the thought of the oncoming pain.

She dispelled *Levitate* and sprinted past the monster, trusting her speed to help her skate by. On the way past, she struck with her dagger. The point glanced off.

Ponderously, the monster turned to follow her movement. She tried to *Freeze* it. The icy prison held for one second before shattering. The golem's hitpoint bar dropped by another 1%. If that.

There had to be something she could do. Devon ran for the far side of the chamber as the mini-guardian sped up, its footfalls slamming the stone floor. She cringed, imagining a stone fist raised above her head. When she reached the far wall, she cast *Fade*.

The monster hesitated, but only for a moment. With a growl that sounded like a landslide, it squinted glowing eyes and paced straight for her. The fist came up, pulled back, and slammed into the wall as she ducked to the side.

The monster was slow. But with every step Devon sprinted, her fatigue rose. She could stay ahead of it for a while, but she didn't have enough mana to chip away at it with her sorcerer spells.

She wracked her brain for ideas as she ran along the wall of the chamber.

What about her new spell, *Simulacrum?*

With a mental twist, she poured mana into creating a passable copy of herself. At her command, the conjuration yelped and ran for the golem. It worked, insofar as the monster aimed a massive swipe at the running duplicate. When its hand connected with the figure, her casting disintegrated.

She quickly raised another and sent it running toward the beast. But this time, not so close.

The *Child of the Stone Guardians* crouched down and peered. It seemed to scoff. Moments later, it turned from her doppelganger and started stomping toward her.

So much for that.

Devon cast another *Freeze*, halting the beast's advance long enough for her to cross the chamber. She arrowed for the doorway where she'd entered, reasoning that the golem would have to tear down the wall to chase after her.

When she was about twenty feet away, the door slid shut with a crunch and a thud.

Devon whirled. The golem let out a noise that was something between a growl and a laugh.

Desperate, she glanced at her mana pool. It was around two-thirds full. Her in-combat regeneration had recovered some of the mana she'd dropped into her *Shadow Puppets* and the sorcerer spells afterward. But not enough. The stone giant's health bar was still nearly full.

Two massive steps brought it almost within melee range. Frantically backpedaling, Devon went through the motions of casting a tier 2 *Flamestrike* and then *improvised*. As the energy left her body, she imagined fanning the flames wide, creating not a column of flame, but rather a curtain standing between her and the golem.

You have learned a new spell: Wall of Fire – Tier 1.

You conjure a fiery barrier that inflicts double Flamestrike damage on any creature trying to pass through it.

Cost: 20 mana

Duration: 3 minutes

You have gained a special skill point: +1 Improvisation.

The golem hesitated. Devon's hope flared.

Moments later, the stone beast roared and plunged through the blaze. Patches of magma formed on its surface as its health dropped by maybe 4 or 5%. Working in a flash of inspiration, Devon cast *Freeze*, and the molten patches popped and exploded in a sudden release of steam. Another couple percentage points fell away from the monster's health.

She looked at her mana. Approaching 50% remaining. Still not enough, but maybe she could kite the beast, slowing its movement and dashing around the chamber while slowly recovering mana.

Distracted by her sudden success, she didn't notice how close the golem had come. A blow from its footstool-sized fist sent her sprawling. Agony seared her weapon arm and rib cage. Scrabbling, she barely managed to get clear before the monster's foot slammed down, sending grit and chips flying.

She whimpered as she stood, her arm limp at her side.

The golem advanced and wound up for another massive punch.

Gagging on the pain, Devon cast another *Wall of Fire*. The monster roared as it stepped through the hungry flames. More molten patches glowed on its arms and torso, and a *Freeze* exploded the regions, sending sheets of stone sloughing off the giant's body.

Devon limped away. Her hip didn't feel right.

With two steps, the creature was almost on her again.

This wasn't going to work, not when she couldn't stay ahead of it long enough to regenerate mana.

As she spotted a shadow wavering on the floor in front of her, an idea struck full force. What she really needed to do was cause a steam explosion *inside* the golem, blowing it to smithereens. Even more insubstantial than moon-cast *Shadow Puppets*, lightning-based shadows passed straight through creatures' flesh. That was her way in.

Staggering forward just paces ahead of the golem, she poured mana into a pair of shadows cast by the orbs decorating the wall near the chamber's entrance. The dark figures rose and kept pace with her.

Whirling, she commanded one to penetrate to the core of the golem. The timing had to be just right, because her creation couldn't survive the contact for more than a pulse or two of damage. As it disappeared into the stone giant, she cast *Flamestrike*, not on the golem, but on her own *Shadow Puppet*.

The golem glowed from within, cracks in the stone flaring red as 20% of its health fell away. But Devon wasn't done. Before the ruddy light faded, she sent the second shadow after the first.

Her *Freeze* spell hissed as it struck her shadow, and for the barest instant, she worried that her ploy hadn't work.

The *Child of the Stone Guardian* detonated. Fragments of rock slammed into her, knocking her flat yet again.

Devon's health fell to 30% as ejected stone shards hit the far walls.

She lay on the ground, paralyzed by the pain.

And then, as abruptly as the agony had come, it vanished in a wash of blue light. Her health bar flashed as it filled to 100%.

She sat up, disoriented, as an area in the center of the room shimmered. A set of pillars wavered and then slowly vanished.

In their place, a flight of low stairs led to a raised dais. Upon it was a throne and sitting in the throne was a skeletal creature.

Ancient eyes rose from the floor to inspect her. Deep within the cavernous eye sockets, flecks of light caught the glow of her orb. A robe hung in tatters on a frame more bone than skin. Power flowed off the figure in waves. Devon swallowed and laid a hand on her blade. Almost afraid of the answer, she tried her *Combat Assessment* skill.

Ancient Lich of the Khevshir - Level 350
You're smart enough to know what that means for your chances, right?

Devon raised a hand. "Sorry, I think I took a wrong turn," she said as she stepped toward the wall.

"Come closer," the lich commanded in a voice that sounded like a blade on a whetstone. Trying not to barf, Devon put her dagger back in its sheath—yeah, no need for that—and started forward. She clenched her fists, preparing for bone-shattering pain and a brief moment of nonexistence before her respawn.

Her thoughts whirled as she advanced. *Ancient Lich of the Khevshir. Khevshir... Khevshir...* Where did she know that name from? Oh, right. The Khevshir Vassaldom. Weren't liches crazy wizards that somehow became immortal and really creepy? Was this guy the last remaining member of the vassal society?

358

As she neared the throne, a massive thing carved of black marble with dragons rearing up on either side of the lich's head, she glimpsed something on the far side of the chair.

A wisp, bobbing lightly in the air.

The lich noticed the direction of her gaze.

"I believe you've already met my pet," he said.

The wisp detached from the throne and spun a playful circle around her before bopping her on the nose. It let out a tinkling laugh, then spoke.

"She wasn't sure what to think of me back then. I thought I'd give her some time to come to terms with her destiny."

"You made it here with remarkably little help," the lich said. "Your unique strengths allowed you to bypass the defenses I and my people put in place nearly 1000 years ago."

"Uh, thanks. So why am I—"

The lich raised a finger to silence her. "You see, the fall of Ishildar was tragic. The ruler, a kind woman with a weakness for animals, was mauled by a bear brought to her court as a coronation gift. Though it was never proved, many suspected the bear had been magicked into attacking. As Evelvashi was new to the throne, she hadn't yet arranged an heir. Together, leaders of the vassal societies searched for a new ruler. Those candidates who were noble couldn't be merciless enough to hold the city together during times of strife. The strong were too cruel. Others were too sickly or too old. Even if some vassaldoms agreed on a candidate, others did not. And so Ishildar fell under the Curse of Fecundity and quickly became uninhabitable.

"The Greenscale Pendant was our legacy. Before my people migrated away, we built this Temple of Sorrow. I alone agreed to stay and protect the relic which had been given into our guardianship. It took all my power to extend my life until this point, and now you are here. I've never known a home besides these humble shadows of wondrous Ishildar. And soon, I will move on."

Devon had to work not to fidget while the guy got his nostalgia on. Finally, he seemed to drag himself out of his memories. He turned his attention back to her.

"I imagined my solitude would last a century. Instead, it's been nearly a millennium. Some of the magic I used to defend this temple and the relic it guarded has become corrupted."

"Yeah," she said. "About that. What's going on with the animals?"

"Alas, the charms I created were intended to grant valiance to the wild creatures of the forest. I hung pendants around their necks and made them my defenders. Unfortunately, that only lasted a generation. Such is the way of life; the predator consumes the prey. Carrion-eaters devour corpses. My pendants traveled through the digestive system of countless animals, and in doing so, their power became tainted."

Was this guy serious? His super-duper defend-the-relic plan got defeated by the food chain?

"Were your pendants made of carved bone?"

The skeletal face crinkled in shock. "How did you know?"

Quest Completed: What's Wrong with the Wildlife?
Well, now you know. Probably a good idea to run a sweep for "stomach contents" in the carnage you left behind while clearing the city.

Reward: Other than the satisfaction of a job well done, 15,000 experience.

"I've encountered a few of the creatures, no big deal."

"Pssst! Ask her about the champion thing..." the orb said, bopping the lich on the nose.

The lich seemed to raise his brows at her. Kind of hard to tell with the shadowy cowl and shriveled skin. "Well? Are you the champion Ishildar has waited for?"

Devon shuffled. "Well, I can't promise to succeed, but I'll try my hardest. I'm determined to stay here and carve whatever home I can from the jungle. If finding the other relics and restoring Ishildar helps out that plan, I'm all for it."

The lich seemed to accept this, though within the folds of dried out flesh that hung from his cheeks, she detected no change in expression.

"Then I give this to you with my blessing. And if you'll accept another gift, I'd like to offer my pet as an adviser. I've long waited to lay down my burdens and continue my journey toward communion with Veia."

He held out a trembling stick hand draped with a golden chain and a single, glittering pendant.

You have received: Greenscale Pendant
One of five ancient relics created to bind the inheritance of the great city of Ishildar, this relic hums with power. Already, you feel a kinship with the city and a sense that, as you attune your awareness to the necklace, some of Ishildar's power will become yours.

Quest Completed: Find the Greenscale Pendant.
Grats.

Devon clasped the pendant to her chest and carefully slipped the chain over her head. She tucked it into her shirt for safekeeping.

The lich nodded, bones crackling. "Now, I'll ask you to leave. The path to the exit should be straightforward to follow. Go quickly, please. When I depart the area, the magic which preserved the temple all these years will vanish. You don't want to be here when it comes crashing down."

"Thank you, uh, sir," Devon said with a quick curtsy before spinning around. The wisp followed on her heels as she trotted from the lich's hall and into the outer passages. As advertised, the exit corridor was as obvious as the nose on her face. Dawn light fell through the archway. Had she been inside so long?

From the recesses of the temple, a low grating sound shook the floor. Devon broke into a run as blocks shifted and dust filtered down. Within a few seconds after she burst through the door, the temple came crashing down in a cloud of dust.

Chapter Forty-Two

DEVON'S CHEST FELT warm with satisfaction as her friends ran toward her. She searched their faces and saw relief—but something else, too.

They were worried.

"It's okay," she said, pulling out the pendant.

Dorden stopped in his tracks and seemed to forcibly change his train of thought. "Is that what I think it is?"

She did a little fist pump, then felt strange and dropped her hand to her side. "The Greenscale Pendant. We're on our way to restoring Ishildar."

Dorden grinned, but it seemed strangely forced.

"What is it? What's wrong?"

The flash of excitement over her news fled the group, replaced by a darker emotion.

From the back of the crowd, Hazel stepped forward. "There's a problem, You Gloriousness."

Devon's throat clenched down at the sight of the scout. She wouldn't have come unless there were an important message to deliver. "The village? Is it okay?"

Hazel nodded. "For now."

She searched the others' faces as the weight of her choices settled heavily on her shoulders. She'd pulled her fighters away from the camp and brought them an hour out into the wilderness. Aside from Greel, the camp was undefended.

"We have to hurry back. Explain on the way."

Hazel chewed her lip. "Actually, I should explain here. You see, late last evening, Grey noticed something that brought back old memories. He nudged me and pointed to Greel. The man was slipping toward the edge of the village, just like he used to leave Uruquat's camp when night fell. Back then, I was just a simple worker. I couldn't follow. But now..."

Devon clapped her hands on top of her head like a runner just finishing a race. Why had she trusted the man?

"I'm guessing you followed him."

Hazel nodded. "He headed back toward the old camp. I followed long enough to see him meet with a small group of men. I counted four, though there could have been more."

"Did you get their names?"

"One of them, at least. The one I knew you cared about. Henrik is here. And he told Greel there's an army on the way. The lawyer just needed to show him where to march it."

Devon felt sick. After everything she'd done, she'd been betrayed by one of her own. She swallowed hard and tucked the pendant back beneath her shirt. "Take me to them. If we can take out Greel and Henrik before they reach the village, maybe we can save Stonehaven."

***

Devon crouched in the brush. She watched as Greel walked at the front of a small procession, hacking his way through foliage with the *Superior Steel Knife* she'd given him. He stepped onto the open ground of the quarry and swiped the sweat from his forehead while he waited for Henrik and the other members of the advanced party.

"We've taken stone from here," Greel said. "But as you can see, there's quite a bit of material remaining. If you come this way—" He gestured toward the foot of the cliffs. "You can see there's also a nice vein of moss agate that will provide additional funding for our search for the relics."

As Henrik broke off from the small group and followed Greel to the base of the escarpment, Devon clenched her fists.

She understood now what people meant when they said they saw red. Just looking at the slimy lawyer made her ready for murder. After showing his boss the quarry, she had no doubt Greel would lead the man through the braided trails that now led between the rock outcroppings and the village. Right now, she and Hazel were hidden at the edge of the forest nearest the village. When the small party approached, she'd make her move.

She activated her *Combat Assessment,* focusing on the pair of men. Greel had been practicing, no doubt in secret. He was now level 13. And Henrik was a level 15 rogue. Lovely.

"This is all fine and well," Henrik said. "But the point of this little adventure is you showing me the way to your quaint little village. I can't have competition—however inept—in my hunt for the relics."

A strange expression crossed Greel's face, but he quickly covered it.

Feeling a hint of conscience? Devon wondered.

"If you're so eager, then let's get on with it," Greel said. "But I must ask your men to remain here so that you and I can discuss business arrangements. You see, in exchange for this valuable service, I'll need a much better position in your organization. It's me that's making your plans possible."

Henrik glanced at his men. "My associates are discreet. You need not worry about negotiating in front of them."

"As a legal professional, I must insist on discussing these terms in private."

"Oh for Zaa's sake. Fine. Whatever."

As Greel led the man toward Devon's hiding spot, he cast a triumphant look at the other henchmen. The men bristled and laid hands on their blades.

Devon would need to be quick. Beneath the canopy, her *Glowing Orbs* would give her away. Waving Hazel back, she drew a deep breath and cast *Levitate.* The men stepped into the shade of the forest.

With a yell, Greel drew his blade. He must have glimpsed her.

Frantic, Devon summoned an orb and slapped it against a tree. The others followed. A breath later, six *Shadow Puppets* sprouted from the ground. She ordered them forward as Greel sprang.

And plunged his knife into Henrik's back.

The man staggered, his health cut in half by the sneak attack damage. Devon's eyes grew wide as her shadows dove at the pair. She tried to recall them, but it was too late. Lightning forked and crackled and arced from the dark figures, glowing and sparking across the men's bodies. In an instant, both Greel and Henrik's health bars dropped to zero.

Shouts erupted across the clearing, the henchmen jumping into action.

Devon sent more shadows at them, almost as an afterthought. They died screaming, but she couldn't take her eyes from the sight near her feet.

Greel, reluctant ally, lay unmoving on the muddy trail near the forest's edge. She let the levitation spell drop and staggered forward, laying her fingers on his neck to feel for a pulse.

Nothing.

Tears welling, she stooped and picked him up and began carrying him back to Stonehaven.

Chapter Forty-Three

DEVON LAID GREEL'S body beside the shrine in a shaft of golden mid-morning sun. One hand clutching the *Greenscale Pendant,* the other resting on his shoulder, she listened to the birdsong filling the jungle.

"I'm sorry," she whispered. "I should have trusted you."

Sometime during the stumble back between the quarry and the village, she'd sent Hazel to retrieve items from Henrik's and his henchmen's bodies, then to recruit others to help clean up the corpses surrounding the collapsed temple. The bone baubles would need to be destroyed to keep them from passing the curse on to new creatures. Idly, she wondered how long a body stayed around before the game removed it from the world. Eventually, she supposed, she would have her answer when Greel dissolved into nothing.

After some time sitting in isolated silence, she saw Bayle approaching. The woman held out an item Devon hadn't seen in quite a while.

You have received: Rusty Knife.
This blade looks as if it has opened many letters over the years. Perhaps while in a swamp?
1-3 Damage | 0/10 Durability

"Doesn't really cut anymore," the fighter said. "But it seemed right to return it to him."

"Thank you," Devon said, setting the knife in the grass beside the fallen lawyer.

After Bayle left, it was quiet again until Hezbek hopped over the stream, clothing flapping, muttering to herself.

"Well, child, you accomplished everything I set you to," the medicine woman said quietly.

"Wasn't worth it if this was the cost," Devon mumbled.

"Maybe not. But done is done, and we *are* stronger and safer for your efforts."

"If you say so."

"Listen, I know you're grieving, but I'd like to talk to you about something. Sometimes, a small distraction can help soothe the pain."

Devon sighed and ran her hands through her hair before turning her attention to the woman.

Hezbek glanced toward the small alcove where the captive was bound and sleeping. "Given what we learned about this so-called army Henrik was bringing into the jungle, I imagine we'll find a use for that fellow. He's been softening toward us lately. With the right motivation, I think we could extract useful information. Or better, get him to lead us to where the army might encamp. Of course, that won't work if we have to keep dumping potions down his throat."

"But we don't know how to cure the poison."

Blushing ever so slightly, Hezbek dug into her belt pouch and pulled out one of the *Ivory Fangs*. "You sort of left your stuff scattered around my hut when you unloaded your bag. Might want to consider building your own cabin at some point. Anyway, I've been gaining skill, and with a sample of the toxin, I think I can brew up an antidote. I wanted to ask your permission before I took a scraping off this."

Devon shrugged. "That's fine. Speaking of, I've meant to ask you... How do I identify items?"

"It's not as easy as you might hope. Most cities have a guild of magic scholars who offer the service. A few very powerful wizards can do it as well. I've recently heard that engineers can build a device."

"In other words, I won't know much about those fangs anytime soon."

Hezbek shrugged. "Precise information, no. But I can sense a few things about it—you'll likely develop the same knack as your sorcery improves."

"What do you sense?"

"Well, for starters, the captive's wound was caused by necrotic damage. Nasty stuff."

Like a wet fish to the face, the memory of dying to the bog serpent queen's necrotic cloud smacked her.

Devon groaned. "Please tell me it's possible to gain resistance to necrotic damage..."

The woman gave her a strange look. "I don't see why it wouldn't be...?"

"Never mind. Bad experience in another... another life I suppose."

Hezbek looked down at Greel's body and gently touched the man's brow.

"You know," she said, "Greel is with Veia now. Perhaps it would give you some peace to commune with the shrine. Not really the same as sharing a mug of ale with the man, but he was never one for camaraderie anyway."

As the woman stood to go, she planted a kiss on the tips of her fingers and pressed them onto the crown of Devon's head. "You did good," she said. "And it will get easier."

"Thanks, Hezbek," Devon said as the woman walked away.

Standing, Devon laid her palms on the sun-warmed stone of the shrine. As she closed her eyes, an interface popped up. The text on the popup was echoed in her mind in a soothing female voice.

Welcome to the Shrine of Veia, offering blessings and boons to the faithful.
What is your desire?

The idea flashed to mind immediately. Devon was almost afraid to say it.

"I seek resurrection."

The interface disappeared, replaced by a field of glowing motes that swirled as the voice continued to speak.

"You wish to restore a non-starborn, the recently deceased Greel, I assume."

"Yes, please."

The motes circled and danced. "Occasionally, an advanced NPC can be brought back to the world if the death was sudden and of unnatural causes. But you should know, many who have passed on do not wish to return."

"Greel had friends here. We miss him. Can you tell him that?"

"I can convey the information, and perhaps the rebirth can be accomplished. But you must bring specific offerings to the shrine.

For magic this potent, the required items will be more notable than a couple of coppers or a whispered prayer. Are you prepared to submit the offerings?"

"I—I think so." She clutched the *Greenscale Pendant* tight, hoping desperately that the shrine wanted something else.

"Very well then. Sometimes a boon requires sacrificing things dear to yourself. In this case, they are dear to the deceased. I require a rusty knife, a sample of Carpavan Legalese, and a sincere apology from Devon Gloriousness for being such a jerk and not trusting Greel."

Devon laughed. "Are you in there, Greel?"

"I am a shard of Veia, and all who have died are now in communion with her. So yes."

Animated with more energy than her fatigue bar should have allowed, Devon dashed back to Hezbek's hut to grab the *Folded Parchment* she'd looted from Uruquat's corpse. Hezbek looked up from her inspection of the fang and started to speak.

"I'll explain later," Devon said as she shut the door and ran for the shrine. On the way, she opened the parchment and verified it was the document describing the ownership of Ishildar.

"All right," she said, setting the knife and the parchment on the shrine. "One rusty knife, a sample of Carpavan Legalese, and an apology. Greel, I am truly, deeply sorry. I acted too quickly when I should have trusted you. It won't happen again."

"Now dance like a chicken," the shrine said.

Rolling her eyes, she glanced toward the village to make sure no one was watching. She flapped her elbows and let out a few bawks.

The shrine glowed. At her feet, Greel's corpse jerked to life. He glared at her as he sat up. "If it's not obvious, I saw smoke from their campfire. Went to check it out and figured I had to do something to get Henrik alone and take care of him. But then you decided to murder me."

"It's good to see you too, Greel," she said with a smirk.

***

Devon logged out for some much-needed sleep, but when she next entered the game, the Stonehaven League was waiting for her.

And they were ready for a massive kegger.

It was the first time she'd tried dwarven grog, and she took an unfortunate tumble into the stream. Wet *Superior Medium Armor* was not very comfortable.

After that, she kept her *Everfull Waterskin* close at hand, holding it up and shaking her head whenever someone offered her a mug of ale. The party lasted from late afternoon until well into the night, the flames from a bonfire pulling the villagers close as the moon rose over the jungle.

Devon sat on a stump, glad for the heat and the companionship. She slipped the <u>Greenscale Pendant</u> from beneath her tunic and examined it. Over the last day, it had gained a new stat: *1% Attuned.* Seemed she had a while before she learned what power it would offer.

In the late hours of the night, Hezbek approached with the captive. The man gave a grudging thanks for healing his wound then sat and held his palms before the fire. Devon examined him and learned that his name was Jarleck, he was a level 13 Brawler, and surprisingly, he held her in slightly above neutral esteem. Maybe she could make an ally of him after all.

As she watched the dancing flames, she wondered what the coming weeks would bring. A search for another relic? An invading army? An influx of players?

"Hey, wisp?" she called.

The glowing ball descended from the canopy and circled her head. So far, it seemed to hover close enough to hear her, but far enough that it wasn't annoyingly in her vision all the time.

"Do you have a name?"

"The lich only ever called me Pet."

"Hmm. Not really my style. Is there a name you'd like to be known by?"

"Not really."

The orb bobbed in the air, dancing back and forth.

"Well, then I guess I'll have to call you Bob."

"If it makes you happy, sounds good to me."

"So, Bob, how do we find the next relic?"

"Not a clue."

With a shrug, Devon straightened her legs and went back to watching the fire. For tonight, that was enough.

Chapter Forty-Four

EMERSON LEFT *ANOTHER* text message for Devon. She hadn't been answering, probably because she was spending every waking moment in the game. As far as he could tell, she hadn't even connected to the messaging program in the past week, though he couldn't be as certain about that as he was about her play time, something he'd verified with customer support.

He was about to break his own rules and create a character just to get her to answer him.

Or worse, hack into a device in her apartment and take control of a speaker.

He brought up the report from customer service and read it again.

A handful of players were now reporting increased pain. All power-leveled or otherwise distinguished. All hardcore gamers.

All living alone.

He flipped to the other disturbing message, the note from one of his all-stars, Owen.

Or rather, from Owen's girlfriend who had connected to the messenger program with Owen's mobile phone. She'd come over to meet him for dinner and had found him non-responsive.

Owen was now in a coma in an Atlanta hospital.

He sent Devon another message, peppered with enough attention-getting emoji it almost hurt his eyes to read it back. The text part was simple: *Please log out and call me.*

He waited for five minutes, pacing back and forth.

"Emerson?" Mini-Veia asked through his condo speakers. "You seem agitated. Might I suggest a gym membership to promote relaxation?"

"Deactivate home assistance," he snapped.

After another ten minutes, Devon still hadn't responded. Emerson balled his fist, smacked the door jamb, then winced and shook his hand.

"Actually," he said. "Activate home assistance. Veia, please buy me a hyperloop ticket to Las Vegas and order an autocab to take me from there to St. George, Utah."

He already had one comatose player on his hands. He would not let Devon become the next victim.

Dear Reader,

Thank you so much for reading *Temple of Sorrow*. I really hope you enjoyed it! As a working writer, I utterly depend on readers to spread the word on my books.

Please consider leaving a review on Amazon for this book and for other authors you enjoy. I promise that I read every review (yes, even the critical ones). Sometimes, they help me shape the story to come, and often, they are the reason I get out of bed and in front of my computer long before the sun rises. Thank you!!

If you would like to grab free books and participate in my reader community, head over to www.CarrieSummers.com and join my reader group. We have a lot of fun writing collaborative stories over email, talking about books, and other great stuff. Plus, the group is how I let readers know when new books are out.

So, what's next? Devon has her work cut out for her. The second book in the Relics of Ishildar series will be out Summer 2018, so keep an eye out. In the meantime, you can check out my other fantasy series, *Chronicles of a Cutpurse*, *The Shattering of the Nocturnai* and *The Broken Lands*.

Once again, thank you for reading!

All best,

—Carrie

carrie@carriesummers.com

BOOKS BY CARRIE SUMMERS

Shattering of the Nocturnai
Nightforged
Shadowbound
Duskwoven
Darkborn

The Broken Lands
Heart of the Empire
Rise of the Storm
Fate of the Drowned

Chronicles of a Cutpurse
Mistress of Thieves
Rulers of Scoundrels
Queen of Tricksters (coming May 2018)

Relics of Ishildar
Temple of Sorrow

Made in the USA
Middletown, DE
05 November 2018